Elaine Faber

Black Cat
and the
Accidental Angel

A tale of memories lost and love found with a touch of the divine.

Elk Grove Publications

Black Cat and the Accidental Angel

Published by Elk Grove Publications

© 2015 by Elaine Faber

ISBN-13: 978-1-940781-11-2

A portion of the proceeds from the sale of this book are donated to support feline rescue projects.

This novel is a work of fiction. Names, characters, places, and incidents either are the product of the author's imagination or are used fictitiously. Any resemblance to actual events, locales, organizations, or persons, living or dead, is entirely coincidental and beyond the intent of either the author or publisher.

Cover photo *Black and White Cat*: © vivienstock, http://us.fotolia.com/id/46333972

Cover layout and book formatting: Julie Williams, juliewilliams.us
Printed in the United States of America

A Special Thank-You

To Elk Grove Publications, for making the Black Cat mysteries possible. Thanks, Michael.

To my editor, Julie Williams, my mentor, formatter, book designer and confidant. Your assistance and advice adds so much to the Black Cat mysteries.

To my beta readers who help with edits before publication. Sherri Bergmann, Sandy Lassa, Lois Parrish, and Sharon Prewitt.

To my long-suffering husband, Lee, who brings me coffee in bed every morning and patiently listens to every agonizing decision and heart-wrenching twist until the novel is complete.

To my precious children, Michael and Londa, for their continual encouragement and praise.

To my readers who ask for the next Black Cat adventure.

And lastly to Boots and Amber, my living, breathing muses for Black Cat and Angel (aka Thumper and Noe-Noe). Without their inspiring personalities and antics to influence my writing, Black Cat and Angel would just be two more cats with six toes on each foot.

Chapter One

Thumper lifted his head to peer through the wires of the carrier. For as far as his eyes could see—nothing but the tops of apple trees. Where were they? Last time he'd looked, they'd been on the freeway, somewhere between San Francisco and Fern Lake, headed home. They couldn't get there fast enough to suit him.

"*Oww!* You've stepped on my tail." Noe-Noe twisted her fetching furry head and glared. "When can I get out of this wretched thing?"

Thumper shifted his weight in the carrier they shared, trying to give her more space. "Sorry, my precious. It won't be long now."

The SUV hit another pothole, rocking the cat carrier against the passenger door and the seat cushions.

Thumper lifted his nose and sniffed. He pulled his ears back. *Dog!* How long had it been since Kimberlee's cousin, Dorian, gave Sam a bath? Probably before they left Texas. Dog smell swirled through the car, stirred by the air conditioner. Would it hurt someone to crack a window?

Sam's panting sounded behind the seat. He was probably drooling all over the luggage. Noe-Noe was right. This trip couldn't be over soon enough. "We should be home in an hour, my sweet."

His companion, appearing less than impressed, turned her head away. "*Oww!* Move over. Now your foot is in my stomach." Noe-Noe laid her head on the blanket and closed her eyes.

Poor thing. She's exhausted. She certainly wasn't the sweet kitty he'd fallen in love with in Texas this past week. But, how could he blame her for being cranky after five hours on the plane and another hour and a half jammed together in a carrier meant for one cat. Thumper scooted closer to the hard side wall and tried to find a comfortable position.

Noe-Noe's eyes slit open. "I had no idea how far Texas was from Fern Lake. I've changed my mind." She stood and rocked as the carrier swayed. "Tell Brett to stop this car and let me out this instant. I want to go home!"

Thumper's gaze moved from her golden stripes to the front seat where Brett drove with one hand on the steering wheel and his other arm across the back of the seat. He reached up and twirled his finger through one of Kimberlee's dark curls.

Kimberlee glanced at Brett and smacked her lips, sending him an *air-kiss*.

Thumper turned back to Noe-Noe. "You want to go home now? How do you think you'd get there? Fly? You're a cat, not a bird!" As if he could tell Brett to stop the car, anyway. It wasn't likely his *person* would start taking driving instructions from him at this late date. Nor would he turn the car around and take the cantankerous feline back to Texas.

"Maybe this was a mistake. Why did you make me come with you? " Noe-Noe flattened her ears against her head, reached out a golden paw and gave him a swat.

"What do you mean, why did I *make* you come? You begged me not to leave you behind. It was a lucky break that Kimberlee brought you along at the last minute. Now scoot over. You're already taking up three-quarters of the space."

"Am not. Move your own fat black butt. You're poking me. I'm up against the wall already…"

Kimberlee's voice cut through his sweetheart's muttering. "Is this right? It looks like a levee road. Did you make a wrong turn at the last intersection?"

"Yeah, I think we did." Brett sighed, pulled his arm off the back of the seat and gripped the steering wheel with both hands. "I'm looking for someplace wide enough to turn around."

"Our *persons* sound like they're as tired as we are." Thumper reached up to scratch his left ear. *That blasted dog. I better not have a flea on me.*

"They aren't jammed into a little bitty cat box like we are."

"Go back to sleep. It won't be long now."

Thumper peeked through the wire door. Outside, tree tops whizzed past on both sides of the road. He sighed. Kimberlee was right. This definitely didn't look like the right road. Were they lost? *I'm much too tired to be lost.*

He was at his wits end with exhaustion, after traveling all day with five-year-old Amanda, Brett, Kimberlee, her cousin Dorian and her potentially flea-ridden dog, Sam. Not to mention dealing with his newly acquired cranky *mi amour*. Lost? They weren't really lost. He had faith in Brett. He'd figure it out.

Amanda leaned over her car seat, across Dorian's lap and peered into Thumper's cage. "Hi, Thumper. Are you and Noe-Noe awake? I'm so glad Mama brought her with us. I know how much you *wove* her."

Indeed, he *woved* her. At least he'd *woved* her this morning. This afternoon, he wasn't so sure.

Kimberlee turned to Dorian, squeezed between Amanda's booster seat and Thumper's carrier. "How are the animals?" She peeled the wrapper off a hard candy and offered it to Amanda. The scent of cinnamon momentarily drowned out the odor of sweaty dog as Amanda popped the candy into her mouth.

Dorian peeked into Thumper's carrier, and then glanced back at Sam's cage, wedged behind the rear seat. "Noe-Noe's sleeping. Sam and Thumper are awake."

"Good. We'll be home soon." Kimberlee shoved a curl behind her ear and turned back. She spread the road map across her lap. "Oh, I see what happened. We should have turned right at that last intersection."

Thumper lifted his foot and poked a toe through the wire. *Play with me, Amanda.* As much as he loved all three of his *persons*, Amanda was his favorite. Whenever he was bored, she was the one most likely to entertain him. Like now.

Amanda tickled his toes and giggled, then sat back in her seat.

The SUV swayed in the draft of a delivery van that zoomed past, its wheels edging over the white line.

"Brett! Be careful." Kimberlee grabbed Brett's shoulder. "That truck almost hit us." She twisted again toward the back seat. "Are you okay, Dorian? Are you getting carsick?"

"Oh," Dorian yawned. "I'm fine. I've been napping." She glanced out the window "Apple trees? What is this? Some kind of levee road? Did we make a wrong turn?"

"Okay! Okay! I get it. I'm outnumbered," Brett mumbled. "I'm looking for a place to turn around. It's too narrow here." He slowed the SUV.

Another pick-up truck zoomed past. Thumper's carrier swayed.

"Up there," Kimberlee said. "Turn around there."

"That looks good." The brakes squeaked as Brett slowed the vehicle. "I think there's room to…" He glanced into the rear view mirror. "Watch it!"

The screech of crunching metal filled the car as the truck behind struck their rear bumper, flinging the back passenger door open. The SUV lurched sideways and swayed.

Thumper pitched forward. He collided against Noe-Noe as the carrier toppled from the car, crashed onto the asphalt and then tumbled down the twenty-foot embankment on the side of the road. Metal grated against metal, drowning out Noe-Noe's shrieks. *Brett! Kimberlee! Amanda!*

The world tipped upside down, then right side up. Thumper's head reeled as the carrier plummeted down, end over end, striking against the wall of rocks. *Wham!* His head whacked against the hard interior wall.

The carrier rocked to the side and then lurched to a stop. The scent of rotten apples made his stomach turn. A fine mist of dust rose up and drifted in through the wire. He moaned and tried to lift his head. *Noe-Noe?*

Then, everything went black.

Chapter Two

rett checked the huge clock on the stark white wall for the sixth time in five minutes—one and a half minutes since the last time he'd looked. He fidgeted in the chair, his stomach churning, fingering the bandage on his hand. The pain in his wrist had eased somewhat, thanks to the pain pill they'd given him for ribcage bruises and a sprained wrist. Had it been over an hour since he and little Amanda entered the waiting room, waiting for word about Kimberlee's test results? What would her x-ray show? Brain damage? Blindness? Remember the movie, *Magnificent Obsession*? The bump on Jane Wyman's head caused her to go blind. *Calm down, Brett. That was just a movie, not real life. Please, Lord, let her be alright.*

And what about Dorian? Off to the orthopedic procedure room to check her shoulder injury.

The smell of antiseptic in the emergency room at St. Joseph's Hospital reminded him of his grandmother's bathroom. Stressed parents walked the aisles, futilely trying to console wailing babies. Other children, likely siblings of the sick and injured, chased each other around the play yard outside, in contrast to other patients inside, some holding their heads in their hands.

Head injury! It sounded so ominous. They took Kimberlee to Radiology first thing, thanks to the diagnosis of head injury reported by the ambulance technicians. *Lord, don't let her die.* Prickles of sweat dampened his forehead. If anything should happen to her… What would he do without her? Because he had Amanda with him, he couldn't go to the x-ray department with Kimberlee.

He shuddered, as the sound of the crash rang through his mind.

They'd been on a levee road one minute and the next, a rusty flatbed truck turned his world upside down.

Amanda squirmed in the hard plastic chair next to him, the third seat they'd moved to over the past hour, driven from one place to another to avoid a vomiting baby on his left and an old man coughing into a bloody handkerchief on his right.

"Why don't you run out there and play with those little girls?" Brett gestured toward the riding toys just beyond the emergency room glass wall. She'd be safer outside in the sunshine, than she was sitting here in the waiting room with who-knows-what germs swirling overhead. *And let me worry about Kimberlee, alone.*

Amanda peered through the window where two little girls peddled plastic cars around the fenced enclosure. "*Nuh-uh.* I want to wait for Mommy." She swung her legs over the edge of her chair. "Will Mommy be alright?"

"The doctor is doing her best to take care of her."

It's my fault. His stomach lurched. The taste of bile soured in the back of his throat. Had his tiredness and frustration contributed to the accident? With nerves frayed from an all-day flight, he must not have paid enough attention to his driving. Getting lost on a levee road with his three favorite women, two cats and a dog wasn't exactly the best way to end their vacation. Maybe he hadn't checked the rear view mirror before he slowed to make the turn. He'd been so annoyed by Kimberlee's gentle nagging and Noe-Noe's caterwauling. The flatbed truck must have come up from behind—

Brett glanced up as a woman in pink scrubs approached. Could it be the doctor? She looked more like a high school kid, but her name badge read *Doctor* and the silver stethoscope around her neck gleamed like a badge of honor, signifying the completion of eight years of medical school. She hardly appeared old enough to hold Kimberlee's life in her chubby hands.

"Mr. Clarke?" She shoved her glasses over the curls on top of her head and extended her hand. "Dr. Smythe."

He stood. "My wife. Is she going to be okay?"

"Your wife is back from Radiology." She flipped the pages on her clipboard. "Good news. No broken bones, but she has a pretty nasty lump on her head. I'd like to do an MRI and admit her for observation. If the results look good, we'll release her in the morning. You and your daughter can go up to the second floor and see her. She's in room 212. Check with the floor nurse." She closed the clipboard file and smiled.

Thank God. She's going to be alright. "That's good news. How's her cousin, Dorian Dilman? She came in the ambulance with us."

Dr. Smythe shook her head. "I'm not her attending, but I know she's in the Orthopedics wing. They should be about done by now. The receptionist can arrange for her doctor to speak with you."

"Do you know where they took our car? I'll need to pick up our luggage and make…whatever arrangements."

The doctor checked her clipboard again. "There's a note here that says the Redi-Care Ambulance brought you in and your car was taken to…O'Reilly Towing Company."

Brett pulled a notebook and a pen from his pocket. "O'Reilly Towing. Thank you. How about the SPCA? Our pets were in the car with us. They said the SPCA would take the animals."

The doctor pointed north. "You'll find the SPCA three blocks north, on Old Redwood Highway."

"Thanks." He turned to Amanda, "Come on honey, let's go see Mommy."

The elevator doors opened on the second floor. Brett checked left and right. "Two-ten, two-eleven…here it is. Two-twelve." He tiptoed into the room, his finger to his lips. "*Shh.* Mommy's sleeping."

Amanda stopped halfway across the room and put her hands over her eyes. No wonder the kid was scared. He'd gulped down the same panic when he first stepped through the door. A large bandage swathed Kimberlee's head. Black circles under both eyes made her pale face resemble a marshmallow with two raisins for eyes.

Brett leaned over and kissed her forehead.

Kimberlee opened her eyes and reached toward Amanda. "Come here, sweetheart. Don't be afraid."

Amanda shook her head and backed away.

"It's okay, honey." Brett reached out his hand. "Mama bumped her head. See? She has a big bandage on her head. Come and give her a kiss."

Amanda crept to the bed and gave her mother a hesitant kiss.

Brett brought Kimberlee's fingers to his lips.

She touched the bandage on his hand. Her eyebrows rose. "And you?" Her voice was just a whisper. She cleared her throat. "How are you holding up?"

"I'm fine. Just a scratch. Amanda passed her exam with flying colors."

"Oh, Brett." She blinked back tears. "How is Dorian? Is she okay?"

"Now, take it easy. She's nearby. I spoke to her doctor. They're treating her for a shoulder injury. They want to keep her overnight, too. I'll see about getting both of you out of here in the morning, just as soon as they say you can leave."

"The car. How will we get home? What about Sam and the cats?"

Brett laughed. *She's going to be fine.* "Listen to you. You're worrying about everybody but yourself. Your job is to get better. Let me worry about the car and the animals. The local animal control took them. I'll pick them up in the morning before I come back for you and Dorian. Now, get some rest. Amanda and I will get a motel tonight. Everything's going to be fine."

Kimberlee gripped his hand and smiled.

"I'll check on Dorian before we go." He kissed her cheek and took Amanda's hand. "Give Mama a kiss. We'll see her in the morning."

Brett lifted Amanda up for another quick kiss. "Bye, Mama. See you tomorrow."

"Bye-bye." Kimberlee waved.

Brett located Dorian's room. He reassured her that Sam and the cats were at the animal shelter. "Kimberlee's in Room 212 if you want to call and coordinate your release time in the morning. She can call my cell and let me know when to pick you up. I need to find a motel and get this little girl to bed."

Within an hour, he had arranged for a rental car and booked a room at Howard Johnson's. He put Amanda into bed and pulled the covers up to her neck. "Nighty-night, sweetheart."

"Daddy Brett? Won't Thumper be scared with all the other cats and dogs?"

"They'll be okay. The people at the SPCA are there to take care of the animals."

"Can't we call and tell Thumper we'll come in the morning and get him?"

"That's a good idea, sweetheart." He kissed her cheek. "I wish we could."

Chapter Three

OMEWHERE BELOW THE LEVEE ROAD—

He opened his eyes and blinked. *Where am I?* He lay sprawled in the doorway of the cat carrier, leaned against an apple tree, the door hanging at an odd angle. Beyond the tree, a steep embankment, barely visible in the darkness, rose up to God knew where. Maybe a road, if the occasional roar of cars approaching and then receding were a clue.

Overhead, a million stars surrounded a bright quarter moon. *What is this place?* He shivered in the cool night air. Pain shot through the back of his head. *What happened?* He tried to move. His head whirled into a sense of falling, tumbling end over end. He leaned back against the hard carrier door. Something soft pressed against his lower body.

Maybe it's all a bad dream. Surely, he was in his own bed. He could almost imagine the smell of fried chicken. He lifted his head, opened his eyes and sniffed. No. It wasn't fried chicken. It was rotten apples and cow manure. Instead of his favorite fuzzy blanket and his soft donut bed, he laid half in and half out of his carrier among a stand of weeds.

Flexing his legs, he tried to stand. *Everything seems to work.* Then he saw *her* curled against his side. Her creamy gold-colored body gleamed in the moonlight. A gentle breeze ruffled a tuft of hair on the back of her head. *Who?* Another wave of pain shot through his head. His eyes refused to stay open, and he fell back against the body of his companion, lying motionless inside the carrier.

Sometime later, he woke again, roused by something rough, wet and sticky stroking the side of his face. He blinked into the early morning light. A sliver of a moon hung low in the sky.

"Oh, wake up. *Slurp*. Please wake up. *Lick, lick*. Oh, please, don't be dead… I hate blood, oh…oh… *Slurp*. I can't be a bride one week and a widow the next… You can't be dead…" *Lick, lick, lick!*

A wet tongue slathered the fur between his ears, each lick sending tiny electric shocks through his skull. He opened one eye a slit and looked into the most beautiful pair of golden orbs. A furry amber goddess.

"Oh. Oh. You're alive. Thank goodness…" *Slurp*. A strand of black fur hung from her mouth from where she'd licked it off his shoulder.

Alive? I think so. He tried to lift his head. *Bride? What does she mean…bride? Is this a dream?* He reached out a big white paw and touched the side of her cheek. Yep, real.

"Are you okay? You have a big lump on the top of your head. I did the best I could to clean off the blood." She blinked.

Whoa! What a babe. His heart skipped a beat. He took a breath and pulled his whiskers back. "Thank you for helping me, but…*um*…I'm not sure… Who are you? I can't seem to recall…" He tried to bring the quivering outline of her delicate face into one firm image, but her features slid from side to side. He shook his head to clear his vision. "*Ouch*…oh…I shouldn't have done that." He dropped his head and counted to six. The pain receded and her face shifted together into one image. "Oh…oh…that's better."

He stared into her enchanting face—the angle of her teasing whiskers—the slant of her taunting ears—her voluptuous eyes, tinted ever so slightly with green, glittered in the early morning light. The rims of her eyelids were dark, like circles of onyx around a citrine gemstone. Her fur, like rows of buttercups set in a field of marigolds. Her teeth were small and straight. All her curves were all in the right places.

"You don't know me? I'm your soul-mate, the one you promised to love and cherish till *death do us part*," she whispered, the faint whiff of tuna on her breath. "Though, I must have heard that line a dozen times." She patted his foot with her paw. "I suppose I'll forgive you since you did get quite a clunk on your noggin. I expect everything will be clear soon and you'll remember the accident—"

"Accident?" His heart pattered a bit quicker. *Yes, the falling, the darkness, and then the nothingness.*

She stood, stretched, and shook her body, giving him a better glimpse of her fetching figure, and then lay down again beside him. "You really don't remember anything?"

Over the next half hour, she told him all the gory details of the accident. "Now, aren't we just the poster children for exactly why riding without a seatbelt is a bad idea, even for animals? In the confusion, the ambulance left and since no one saw our carrier, we were left behind."

He lowered his eyes. "I don't remember much about it. I can't even recall my own name…much less yours." He pulled his ears down and twitched his whiskers. She'd think he was a real basket case. Not a very good impression on a first date.

"Give it time. It will all come back to you." Her voice was soft and reassuring. "In the meanwhile, you can call me Angel. I'm here to take care of you."

He jerked back. "Angel? So, that's it? I'm dead." He closed his eyes and shuddered. Wasn't it just too good to be true? Left behind on a deserted road with a beautiful female and he was already dead. *Just my luck.*

"You're not dead, silly. Don't worry." Her laugh tinkled like a silver bell.

He sighed and glanced up at the rock-covered embankment. The whoosh of a car passed, out of sight beyond the weeds. It was time to take control of this miserable situation, if he could just hold his head up straight.

He stepped out of the carrier, his black legs wobbly and weak. "There's a road up there. Maybe someone will stop and help us."

"I don't think so, dear. It's not safe up there. You've lost a lot of blood and I'm tired. I doubt we'd even make it up the hill and I've no intention of leaving you here alone." She snuggled next to his side. "Just stay close to me. I'll keep you warm. Let's wait. They're bound to miss us and come back pretty soon."

Why *hadn't* someone missed them and come back already? He must have a *person*, although, as hard as he tried, he couldn't think if it was a *man person* or a *woman person*. Or was it because his *person* was dead? He shuddered at the thought.

The cool morning air rippled across his face as he lay beside her, licking the back of her ears. He tried to remember something, anything before the accident, like, his name or his *person's* name. But, his eyes were heavy and his head felt like a chunk of lead. *What is my name?* Too tired to ponder the problem further, he rested his chin on his white paws and fell asleep, lulled by the sound of Angel's purr.

"Let's stop on the way to the animal shelter and pick up some breakfast." Brett sipped his Styrofoam cup of motel coffee. He grimaced and set the cup in the rental car's cup holder. The sun had yet to burn through the cloud cover, as he and Amanda drove across town. "The pets won't mind waiting a little longer." He glanced at his watch.9:00 A.M. "The shelter may not even open until 10:00 A.M."

"I can't wait to see Thumper." Amanda bounced in her booster chair.

Thirty minutes later with a cup of Starbucks coffee in hand, Brett parked in front of the pink brick building where stray and unwanted animals waited, in hopes of finding a forever-home and establishing a mutually rewarding relationship with a human.

Amanda stopped to point. "Look at the doggies."

Several dogs dragged human attendants around shrubbery, trees and trails, frequently stopping to mark a bush or squat and do their business. Obliging, subjective *two-leggers* knelt and gathered up the canine's deposits.

Brett took Amanda's hand. "Yes, I see them. Let's go in and get Sam and your kitties." He pushed open the door. Off to the right, faint barking and an occasional meow echoed down a corridor. Off to the left, a glass window opened into a room where a lady sat on the floor with a couple of kittens, leaping and pawing at a feather tied to a stick.

Posters covered the walls, advertising dog and cat food. Other posters advocated the joys of pet ownership.

A woman behind the reception desk looked up from her computer and smiled. "Good morning. Can I help you? Are we here to adopt a puppy today?"

"Yes…no…I mean…no puppy. I'm Brett Clarke. We've come for our pets. We were in a car accident yesterday afternoon. They told us our pets were brought here." He glanced at a poster over her head depicting a happy family with their newly adopted dog. Wasn't it just like the SPCA to take every opportunity to encourage pet ownership?

The woman checked her computer and picked up the phone, dialed a number and waited. She nodded. "Will you bring up the Clarke rescue dog?"

Brett raised an eyebrow. *Dog? What about the cats?*

He picked nervously at his fingernail. How many times, over the years, had the SPCA wheedled donations from him? When he wrote the checks, he never thought that one day he'd be on the receiving end of their services.

Amanda walked to the glass walled room where the lady and the kittens cavorted on the rug.

A side door opened and a young man came into the lobby, pulling a dolly holding Sam's large carrier.

"Here he is, Mr. Clarke. He's a great dog and so well-mannered. He made quite an impression on the staff." The young man hefted the carrier off the dolly and set it in front of Brett.

Sam wiggled inside, likely relieved to see a familiar face.

Brett leaned down and scratched Sam's nose through the wire. "Great. Will the cats be here soon? We had two cats with us, too." He glanced up at the attendant.

"Cats?" The attendant peered into Sam's cage, as if looking for some elusive cat, maybe hiding under Sam's feet. His brow furrowed and he glanced at the lady behind the counter.

She shrugged, her face a shade paler than before. She rifled through her paperwork. "They only brought the dog to the facility. There weren't any cats."

A muscle in Brett's clenched jaw twitched. It didn't make any sense. How could they have overlooked the cats' carrier sitting right in the back seat next to the door?

Brett ran his hand over his face, trying to erase the terror he'd felt with his family trapped, the car crunched and broken, and him—helpless. He closed his eyes, visualizing the scene of the accident. The grind of metal as the rusted flatbed slammed into the rear of the SUV. Sparks flying across the pavement as the SUV careened across the road and flipped onto its side. The sound as the truck struck the bottom of the SUV. Kimberlee lying crumpled against the door. Amanda's car seat hanging sideways. The smell of gasoline…

His forehead prickled with perspiration. He couldn't forget how the firemen forced open the door with the jaws-of-life, pulled Kimberlee from the car, unconscious, her head bruised and bleeding… Dorian hunched over the seat, her shoulder jutting at an odd angle and…*the empty seat beside her!*

The cats' carrier must have fallen from the car and rolled down the embankment!

How had they not realized it was missing? Just before they left, he spoke to the fireman. 'By the way, what's the plan for the animals?' and he'd answered. 'Don't worry. I saw the carrier. The local animal control is sending a truck. They'll be taken to the SPCA. Here's their card.' He'd seen Sam's carrier, the only carrier in the car and must have assumed it held several animals.

"Oh, no!" He'd been too worried about his family to notice the missing carrier.

"Daddy Brett? Where's Thumper and Noe-Noe?"

Three pairs of eyes swiveled toward the little girl.

"There's been a terrible mistake." Brett knelt beside her and gripped her shoulders. "Thumper and Noe-Noe…" What could he say? Were they dead? Or, were they trapped inside a fiberglass prison, somewhere over the embankment, twenty miles out of town?

"Where are they, Daddy Brett?" Her gaze traveled around the reception room.

"I think they're lost, sweetheart, but we're going to find them, okay?"

He stood, pulled out his wallet and tossed several large bills onto the counter. "Is that enough to cover Sam's expenses?"

The receptionist nodded. "I hope you find your cats, Mr. Clarke. I'm sure sorry about the mix-up. We had no way to know—"

"Thanks again." He hefted Sam's carrier through the front door, opened the van's tailgate and shoved it inside.

He lifted Amanda into the booster seat, jumped behind the wheel and gunned the engine. The tires spun in the gravel as Brett's rental van turned onto the road. "Ready, Amanda? Let's go find us some cats!"

The sun peeked through the apple trees and reached across the patch of dirt where the carrier lay, warming the side of his face. He lifted his head. *Where am I? Oh, I remember.* He rolled his head from side to side, holding it in a relatively upright position. Thank goodness, the pain in his head was almost gone.

The little orange female still snuggled close to his side. She'd kept him warm through the night. God bless her. If he had to be left for dead in the middle of nowhere with a lump on his head, he couldn't think of anyone he'd rather be with than this lissome creature. She said she was here to take care of him. If anyone was going to be doing any *taking care of* around here, it would be him, not some mysterious female claiming to be his bride. Just exactly how and when did that happen? He felt as if he was a determined bachelor, though one could not be sure, in his present state.

He stretched, stepped outside the carrier and licked his left paw.

She woke, came alongside and shook herself. "Good morning."

"Looks like it." His gaze traveled the length of her golden body. *What a body.* Whoa! Better keep his mind off the babe and on more important things. "So, where did you say we met and why did you say you were my bride?"

"Oh, never mind all that now. Plenty of time to talk about such things later. We should try and find help. It doesn't look like anyone is coming back and I'm starved."

"My thoughts, exactly. I think I'm feeling well enough to travel." He twisted his neck from side to side, lifted his left foot, then his right. *Good! Legs still work. Head doesn't hurt.* "I'm as ready as I'll ever be. Let's go this way. I feel as if home is north."

"It might be easier now to climb the bank and go along the road." Angel picked her way through the dirt clods and stickers, headed toward the rock wall.

He shook his head. "It's too dangerous on the road. We could be hit by a car or worse, picked up by the local animal shelter. For some reason, our *persons* left us behind and didn't come back. If they're dead…" He lowered his ears and pulled back his whiskers. Where did that come from? He hadn't allowed himself to think about that possibility. The thought was mind-boggling. *Scratch that thought from your head.*

How was it that he could know anything about animal shelters or dangerous cars when he couldn't even remember his name? Memory loss must be selective. Well, best to work with what you had and hope the rest would come later. "Follow me." He led the way through the orchard below the levee road, searching for something, anything to point the way home. He could do this. He had to do this. Cats have some kind of built-in homing device, right?

Chapter Four

"Quick, Daddy Brett!" Amanda clutched her carton of Starbucks orange juice. Wrappings from her breakfast sandwich lay crumpled on the floor mat.

"Don't worry, honey. We'll find them." Checking a local map, Brett determined the accident had occurred on the Johnson Levee Road. He drove toward the north side of Cloverdale where the levee road branched off the freeway toward Lake County. At the cut-off, he popped in his ear bud, and keeping an eye on the road, punched in his friend, Jack's, number on his cell phone. It rang several times. *Pick up. Come on Jack, pick up.*

"Herman's Motor Lodge, Jack—"

"Hey, it's me, Brett. I need your help."

"Brett! Where are you? I expected you folks back yesterday. What's happened?"

"What didn't happen? We were rear-ended outside of Cloverdale yesterday afternoon. Dorian and Kimberlee are in the hospital and—"

"Are they alright? How's Amanda?"

"She's fine. Kimberlee has a bump on her head. Dorian dislocated her shoulder. They were both kept overnight for observation, but they should be discharged this morning. Listen, something else. Animal control came out and got Sam. I just picked him up at the SPCA. He's here with me now, but—"

"What about Thumper? He's not… He didn't…"

"No. Here's the thing. Look, I can't explain right now. Thumper's carrier was thrown from the car when the truck hit us and in the confusion, we didn't even realize…" He put his hand to his forehead.

He wasn't explaining this very well. *Read between the lines, Jack!*

"Good Lord. Where the heck is he?"

"He and Grandmother's cat are still in the cage out at the—"

"What's Grandmother's cat got to do—?"

"I'll tell you all about it when we get home." Brett glanced into the rear view mirror. Amanda's eyes stared back. "You know… They could be… *Umm*… Amanda's here in the car… I can't really go into details… You know…" *Fill in the blanks, Jack. I'm such a jackass. Our pets were left on the side of the road and I didn't even miss them until this morning. Get it?*

That wasn't exactly true. He had assumed they were being cared for at the SPCA, but he felt guilty, knowing what had really happened. Now, pray God, they were alright.

"What do ya need me ta do?"

"Can you drive down and help me look for them? I'll be on the Johnson Levee Road, about thirteen miles north of Cloverdale."

"That's all ya gotta say. I'll gather a few things and I'll get there as soon as I can."

"I'm beat up pretty bad from the airbag… My wrist… I don't think I could crawl down the embankment and bring the carrier back by myself. I'll need help."

"Gotcha'. I'm on my way out the door. I'll meet ya on the levee road in about an hour. Now, Brett, don't ya worry. I'll take care of everything. We'll find em'. Ya need anything else?"

"We ate before I went to the SPCA. Jack. I feel awful. What am I going to do if…" He glanced back at Amanda.

"I know Thumper. He's a trooper." Jack chuckled. "I think he's still got six or seven of his nine lives left."

"We're turning onto the levee road now. I'll locate the crash site and we'll wait for you there. Hurry, Jack, and thanks."

"No need… See ya' in a few."

Good old Jack. He was the kind of friend you could always count on, no matter what you needed.

Brett's hand shook on the steering wheel as they neared the accident site. Where was that wide place in the road where he tried to turn around? His stomach churned when long streaks of dark skid marks and shards of broken glass appeared on the asphalt. No need to look further. This was the place.

Brett pulled his car off the road at the widest point and switched on the hazard lights. What if they found the cats seriously injured, or dead? The carrier could have been crushed. At best, they'd been without food and water for almost twenty-four hours. What would he tell Amanda if… *Oh, Lord, please let me find them alive.*

"Now, will you promise to stay here in the car, Amanda? I need you to take care of Sam. I'll just be a couple of minutes. Promise?"

Amanda nodded.

Brett walked back several hundred feet to where the skid marks started. This must be where the truck hit the SUV and the rear door sprang open. "Thumper! Noe-Noe! Where are you?" He looked over the side of the embankment and then crossed the road to check the other side. Would he even be able to see the carrier through all the weeds down there? Probably not. He'd have to crawl down the embankment. "Thumper! Can you hear me? Here, kitty, kitty!"

No sign of the carrier.

Rocks covered the edge of the steep embankment and thick shrubs and weeds blocked his view of the area directly below the road. Getting down over the rocks would be a trick. Even if he could climb down and find the cats, he couldn't hoist the carrier back up the embankment with his bandaged hand. He had to wait for Jack. He walked back to the rental van.

Just short of an hour later, Jack's green pick-up pulled behind Brett's rental vehicle. Jack and his dog, Chance, hurried toward Brett's car. "We got here as fast as we could. Any luck?" He waved to Amanda and tipped an open box filled with a bottle of water, a can of cat food and a plate toward Brett's open window. A revolver peeked out from under a paper plate. Jack moved the paper plate, covering the revolver, an answer to Brett's unspoken request on the phone, not wanting Amanda to hear.

Brett waved his bandaged hand. "I couldn't go down the embankment. It's too steep. Thanks for coming." He stepped out of the SUV, and opened the door on Sam's carrier. They walked to the edge of the road.

Jack set the box down a ways from the vehicle and tucked the gun into his waistband. He pulled his shirt over his jeans. "I'll take care of things, if…" He climbed down the rocky embankment. Chance and Sam, hopping from rock to rock, followed him down.

"Be careful," Brett called. *Hope he's got that gun on safety. God forbid he has to use it.*

Nimble Jack scrambled to the bottom of the embankment. He jumped the last several feet and walked through the orchard, swishing aside the long grass.

He hadn't gotten far when he called. "I've got it. It's here, in the weeds."

"Are they alive?" Brett's stomach knotted. He hurried back along the road until he was parallel with Jack. *Please, please, let them be alive.*

Brett turned at the sound of the car door slamming.

Amanda rushed down the road toward him.

He put up his hand, wanting to keep her back, wanting to keep her from hearing Jack's answer, if the worst of his fears were realized. "No. Amanda, go back!"

Amanda ran on, until she was beside him. "Did he find them, Daddy Brett? Are they okay?"

Brett put his hand on her shoulder and squeezed, his heart pounding. "Jack! Are they alive?"

"They're not here." Jack turned and looked up, his face pale. "The carrier is here and the door's open. It's empty…"

Jack returned to the top of the bank. He shook his head, his heart wrenching. "There's not a sign of them anywhere. They musta wandered off somewhere. I'll take the two dogs back down. They can follow the trail. That's what Search and Rescue dogs are trained to do."

He stooped beside Amanda and stroked her hair. "Uncle Jack is going to find your kitties, honey. Now, don't you worry." He gave her a hug.

Amanda ducked her head. "Okay."

Brett nodded. "Amanda and I will wait here in the car. Kimberlee called from the hospital. If you're not back in an hour, I'll need to go back to town and pick up the girls and take them home. Good luck."

With Thumper's blanket stuffed into his backpack, and the other supplies, Jack climbed back down the ridge with the two Golden Retrievers.

Chance darted ahead, her golden fur flying. Exuberant barks broke the morning stillness.

"Come on back, girl," Jack called. *Can't expect too much from her, yet. She's still a puppy. She's gotta learn the business. Lucky for her, she's from champion stock and Sam's a good teacher.*

Chance scuttled back, hopping from side to side as Sam sniffed the cat's blanket and the weeds surrounding the crumpled carrier.

Jack shoved the blanket into Chance's face. He gave the hand signal, "Okay, kids. Search!"

Sam took off in a blur, heading north, with Chance three paces behind.

"Sam! Chance! Slow down. I can't run as fast as you."

Sam stopped and sat until Jack caught up to him. Chance danced, tongue lolling, and tail a-wag. "Okay, kids, I know you're anxious. Let's go." He gave Chance's head a pat. "Show me what you've learned, girl. This isn't a game. It's for real. Find the kitties and make Daddy proud." Jack whistled to the dogs. "Search!"

The dogs took off through the orchard below the levee road.

For the next hour, Jack stumbled along behind, tripping over clumps of plowed dirt and weeds. If anyone could find those cats, Sam could. Sam kept up a steady pace, padding through the orchard. From time to time, two sets of paw prints were visible in the soft dirt. Jack grinned. He was on the right trail and from the paw prints, neither cat was limping. They were together and must be in relatively good condition.

Jack trudged through the orchard, keeping the dogs in sight. Wouldn't Amanda's face light up when he brought Thumper home? He imagined the scene. 'Here ya go, honey,' he'd say. 'Uncle Jack brought your kitties home.' Jack smiled. Yes, he'd be Amanda's hero, alright.

He wiped his brow. *How far did those darn cats go, anyway?* He checked his watch. Brett must have left for town by now. They'd walked several miles already and still the dogs surged ahead.

The sun grew warmer. He stopped and pulled a bottle of water from his backpack, drank and tramped on, following the wandering trail, now angling away from the levee road.

Their trek ended at a newly-paved country road. Sam and Chance stopped, searched back and forth, sniffing and rummaging around the weeds beside the road. They'd lost the scent.

"What's the trouble, Sam?" Jack glanced up and down the narrow road. "They musta' walked down the road, but which way?" Jack pulled Thumper's blanket from his backpack and showed it to the dogs. "Here ya go. Get another good sniff. Find the kitties."

Sam whined and paced both sides of the road for several hundred feet, then came back to Jack and lay at his feet. He put his head on his paws.

Chance stood nearby panting, her tail wagging. She lay down beside Sam.

Jack's heart took a tumble. *Don't neither one know which way they went.* "I know how ya feel, Sam. I'm disappointed, too." Failure hurts, even when you're a dog.

"Don't worry, kids. It's okay. I understand." He stroked Sam's head and then gave Chance a pat. "No one's blaming ya. Let's go back now. You've done enough."

Guess he wouldn't be Amanda's hero tonight after all. His heart felt like a lead anchor as they retraced their steps through the orchard. Brett had always come to his rescue. Oh, how he'd hoped to return the favor this time—to be the one to give back.

Even the dogs sensed failure, with their tails drooping and heads down. They'd done their best. No dog could find a scent in all that new road oil. But, how was he going to tell Brett?

The cats were still alive. The dogs had tracked them to the road. Hawks did ride the air currents in that area, hunting small rodents, rabbits, or perhaps a slightly overweight black and white cat and his companion. That was something to worry about.

Fortunately, the cats weren't hurt in the crash and wandered off somewhere to die. Sam would have found their bodies—or some sign of them. He'd trailed the cats a good two miles straight to the road. They were both in good shape to get this far.

In a worst case scenario, maybe when they got to the road, they were hit by a car and scooped away by the animal control people. Sadly, Brett might never know exactly what happened to Thumper and his little friend.

"No," Jack shook his head. Thumper wasn't dead. "I'd feel it if he was dead." Thumper was one smart cat. Hadn't he and his ancestors been part of the lodge for over twenty-five years? Thumper would have figured out which way to go on the road. He'd go north because home was north. And, there'd be a day when he'd see him again. Jack was sure of it.

Brett glanced at his watch. It had been over an hour since Jack left with the dogs. He and Amanda had to leave. Kimberlee and Dorian were waiting.

Back at the hospital, he did his best to clarify the situation to Kimberlee and Dorian. He explained how the cats had been left behind and their carrier broken open.

"But Brett…what about—?" Kimberlee protested.

With Amanda at his side, he cast her a warning glance. "Jack and the dogs are following their trail, even as we speak."

"How is Sam?"

"Now, Dorian, don't worry about him. He's just fine. I saw him this morning. Jack will probably be waiting at home with the cats before we get there. You know, Sam has dozens of successful rescues under his collar. He'll track them down."

"I'm not worried. I'm just anxious to get home and see Sam."

The drive home in the rental car was relatively silent. With Amanda in the back seat, the adults could not verbalize their concerns about the accident.

Brett pulled into the driveway. He helped Kimberlee and Dorian into the house. "You gals sit down and rest. I'll make some coffee and unload the car. Jack should be here any minute with the animals. Amanda, stay here with mommy, in case she needs you to fetch something."

"Do you think Sam's going to be alright out there? Are you sure he wasn't hurt?" Dorian eased her arm onto the edge of the sofa, adjusting her sling. She leaned back against the cushions.

"I told you, Dorian, he's fine. He's doing his Rescue doggy thing. He'll be your hero when he finds the cats. Relax."

Brett propped pillows behind Kimberlee and left the girls with coffee in hand. He hustled back, carrying the last two suitcases when someone knocked on the door.

"It's Jack! See? He's here already. Didn't I tell you?" He hurried to the door. Wouldn't Amanda and Kimberlee be pleased? They'd been through a lot over the past twenty-four hours, were bruised and battered, to be sure, but safe at home. Now, with the cats back, they'd put the accident behind them. In a few days, it would all be forgotten.

He opened the door, a smile crinkling the side of his mouth. "Jack!"

Jack shook his head ever so slightly. "Hey, Brett."

Brett's smile evaporated. Jack hadn't found the cats. What could they tell Amanda?

"Uncle Jack!" Amanda ran to the front door. "Did you find my kitties?" She gazed around the porch and out toward the car. "Where are they? Are they still in the car?"

Jack looked over her head toward Kimberlee, lying on the sofa.

She turned her head and put her hands over her eyes for just a second. "Amanda, sweetie, come here. Mama needs you."

Brett glanced between Jack and Kimberlee.

Sam pushed through the door past Jack's legs and headed straight to Dorian. He wiggled as she stroked his head. "Sam! Here you are. Are you okay?" She rubbed his ears and pulled his head up to her chest. "I'm so happy to see you. I've been so worried." Tears sparkled in her eyes.

Chance followed Jack across the room to the rocking chair and lay beside her master.

Jack held out an inviting hand. "Come here, Amanda. Sit on Uncle Jack's lap."

Kimberlee gave Amanda's hand a squeeze and turned her toward Jack. "Go on."

Amanda shuffled across the room. She crawled into Jack's lap and ducked her head onto his shoulder. "Where are my kitties, Uncle Jack? You said you'd bring my kitties home."

Jack leaned back and closed his eyes.

Brett's heart wrenched. Amanda's heart would break when she heard the news. *Give him the right words, Lord.* His throat tightened. He swallowed a lump in his throat. *Remember. We're all safe. That's the important thing. They're just cats.* But, it wasn't true. Thumper was gone and the place where he lived in Brett's heart left an empty hole and *just cats* or not, it hurt.

Jack ran his hand over his face, opened his eyes and looked down at Amanda. "Do ya remember the story of the three little kittens what lost their mittens?" He stroked the curls off her forehead.

She nodded. "Mama reads the story sometimes."

Jack locked eyes with Brett. "Maybe a little help, here?"

Brett stooped beside the rocking chair and took Amanda's hand. "Uncle Jack and Sam searched for Thumper and Noe-Noe for a long time, sweetheart. Chance helped too, but they couldn't find them. Your kitties are lost, like those kittens that lost their mittens. But, we'll keep looking, okay?"

Amanda's eyes sparkled with tears and then she smiled. "I'm not going to cry, Daddy Brett. Mama says the three little kittens found their mittens. We'll find Thumper. When I say my prayers tonight, I'll ask God to help them find their way home."

Chapter Five

igh in the late afternoon sky, the sun beat down on their backs. Just ahead, the cats came to a country road.

He looked left and right. Not a car in sight. It would be easier walking on the road, than through fields overrun with weeds and stickers. They stepped onto the pavement. Good. Warm enough to feel good on tired feet, but not too hot to burn. "We'll follow this road for a while. There's no traffic and it must lead somewhere. It's headed the right direction. I think *home* must be just up ahead a little ways."

The cats traipsed along the pavement for about a half mile.

"Excuse me for bringing this up again, Angel, but I've asked several times and you haven't answered. Why won't you tell me where we came from and about my *persons?* I can't remember anything before the accident. I don't even know my name. Isn't it about time you answered my questions? What is my name?"

Angel stopped and sat in the middle of the road. "I know it must be hard for you, dear, but there are reasons why I can't tell you. I can't explain, but, you'll just have to trust me. In time, you'll remember everything. In the meantime, I'll be here to take care of you. Isn't that enough? Can you do that? Just trust me for a while? Please?"

He stared at her golden head. She had closed her eyes and lifted her chin, as though she was at prayer. She looked so serene and lovely, he couldn't find it in his heart to argue. "I…I guess so, but I don't understand. Are you ready to go on now?"

"My paws hurt." Angel licked her foot. "I'm so tired. Can we stop soon?"

He scanned the terrain. Off to the right at the end of a winding driveway, a small ranch house was visible through the apple trees.

"Maybe we can find water at that house." His stomach rumbled. *And food.* How long had it been since they last ate? His macho plan of leading her home had long since been replaced by *fear of failure* and the need for food and water.

Angel rubbed against his shoulder. "Whatever you think, dear. I'm sure you know best."

They trotted down the driveway. He put up his nose and sniffed. "This way. I smell food." Around the house they scurried, following the delightful scent of kitty kibble. There! Not ten feet away. A bowl of cat food on the porch! He pranced toward the steps, his mouth tingling and saliva dripping down his chin. "Someone's breakfast. I'm sure he wouldn't mind sharing it with us."

"I'm sure *she* wouldn't mind sharing with us. After you, my love—" Angel shoved the pink bowl with the name *Rosie* on the side toward him.

The tantalizing aroma of chicken gizzards and fish entrails drifted up from the bowl. He dove into the kibble, swallowing whole mouthfuls of crunchy morsels, without stopping to chew. *Rmm...rum...* He glanced up.

Angel lay nearby, her front paws tucked delicately under her breast, her svelte tail wrapped around her toes.

I'm such a pig. She's hungry too. He backed away from the bowl, turned and leaned over the fishpond. His ears warmed. "Please, Angel, you should eat something. I've had enough." He lapped at the water. Thank goodness she couldn't see his face.

"Thank you, dear." Angel nibbled delicately at the kibble.

A chilling snarl came from the direction of the house. "What are you doing here? Who are you?"

He lifted his head. Drops of water dribbled down his chin. The biggest Siamese he'd ever seen hunkered on the top porch step. *Busted!*

He swallowed a knot in his throat, taking a measure of the threat.

Was this Rosie? She looked way too mean to charm and way too big to fight.

The large Siamese oozed down the steps, her dark ears lowered, heading straight for Angel and the food dish. Her sapphire eyes snapped a warning. Dark smudges streaked her cream-colored forehead like arrows of death pointed toward her sharp teeth.

He bounded across the yard, ears flat, tail bristled like a bottle brush, head cocked to the side. He stopped several feet from the Siamese. "Leave her alone. It's my fault. If it's trouble you're looking for, trouble's my middle name." *At least it's as good as any.*

Well, here it was, even sooner than he expected. Nameless, homeless and practically friendless, he'd have to fight for the first meal they came across. If this was any indication of how hard it would be to find their way home, they were in a real patch of *dog doo-doo*. In his weakened condition, the Siamese would likely beat him to a pulp, but he'd give it his best shot. He wasn't about to let Angel down after she'd taken such good care of him. *Grr-wow-wow-wow!* "Bring it on, lady…"

He pulled up short when Angel stepped in front of him, her head lowered. "Rosie? May I call you Rosie? I'm sorry we ate your breakfast. We're in trouble, you see. We're lost and hungry. We saw your food dish and hoped you wouldn't mind sharing. There's plenty left for you. You wouldn't turn away two hungry travelers, would you?"

Angel flopped on the ground and rolled, presenting her unguarded tummy to her potential killer…or benefactor…as time would tell.

Now, wasn't that just like a female? Just when he was about to beat the Siamese to a pulp with one eye shut and one paw tied behind his back, Angel had to go all *Gandhi* on him and offer a peace treaty.

The big Siamese sat and stroked her beige chest with an oversized pink tongue. "There, there, my dear, when you put it that way, of course I'd never turn away a fellow cat in need. Lost, you say? That's harsh. You poor things! What happened?" She leaned forward and licked her dark front paw. Wasn't she the epitome of a female? Hard as nails and ready to kill one second and a jelly-donut the next.

Angel's proffered tummy of friendship had been accepted—terms of surrender proposed and peace declared. Angel had turned a potential enemy into an ally.

His fur slipped back into place on his back. His puffed up tail hairs relaxed and his heartbeat slowed. "We got left behind when our *persons'* car got *smooshed* in an accident. We're going home. You wouldn't have any idea which way is home, would you?"

"Depends. Where do you live?" The cat's big blue eyes slid shut, and then opened.

"Well, that's the problem. I whacked my head and I don't quite remember which way… Oh!" As hard as he'd tried to ignore the truth, it stuck out like a blister on a bunny's butt.

Reality check! He had no idea where home was. Angel must have known the truth, but she'd let him lead her north all day, knowing quite well he didn't have a clue where he was going. She'd been *handling* him, humoring the guy with the conked noggin.

He turned and glared at Angel. "You knew. All day, you knew we were lost. Why—?"

"Yes, dear. I knew. It was important for you to feel in control. You see, it didn't really matter *which* way we went today. Finding food and water was the goal. And you're so clever, you found this lovely place. We've had a splendid dinner and we've made a wonderful friend. Everything will be okay now, won't it, Rosie?"

Rosie scratched the side of her ear. "Sure, kid. Anything you say. If I can help, just say the word. What do you need?"

"Let's see." Angel glanced at him, her gold eyes wide. "Dear, about tonight…perhaps we should find a place to…*umm*…sleep?"

"*Uh*…yeah…right. Any thoughts about where we could sleep, Rosie?"

Rosie jerked her head toward a battered pick-up truck parked under an apple tree. "Over there. It gets cold here at night. How about under that tarp? You can sleep in the truck tonight. I'll share my breakfast with you in the morning."

"Thanks, Rosie." He jumped into the pick-up. "Come on up, Angel." His voice sounded muffled from under the tarp. "It's warm and dry. And, there are blankets up here."

Angel leaped up. "This looks nice. Thanks, Rosie." She stretched and then crawled beneath the tarpaulin where she kneaded the blankets into a soft nest.

Snug and warm with Angel curled next to him, he slept. He woke once, only for a moment. The truck rocked gently from side to side. *Must be the wind.*

In the morning, they'd have to move on. But, which way should they go? How would they ever get home? They would have to make some decisions in the morning. It was too much to think about just now. He yawned and drifted back to sleep.

Chapter Six

Awakened by the squawk of a blue jay, he peeked out from under the tarp where he and Angel had passed the night. The tasty morsel hopped on a low branch overhead. *Hungry! Bird! Breakfast.* He blinked to clear the sleep from his eyes, flexed his muscles and did a quick equation to determine wind velocity versus thrust between the truck and the blue jay…too far…no point in exerting himself. The thing was too skinny to feed two of them anyway, and—

"Daddy, come quick. Look what I found." A cherub-faced little girl leaned over the bed of the pick-up truck bed.

His heart did a flip-flop. *Who…?* He looked up. Where were Rosie's apple trees? Where was her back porch? Instead, a canopy of tall pine trees towered over the truck. Pine needles lay scattered across the tarpaulin. *Uh-oh, Toto. I don't think we're in Kansas anymore.*

The child's brownish-blonde ponytail fell over one shoulder. Her eyes twinkled when she smiled. "Daddy. Look. There are kitties here." She reached and touched his head.

Ouch. Her touch reminded him of the knock on his head. *Meow!*

The tarp jiggled and from deep inside, a faint hiss. Angel!

The little girl jerked her hand back, the tips of her fingers streaked with blood. "Daddy, his head is bleeding." She wiped her crimson fingers on her blue jeans.

A shadow moved across the truck bed. "Stand back, Cindy. If he's hurt, he might bite. Here, let me see."

He peered into the daddy's face, taking measure of the man. Was he cruel? Would the man feed them? His tummy rumbled again.

Calloused hands reached into the truck and caressed his head, but the man's touch assured kindness as he felt the wound.

The daddy's cheeks were dark with several days' stubble. Worry lines crossed his forehead, though his firm jaw suggested courage and determination. Smile lines framed his lips. He looked like an okay guy. *I think we could be friends.*

"That gash on his head must hurt, but I don't think it needs stitches. We'll take the cat inside and clean him up. Look. Here's another one." The daddy reached down and pulled Angel out from under the tarp into the truck bed.

She hissed and struggled, then twisted her body into a helpless fetal position.

Don't be afraid, Angel, he's okay.

"Here, kitty. You're going to be alright." The daddy stroked her head.

Angel nuzzled into his red-checkered shirt. "There now, that's better. We won't hurt you." He set her in Cindy's outstretched arms. "That's right, hold her real gentle and talk nice. She's scared. I'll bring in the tom."

"*Shush, shush,* now kitty," Cindy murmured. "Are you hungry? I'll get you some milk."

Milk! The magic word. The promise of milk sounded like a fine idea. A purr rattled in Angel's throat.

The daddy's feet scrunched through the gravel on their way to the cabin. Cindy followed with Angel.

As they stepped onto the porch, a dull thrumming sound rumbled beyond the nearby shed. Despite an attempt to sniff for a clue to the identity of the sound, the only discernible scent was damp pine needles and trees.

"Now, lie here on this blanket by the wood stove." Cindy smoothed the corners of the blanket and patted Angel's head. "Here's a bowl of water if you're thirsty."

After a good breakfast, a warm cloth and ointment applied to the top of his head, a nap seemed an excellent idea.

With Angel snuggled by his side, he studied the layout of the log cabin. The main living room extended into a small kitchen at one end. Two doors led off the living room on the far wall. A kitchen table and chairs and a small sofa faced the potbelly stove. "Well, this is nice." He curled his tail around his front feet. "A little rest in the woods for a few days will be good for us. Give me time to get my strength back, but we can't stay long. We've got to get home. It can't be far from here, do you think? Angel? Angel? Are you awake?"

Angel lay with her eyes closed and her nose turned up. "*Ahhh…* This feels so good. Milk and a warm fire. *Persons* to feed us—that's what I'm used to. Don't talk about *leaving*. I don't want to think about it today. I'll think about it tomorrow." She twitched her whiskers. "Oh. Did you see that movie? It's a line from one of my favorites. *Gone With the Wind.*"

"Gone with the what?" His eyes flew open. "How can you expect me to remember lines from a movie when I don't even remember my own name? Listen, they're talking about us. This can't be good."

"Where do you suppose they came from?" Cindy sat at the kitchen table, a sketch pad and colored pencils strewn across the tablecloth.

Her daddy lay stretched out on the sofa, reading the newspaper. "I'll bet they crawled into the truck when we stopped at the grocery store, on the way home from Grandma's house last night. They must have come from somewhere down near the store." He flipped the page of his newspaper.

"Can we keep them, Daddy?"

"What? The cats? I'm sure someone will want their pets back. You can take care of them the rest of the day. When we go back into town tomorrow, we'll take them to the animal shelter."

There were those cursed words a cat never wants to hear! The *AS words*. They'd have to make their get-away during the night if they were to avoid the animal shelter.

Cindy gazed toward the blanket. A little pout clouded her face, and then a smile. "Isn't he pretty? He looks like he's dressed up in a wedding suit—all black with a white bib and big white feet. He has such a cute little white mustache. What shall we name them, Daddy? We have to call them something while they're here."

It wasn't polite to eavesdrop, even if *inferior humans* didn't realize that cats understand every word they say. Cats had kept that particular secret for a thousand years, and he wasn't about to let the proverbial cat out of the bag…so to speak.

Angel sighed softly in her sleep. With her paws curled delicately into her breast, her eyes shut tight and her little nose pointed up, she looked as though she might be saying a prayer.

"Look, Daddy. She looks just like a little angel. I'll call her Angel."

Now, wasn't that strange? Was it just a coincidence that Cindy should name her Angel? The exact name she'd said he should call her? Prickle bumps scattered across his back.

"I'll call the boy cat…oh, I can't think of a good name," Cindy said. "I'll just call him *Black Cat* until I think of something better."

Black Cat… Black Cat… The prickle bumps raced across his cheeks. Something about the name sounded familiar, though he supposed all *person*s might refer to him that way, since he was black… almost all black. But, it was more than that. The chill bumps spread from his cheeks down across his chest. It felt as though at some point in his life, *Black Cat* might have been his *real* name. It was odd that Cindy had guessed Angel's name, but how could she have guessed both their names? A coincidence? He shivered.

The daddy's voice sounded as scratchy as his cheeks with a three-day-old beard. "Run on now and straighten your room. Black Cat needs to rest. He's been hurt."

Cindy nodded. "You go back to sleep, *um*…Black Cat and…and Angel. I'll be back in a few minutes and tuck you in." She stroked both their backs and left the room.

With the warm stove, a full belly and Angel's purrs sounding like a Lilliputian lawn mower next to his head, Black Cat laid his head on his paws. Within minutes, he began to dream.

A little girl jumps from a swing and drags a stick in the dirt. "Get it, Black Cat! Snake! Snake!" I pounce. The imaginary foe is dead. I turn my back on the wretched beast and stalk down the flower-lined path, toward the house. The scent of wisteria and roses fills the air. A lady opens the front door and I dart into the house, as though I belong…

Black Cat woke with a start. Was it a dream or a memory? Who was the little girl with bouncing curls and the beautiful lady? He'd ask Angel when she woke up. Maybe after a good nap and a full belly, she'd be more inclined to tell him about his family. Or, was it something too terrible to bear? Was she still protecting him? Was that why she wouldn't tell him? He shuddered. *Don't go there…*

Chapter Seven

addy John folded his newspaper and laid it on the coffee table. He stood, crossed the room to the china cabinet and picked up a framed photograph of him, Cindy, and his ex-wife standing near a mature vineyard. How happy they were—back then.

Cindy had grown so much since that day, her head not even reaching the top wire on the grapevines in the background. Those were better days, when the vineyard his father planted grew strong and tall and produced some of the finest grapes in the valley. Back when they were still a family—before Iraq—before the fire in the vineyard. Before the divorce and Carolyn left.

With a sigh, he replaced the photograph. Best not dwell on things from the past. Things change. People change. Every day held a new challenge. *But, Lord, how much more can I take?*

When do I catch a break? John wiped his hand across his face and crossed to his desk.

The stack of envelopes hadn't shrunk since last he looked. What did he expect? Leprechauns prancing through the night, paying the bills?

He opened the top envelope. Phone bill—two months late. He shoved it back in the envelope and opened the next. Mortgage—three months behind. A red stamp across the top read *Overdue, Foreclosure Pending.*

No way could he lose the ranch his father built forty years ago. No way could he allow the bank to foreclose because of the mortgage he placed on the property after the fire. No way would he be forced off his land. But, how could he make the payments when the newly planted grapes wouldn't come to first harvest for at least another year? His secret weapon wasn't ready to spring on the world yet, either.

It was all he could do to keep food on the table and gas in the truck, selling firewood, much less meet his other financial obligations. Now, Cindy wanted him to keep a couple of cats? What a sad day when he couldn't afford to feed two little cats. Nope. They'd have to go to the animal shelter. First thing tomorrow.

His heart wrenched as he watched his daughter washing the breakfast dishes by hand since the dishwasher had broken and he couldn't afford… Just one more example of the state of affairs around here.

Cindy asked so little. She'd shouldered a good share of the housework since her mother left. Much more than a ten-year-old should have to handle, but under the circumstances, what choice did he have?

He slumped into his chair and pushed the remaining envelopes back in the drawer. They were all pretty much the same. Overdue—in arrears—collection pending. He shoved the drawer closed.

Meow! The little orange cat pawed his leg.

"Hey, Angel. What do you need?" He reached down, ran his hand down her back and up her thin tail. "What's this? A kink at the end?" He smiled.

She pushed her head into his hand.

He stroked her back again, and again, and again, and then lifted her into his lap. His smile worked its way into the crevices beside his mouth. Felt good to smile. It had been a while. He rubbed Angel's velvet soft ears. "Nice kitty. Did you get enough to eat?"

Angel tipped her head and peered into his eyes. She blinked and purred. The purr flowed through her body, vibrating into his hand and up his arm. Why did petting a cat feel so good? Something about the feel of her fur filled him with peace. He couldn't stop smiling.

An idea! He *could* bring a spot of sunshine into Cindy's life. How much could two little cats eat? Cats were good hunters, right? They'd probably pay for themselves, and keep the rodents in check around the ranch. Should have thought of it sooner.

"Hey, Cindy."

"What?" She turned from the sink. "Oh, you've got Angel."

"Yeah, I've been thinking. Why don't we call the animal shelter and let them know the cats are here. We can keep them until their owners show up. How about that?"

"Oh, Daddy!" She dried her hands on the kitchen towel and dashed to the desk, pulling out scissors, paper and colored pencils. "I'll make lost and found posters. We can put them at the little store and on the telephone poles down town. It'll be fun."

"Remember. They're just visiting until we find their owners."

She tipped her head and smiled.

Her happy face clutched at his heart. Who needed a leprechaun when his daughter's smile was worth more than a pot of gold?

"But, in the meantime, we can pretend they're ours." Cindy carried her art supplies to the table.

John stood and dropped Angel to the floor. He swallowed the lump in his throat and headed for the door. "I'm going out and feed the Emus."

Black Cat rolled toward the edge of the blanket as Angel flopped down alongside. Mountain air made him so sleepy. He closed his eyes. "What's an Emu?"

The fur across Angel's shoulders rippled in a shrug. She yawned, exposing all her sharp little teeth. "I think it's sort of like a chicken."

Cindy glanced toward the stove. "Oh, Black Cat, you're awake." She hurried over and knelt on the blanket. "Daddy's going out to feed the mean old birds. I can't go into their yard because I'm not big like Daddy. They try to bite me."

Black Cat tilted his head toward hers. He tried to pretend he was listening, concentrating on every word she uttered, when actually his thoughts were a mile away. He jerked his head back and stared dutifully into Cindy's eyes. *Pay attention. Worship and admire.* It would make her feel important.

She beamed, as expected, and prattled on. "Gilbert is sitting on Myrtle's eggs." Cindy stroked Black Cat's back. "The mama Emu lays the eggs and then she goes off and forgets all about them. The papas have to keep the eggs warm. Daddy's going to sell the baby chicks. That's how we'll earn lots of money."

Angel rolled over. "Told ya. They're chickens. I know all about chickens. We had chickens on the ranch—"

"Where? Did you say *ranch?*" Black Cat sat up straight and glared at Angel. She hadn't shared any of their past in spite of his multiple questions and she certainly hadn't ever mentioned a ranch. "Tell me about this ranch. Is that where we lived?"

"*Uh…* Don't bother me now. I'm sleepy." Angel threw her paw across her eyes and rolled on her side.

Black Cat huffed and paced across the room toward the sofa. He'd been uneasy all morning. Something didn't feel right, but he couldn't quite put a toe on it. He and Angel had found a safe haven with Cindy and Daddy, and yet, the vexing itch behind his left ear meant one of two things. Fleas, or the harbinger of trouble. Since he'd groomed every inch of his luxurious fur right after breakfast, he felt safe rejecting the possibility of a six-legged critter.

For a while, he'd thought it might be the daddy's suggestion to take them to the animal shelter, but Angel had worked her magic and now that Daddy was under her spell, his behavior was almost predictable. Apparently, *persons* were easy to manipulate, once taken over and properly trained by a competent feline, as Angel had demonstrated.

A gust of cool air whooshed as the door opened. The daddy rushed in, his face all squinched up and his chin jutting out. He threw his jacket on the sofa.

Angel glanced at him and scooted under the table.

"Something's gotten into the nests again. Gilbert's only sitting on eight eggs this morning. This is the second day in a row eggs have gone missing."

"Did something get into Gabriel's nest, too?" Cindy got up from the blanket by the stove and crossed to the sofa.

"The other four nests weren't disturbed and all the girls look fine. I didn't see a break in the fence. Fox must have climbed the wire." The daddy's cheeks looked flushed, though hard to tell if it was from frustration or the cool morning air. He lifted a .22 rifle from the gun rack by his bedroom door and took a cleaning kit from the buffet drawer. "Think I'd better sit up tonight and see if I can catch—"

Knock. Knock. Knock.

Black Cat jumped onto a kitchen chair. He scratched again at the irritating itch behind his ear. It might have been sixth sense or a premonition, but he knew… The source of the itch was just on the other side of the door.

Angel hunkered lower under the table, her orange stripes blending in a mass of gold, her fur puffed out twice its normal size. She felt it, too.

Cindy glanced at her father. Her eyes were opened wide and cheeks pale. Like Pavlov's dog, reacting to his nod, she ran to her room and closed the door. How odd, they'd all felt it. Why such a reaction to the knock of an unexpected visitor? It could be the Avon lady, or a guy selling cable subscriptions…but not likely.

Black Cat crouched, half hidden under the tablecloth, yet affording him a clear view of the front door. From his position, he had the advantage of surprise, should he be called upon to defend this new household.

Daddy eased the front door open. "Yes?"

"Are you Mr. John Goldstein?"

A hand clutching a briefcase and a bit of dark sleeve was visible just beyond the doorway. *Definitely not the Avon lady.*

"Maybe I am. Who wants to know?"

"I'm Mr. Adams, from Nevada City Mercantile Bank. May I come in for a few minutes? I came to discuss your loan."

One of John's hands held onto the doorknob, the other, knotted into a fist, lay on the jamb. He frowned and motioned the banker inside. "Make it snappy. I've got work to do." He swept the wrinkles from the faded Indian blanket on the sofa. "Have a seat."

Mr. Adams balanced on the edge of the sofa, only the smallest amount of his posterior perched on the edge as necessary, lest he fall on the floor. He gazed around the room, cleared his throat and laid his briefcase on the coffee table, then unsnapped the latch.

Black Cat oozed off the chair and ambled toward the banker. *My. My. So, I see that he doesn't want to get his bottom dirty. How can I further his discomfort?* He jumped onto the sofa and flopped down, and leaned heavily against Mr. Adams's hip. That should do it. Wouldn't it be a shame if he got cat hair on his pin-striped suit?

John brought a chair from the kitchen and sat facing the banker, perspiration pooling in the creases above his eyes. He must have guessed what was coming. He picked lint off his jeans and then looked up. "Can I get you something to drink?"

"No, but thank you." Mr. Adams pulled a stack of papers from his briefcase and laid them on the coffee table, retrieved a pair of glasses from his coat pocket and fit the wire frames over his ears. He cleared his throat again and smoothed out the papers. He looked down at Black Cat, pulled his jacket closer to his body and shifted his rump over a few inches.

Black Cat rolled to the left and leaned against Mr. Adams's hip again. His whiskers twitched ever so slightly as he gazed with feigned adoration into the banker's face.

Mr. Adams rolled his eyes and shifted on the sofa again. "Mr. Goldstein. It gives me no pleasure bringing you these papers. We've tried to contact you by letter and left messages on your phone—"

"I...I've had some business reverses and I've not been able—"

"We do understand, Mr. Goldstein, and I empathize. Things are tough on lots of folks these days, but the bank has a responsibility to our investors. Two years ago, you came to us and took out a loan to replant your vineyard after a fire. Naturally, we wanted to help you, being sympathetic to the needs of the community and all. But, you're three months behind on your loan payment. We can't allow this to continue."

"You must understand—"

Mr. Adams put up his hand. A constrained note came into his voice. "I must add, as the lien holder, we've also received a notice that you failed to pay the second installment of your county property taxes. The bank has no choice but to begin foreclosure." The air whooshed from his mouth as though he'd delivered his message without taking a breath.

John lurched to his feet, knocking his chair backwards. "You can't do that. I spoke to the bank manager about an extension. He said everything would be okay. He said he'd take it to the board and recommend an exten—"

"I'm sorry. The board denied your request, and—"

"No. *You* need to understand. My family has owned this property for forty years. I was born here. Sure, I'm behind on things. The fire… But, you can't march in here just like this and tell me you're foreclosing." John ran his hand across the top of his head.

Black Cat jumped to the floor. He exchanged glances with Angel, still hunkered beneath the table. *Wouldn't you know it?* They'd landed in a hornet's nest.

John paced the short distance between the couch and the kitchen. "All I need is a little more time, Mr. Adams. Next year, I'll be able to harvest my grapes. I invested in the Emus to tide me over until then. I've got twenty-seven eggs due to hatch in several weeks. I have buyers lined up across three states. When I sell the chicks, I can pay the back taxes and the bank. See how close I am? Can't you work with me? Just a few more weeks—"

"My good man, if it was up to me…but, sadly, it's not. Don't you see? It's not personal. It's business. We can't wait another year for your first harvest. And, I hate to use such a tired cliché, but you really can't *count your chickens before they hatch*!" A smarmy grin crinkled Mr. Adams's face, as though he was tickled at his timely pun.

Black Cat looped around the room at a dead run. He skidded to a stop beneath the table beside Angel. How could Mr. Adams make a joke at a time like this? He came to throw a man off his property and makes a stupid chicken joke? What's funny about ripping a man's life to shreds? He was a skunk in a pin-striped suit if there ever was one.

"Anything could happen between the egg and the chicken, *heh, heh*." Mr. Adams stuffed the papers back into his briefcase and stood.

John jerked his head, his pupils like pinpoints, his eyebrows drawn together. His clenched fists spoke volumes of his intentions. No wonder Angel ran under the table.

"Not personal?" The veins in John's forehead throbbed. "Just exactly what would make it personal? It's my home. I've done everything I can think of to meet my end of the bargain. Now, leave before I forget myself and do something you'll regret!" He yanked open the front door.

Mr. Adams grabbed his briefcase. "I'm sorry you feel that way, but, don't for a minute, think this is over…" He scurried out, looking back over his shoulder.

Black Cat leaped to the top of the sofa and peered out the window.

Mr. Adams jumped in his car, slammed the door and started the engine. Gravel spewed from beneath his wheels as his car barreled down the driveway. He turned onto the county road and roared out of sight. Mr. Adams was gone, but, without a doubt—he'd be back.

Chapter Eight

Not a bird twittered. Not even a hint of breeze stirred the leaves as Black Cat's gaze followed Mr. Adams down the driveway. He shivered, chilled to the bone. Mr. Adams's threat of eviction seeped through the room like a damp fog.

John slammed the front door, picked up the overturned chair and sat at the kitchen table. His shoulders slumped. He pounded one fist into the other.

Angel lowered her ears and skittered from beneath the table to the blanket beside the stove.

Black Cat hurried to her side. "Did they scare you, dear-heart?"

"Did you see the look on John's face? I thought he was going to punch the banker." She glanced wide-eyed toward John, sitting with his head in his hands.

"Any man might react the same way. He's lived here all his life. He can't lose his home without being upset, no matter whose fault it is. Where would he and Cindy go?"

"I don't understand how Mr. Adams can take away the ranch." She tapped the blanket with her golden paw.

"It's not really like—"

The door of Cindy's room inched open and she peeked out. She crept to her father and patted his hand. He looked more like the child and she, the parent, comforting him. "Don't worry, Daddy. Everything will be okay."

John slid his arm around her shoulder. He nodded, but his smile was grim and forced.

"Angel, let's get out of here. I hate seeing them so sad." Black Cat tiptoed to the front door, reached up and scratched at the handle. *Meow!*

Angel ambled toward the door, her back to the couch. "Let's stare at the door. Do you think they'll understand? Living with a properly trained *person* makes life so much easier." She sat beside Black Cat, her eyes riveted at the doorknob.

Cindy jumped up from the sofa and opened the door. "Do you guys need to go out, Black Cat? Now, don't get lost again."

Good. The child was learning fast. Too bad they wouldn't be here long enough to fully train John, but no time. They had to get home. Maybe tomorrow?

Black Cat scooted onto the porch with Angel close behind. Just outside, he stopped short and sniffed. The hair on his neck stood on end. A peculiar scent drifted through the trees and circled the porch rails. He sniffed again. "Intriguing. What is that?"

Angel tipped up her nose. "Exotic aroma, rich but evocative, with a palate-pleasing bouquet... Shall we?"

They stole across the yard, one hesitant step at a time, toward the shed. The scent grew stronger. Beyond the outbuilding, an eight-foot high chain link enclosure rose skyward, where huge long-necked creatures covered with coarse feathers milled around inside.

Black Cat crouched, muscles taunt, hair atop his neck doing the *cucaracha*. *Yikes!* These creatures couldn't be the *birds* Cindy mentioned. Birds weren't six feet tall. Birds were black or blue or light tan, preferably with red heads and...and...little.

Angel dropped to the ground, her tail bushed out like a porcupine. She shook her head. "I don't think those things are chickens."

Black Cat stared at the creatures beyond the fence. "Do ya think?"

He scanned the enclosure from left to right and then crept toward the wire. Two Emus approached the fence, emitting a deep-throated drumming sound. *Yark... Yark... Yonk... Yonk!* The mamas!

One of the six-foot tall critters danced to the fence and stuck out her long greenish blue neck. *Yark! Yark! Yark!* She turned her huge eye toward the wire, focusing a paralyzing glare at Black Cat. Her ugly face ended in a pointy beak that could easily pick out a cat's eye. Thick brown feathers covered a rotund body drooping over long skinny yellow legs. Three-toed feet ended in claws sharp enough to rip a cat to shreds. *Holy-moly! So, that's an Emu!*

In the center of the yard, several large males crouched over a pathetic pile of grass spread atop a few random sticks. Dark green eggs peeked out from under the papa Emu's feet. Was this what served as a nest?

Angel sidled closer and dropped to the ground beside Black Cat.

"John said he thought a fox stole Gilbert's eggs. How could a fox get through this fence?" Black Cat craned his neck up toward the top of the wire. "It's too high to climb."

Angel tossed her head. "My dear, sometimes it amazes me how dense the male species, be it cat or man." She stepped back a safe distance from the enclosure and licked her shoulder. "Isn't it obvious? Our thief wasn't a fox or any other four-legged creature. A human opened the gate, stole the eggs and closed the gate behind him. John has more problems than overdue bank payments and taxes." She nodded back toward the house.

Black Cat whipped his head around. "How did you reach that conclusion?" He drew his whiskers back. It was one thing for her to keep secrets about his past. Now, she had a far-fetched conspiracy theory, based on eggs missing from a nest? She was down-right exasperating! But, cute as a button.

"Think about it. John said he thought a fox had climbed the fence. That's not possible. The only way in is through the gate and it's still latched. And, yet, the eggs have vanished."

"I didn't think of that."

"Apparently, neither did John. Whereas, the appalling poultry are accustomed to a man entering the enclosure. Therefore, it had to be a man. It's not rocket science." She licked her foot and drew it over her ear, then waddled down the path toward the vineyard.

"Makes sense the way you explain it." Black Cat paused to sniff a shrub. He drew in a breath and bared his teeth. Some animal had left its scent on the leaves. He scanned left and right. Whatever had passed this way was long gone. They strolled on, circling the far side of the Emu enclosure.

"Oh! You mentioned that John could lose the ranch." Angel stopped and turned back. "How can the bank take away land?"

"It's just called *losing the ranch*. If John can't make his loan payments, they'll make him and Cindy move away."

Angel's eyes darkened, as her pupils grew wide. "How do you know about these things? I thought you had amnesia?"

Black Cat shrugged. Good question. Amnesia must affect the mind in different ways. Like knowing how to walk and talk and which way is north and about finances, but not being able to remember your own name. Frustrating at best, and frightening. Did one ever recover from amnesia and remember everything? Would he ever remember his family and former life? Why wouldn't Angel answer any of his questions about his past?

Yark! Yark! Yonk! The mama Emus stalked toward the fence again. He backed away, caution being the better part of valor when dealing with a six-foot-tall bird. "Let's leave the beasties and go for a walk."

Angel trailed beside him, headed toward the vineyard. "We should try and come up with a plan to help John."

"What did you have in mind?" Black Cat glanced toward Angel.

"I've been thinking. There must be a reason we came here. I think we're supposed to help John save the ranch. Perhaps that's part of my assignment."

"Assignment? That's just crazy talk. We don't have time to get involved in John's problems. We have to get home."

Angel pointed her nose toward the tallest pine tree and closed her eyes. "You know what? I don't see it that way at all. I'm not stepping one paw off this ranch until I'm sure John and Cindy are alright."

Now, what in the world could she mean by *assignment*? She made it sound like a secret mission. Black Cat rolled his eyes. Big-hearted intentions were always a stumbling block in the face of logic. "We'll give it a few days and see what happens. Then we have to leave. That's it, my final word on the subject."

"Who died and made you King?" Angel huffed down the path.

"Just sayin'…" He lowered his ears and hurried after her, stepping carefully over the stickers.

The trail beyond the bird enclosure moved past a group of trees. Blue jays, robins and brown sparrows with red heads twittered and hopped through cedars, pines, and oak trees—behaving like *real birds*, unlike John's creatures in the enclosure.

Just past the trees, immature grape vines came into view. Rows of wires crawled along the ground covered by young plants—shades of green and yellow against a backdrop of tall pine trees in the distance. At the end of each row, stacks of blackened stumps reached jagged fingers skyward.

"Look there. That's all that's left of John's father's vineyard." Angel stopped to stare.

"Spooky looking, isn't it?"

At the edge of the closest row of grapes, a ground squirrel popped from a hole and streaked toward the tree line. "Squirrel! Catch it!" Black Cat raced past the wires, ducked between the poles and the vines, hopped over rocks and through thickets of grass. He skidded to a stop as the squirrel plunged into its hole. He flopped onto the grass, breathing hard, his sides heaving.

Angel sauntered up to him. "I hope you did that for the exercise. They never run like that unless there's a hole near enough to jump into. Back on the ranch, we couldn't ever—"

"There! You said it again. Is that where we lived? On a ranch?"

Angel ducked her head. "*Um…* Do you remember a ranch?" She tipped her head and swished her tail.

"I remember a little girl and a pretty lady and a house with purple flowers on the porch. At least, I think I remember, or maybe I dreamed it. Was it real? The house on the ranch?"

She turned away, avoiding his eyes.

"Why won't you tell me, Angel? Tell me my name and where we come from."

She shook her head. "I can't. I made a promise. Please don't ask me. If I tell…" She touched him with her paw and licked the top of his head.

He had so many questions and she had all the answers. A lump the size of coal lodged in his throat. He swallowed and then ducked his head. "Why shouldn't you tell? It doesn't make sense. Are my *persons* dead? Is that it? We can't ever go home again, can we?"

She shook her head. "Perhaps, one day we can. I wasn't told. But, it's really nice here." She looked up at the trees and then toward the vineyard. "Would it be so bad, living here with Cindy and John?"

He sighed. He couldn't *make* her tell her secrets. He had to trust her. "It is nice, but how long will it last? If John loses the ranch and has to move away, I doubt he could take us with him."

She shrugged. "There, see? You agree. It's in our own best interest to help John find a way to keep the ranch."

Wasn't that just like feminine logic? If circumstances get in the way of your goal, change the goal. "Just how are we supposed to do that? Hello! We're cats!"

"I'm not sure right now. I have a feeling we're exactly where we're supposed to be. If I'm right, we will find a way… Listen." She cocked her head. "I hear water. There's a creek back in those trees. Race you…"

She took off running.

He raced along behind. What a pretty picture they made—a splash of gold, and a black and white streak sprinting through the green grass. Insects and birds fell silent as they bounded across the field. The chase ended at a creek rushing down the hillside. Water, fed from some mountain stream high in the Sierras raced downhill, tumbling over moss-covered rocks. Shrubs bursting with yellow flowers hung over the riverbank, their branches trailing into the water. From time to time, a petal would tumble off and float down river.

Black Cat's gaze followed the petal until it disappeared into a semicircle of rocks along the embankment. There, the petal gently swirled and came to rest against a dozen other petals, lining the water's edge, like foam on a root beer soda. Tiny fish flitted through these gentle pools, just beneath the surface, sometimes stirring the sparkling sand.

What a lovely sight. Angel was right. If they couldn't go home again, there wasn't a nicer place to live than here on the ranch with John and Cindy. But, didn't that all depend on finding a way to help John save the ranch?

Black Cat leaned down and touched the tranquil water. It rippled beneath his paw in a widening circle until it reached a school of baby fish. At the first ripple's touch, they skittered into the rock crevices, and sent the petals careening into the current, where they tumbled and disappeared beneath the rushing water. "Angel, come and see the baby fishes."

Angel sat straight and tall, her front paws together, her head held high, like an Egyptian goddess. "They're called minnows. When they grow up, our *persons* catch them and eat them. They're quite tasty, once you get around the little bones." She gazed across the stream, like she was remembering a special moment. "Our *persons* slather them with butter and sprinkle salt and spices on top. Then they toss them on a barbeque grill until their outer skin is all golden brown and crispy."

Black Cat could almost hear them sizzle. His mouth watered. The creek bed faded and another scene flashed into his mind.

There was the house with the purple flowers over the porch. The house sat close to the shore of a crystal lake… Boats with colored sails were tied at the dock… Across the lawn, a row of cabins. There! The little girl with bouncing curls and the beautiful lady sat at a table on a cobblestoned patio. A tall blond man moved pieces of fish sputtering on a black barbecue grill. A black and white cat…

Black Cat threw up his head. "I remember a barbecue. It must have been my family…and a lake and boats. I remember! I think I was—"

The sound of feet crashing through the bushes interrupted his memory. *Someone's out there.*

"Here, duck behind this log. Someone's coming." Black Cat crouched beside Angel.

Just beyond the bushes—the faint outline of two people. Tree branches obscured their faces, but their voices could just be heard over the sound of the water as they came closer to where the cats were hidden.

"So, let me get this straight. Just exactly how far should I push him? Things could get ugly." A shock of dark blond hair was visible through the leaves.

Black Cat peeked over the log and strained to hear the muted voices as they moved further away.

"Do whatever it takes. The bank…already…foreclosure. Put more pressure… I need him to see things my way before… With the laws… take five or six months…evict him. I don't want to wait…"

"Trust me…come to his senses. I've got a few ideas…" The blond man laughed.

"Do whatever you…careful…hurt Cindy."

Black Cat glanced at Angel. *They know Cindy's name?* John's troubles were bigger than they had guessed. Why these people were in such a hurry to get control of a non-producing vineyard and a dozen Emus that hadn't yet hatched a chick was a puzzle. Was there something else of value on the land? These two weren't fooling around, and somehow it involved Cindy. How could they think about leaving if she was in danger?

"Come on. Let's follow them and find out what they're up to." Black Cat hopped over the log.

Angel followed on little cat feet behind the mysterious figures.

The tall blond man shuffled along the riverbank, his hands stuffed in his pockets.

The shorter one wore a black sweatshirt with a red star on the back, the hood pulled up. They stopped beside the river and poked a stick in the sandy soil.

The blond man picked up a handful from the riverbank and rubbed it in his palms.

"What is he doing?" Angel whispered.

"Search me. They're looking at the dirt. It doesn't make any sense."

The hooded figure pinched some of the dirt and held it up to the light. "Color. It's all through this area. Didn't I tell you?"

"Is that a good sign?"

The shorter figure's head lowered. The hood obscured the scoundrel's face. "It doesn't concern you. Your job is to bring him around. I don't care how you do it. There's an extra $1000 for you if he's out of here by the end of the month." The two turned back toward the road.

The blond man nodded. "Trust me. He's as good as gone."

Angel and Black Cat sat beneath the bushes long after the couple were out of sight.

"Poor John! Bad enough the bank is after him, now these two."

Angel shook her head. "The least we can do is keep an eye on Cindy and keep her safe. We should get back. We've been gone quite a while. She'll be worried. I'll race you back. Just try and catch me!" She ran, leaving him staring after her retreating figure.

She had more gumption than he thought. By the time he reached the front porch, she was waiting beside the door.

He panted. *I'm getting all out of shape. Perhaps I should lose a pound.* Yes, indeed. He'd start a diet. First thing tomorrow, right after breakfast.

Chapter Nine

Moving slowly up the steps onto the porch, Black Cat gasped for breath, his lungs thumping from the exertion. It was a good thing to let her win once in a while. Bolstered her ego.

Angel sat beside the door, delicately licking her shoulder. She wasn't even breathing hard.

The screen door squeaked open. "Oh! There you are." Cindy shook her finger. "Bad kitties! Where have you been? I thought you were lost again. Wait until you see who came to visit. Come in and say hello to my mama."

Black Cat took a deep breath, his sides still heaving. Cindy's mama? He didn't know she had a mama. No one had mentioned her before. Where had she been all this time? He stepped inside.

Cindy closed the front door.

A lady with short-cropped blonde hair, cut square across her ears, sat on the sofa. She took a drag from her cigarette, tipped up her face and blew smoke toward the ceiling. She sat back, a nervous smile touching the corner of her mouth. Her gaze flit across the room and settled on the family picture on the mantle. She shook her head as though the memory of days gone by was too troubling to remember. She glanced back at Cindy when she spoke.

"Daddy says no one should smoke in the house. It isn't good for you, Mama."

The mama squashed her cigarette into a cup on the coffee table. "Okay. I'll put it out." She fidgeted with her lighter, and then laid it beside the coffee cup.

"This is Angel and Black Cat." Cindy gathered Angel in her arms. "They were in the back of Daddy's truck when we got home from Grandma's house. We're taking care of them until we find their home." Cindy bent down and kissed the top of Angel's head. "I made some lost and found posters and we're going to put them at the grocery store." Cindy flipped Angel onto her shoulder and patted her back. She sat down beside her mother. "You can pet her if you want. She's real gentle."

Angel moved her head away from Cindy's long brown ponytail, turned and looked into the mama's face.

Black Cat's gaze fixed on Cindy's mother. She had blue eyes like Cindy, but different. Not kind, like John's. More intense, calculating, maybe even hard. In an instant, he took a measure of the woman. *I don't like her*. No particular reason. Just didn't. He noticed how Angel's ears tipped back like when something smells bad. She felt the same way about the mama. How odd.

"She's very pretty." The words were right but her tone had a cold insincere quality. Cindy's mama touched Angel's head.

Angel jerked back, as though the mama's fingers had shocked her head.

"I hope you aren't going to feel bad when you find her owner." The mama pulled out a lipstick and mirror from her purse, applied a coat of bright red lipstick and then dropped the items back into her handbag. She smacked her lips and reached for Angel. "It's not a good idea to get attached to strays."

Strays? What kind of a remark was that? How could she call them *strays*? They weren't strays. They had homes and *persons*. He just didn't know who or where they were at the moment.

The smile melted from Cindy's face. Making lost and found posters probably sounded like a good idea—in the beginning. It hadn't occurred to her how she would feel when she found their home and had to give them up.

Her face brightened. "Maybe nobody will call. Daddy says I can keep them if nobody comes." Her ponytail bounced as she emphasized each word.

The mama ran her hands over Angel's back and around her tummy. "Did you know that she's going to have kittens? Your daddy can't afford to keep a passel of cats around here. Maybe it would be best if you took them to the pound before she has kittens and before you get attached to them."

The breakfast tuna in Black Cat's stomach did a summersault. Kittens? Kittens? Guess that was one more thing Angel *forgot* to mention. His heart flipped over. He moved toward the door, his gaze locked on Angel's face.

She turned away from his gaze.

She's embarrassed. She won't even meet my eyes. He walked slowly to the door. *Please. Someone open the door and let me out before I toss a hairball.*

Why Angel kept so many secrets was beyond understanding—and now this! She might have mentioned she was expecting right from the start. It was somewhat pertinent, wasn't it? He lowered his ears and faced the door, his back toward Angel, his heart feeling like a wad of aluminum foil in a campfire.

The mama dropped Angel on the sofa, walked over and opened the door. "Scat!"

Black Cat raced across the yard toward the Emu enclosure.

One of the Emus rushed to the edge of the fence when he ran past. She craned her neck and jerked her head. *Yark! Yark, Yark!*

Black Cat ignored the Emu, turned on his heel and streaked back across the yard toward a pile of firewood stacked near the end of the driveway. Across the front, a sign read *Firewood:$200 Cord.*

Another of John's efforts to put food on the table, but it was doubtful he sold enough wood to meet all his obligations. For a man who tried so hard, he sure had bad luck. Nothing seemed to go right for the guy. Nothing much was going right for Black Cat these days, either.

He and John were two of a kind. The weight in his heart felt as heavy as an iron doorstop.

Here he sat, in the middle of nowhere, didn't know his name or where he came from. Angel was the only link to his past, however grim it might be, and she held the truth locked tight in her heart and denied him access. Now, she had betrayed him. He should run away, that's what he should do. Just march right down the driveway, turn left and keep going. What was Angel to him anyway?

She said she was his bride. Was it the truth? Was he the father of her kittens? Maybe. Maybe not. She hadn't even told him her real name. He'd assumed they had a past together, but for all he knew, she might have been out for a walk one day and wandered past his broken carrier. Maybe she saw him lying in the ditch, felt a *pity-pang* and figured he'd be her missionary project this week. Maybe she was just a pregnant hussy looking for someone to take responsibility for her kittens. How easy it was to string him along with a bunch of evasions and lies and he'd never know the difference in his condition.

Ever since the day they met, he had come to believe they had a special connection. No! More than a connection. He loved her and thought she felt the same. Betrayed! Betrayed!

The ache in his heart swelled. His stomach lurched, like when he had a hairball and couldn't get it up. His body convulsed again and again, until with the last retch, up came breakfast. Nothing left inside now, but an empty stomach and a dark and foreboding sorrow. He felt lost in a deep fog with no way back. If a cat could cry, he would have drowned in his own tears.

The rumble of the mama's car forced him out of his lethargy and back to reality as she cruised down the driveway and turned left onto the country road. He was glad she was gone. She was a terrible woman. She thought John should send them to the pound! She even called them strays. The old witch! Strays? The word made his blood boil.

He sat still, listening to the wind whistling through the pines, mentally probing the pain in his heart, pushing it from side to side.

Like a sore tooth, thinking the next time you touch it, maybe it won't hurt as much. Finding with each touch, the pain is still there, pulsing and throbbing, yet you're unable to stop poking it with your tongue.

Angel! The breeze whispered her name as it swished through the pines. *Angel!* A bird chirped her name from the treetop. *Angel.* Somewhere down the road, a chainsaw hummed, repeating her name over and over until the humming stopped and there was stillness.

He sighed. So, Angel was in the family way. The question niggled at him again. Was he the father? Why would she conceal something as important as that? He hung his head.

Angel! His insides were all squishy and cold and his heart felt like a block of ice in a 1920's icebox.

"Black Cat! Black Cat, oh, where are you?" Cindy called from the front porch. She sounded like she'd been crying.

I don't care. Black Cat hunkered behind the woodpile. He didn't want to see anyone, not even Cindy. From now on, he was on his own. He tried to remember something about his past life. Something! Anything! He had to remember. How else could he go home?

He squinted his eyes, thinking of what he remembered so far.

A car and people screaming…

A lovely lady and purple flowers over the porch…

A little girl with brown bouncing curls and a daddy sitting on a patio…

Wait! There was a lake and a motel next door and a barbecue!

As he visualized the lawn between the house and the motel, he saw a man throwing a Frisbee to a dog with flowing golden hair. Boats tied up at the dock. Where was Angel? Why wasn't she in any of the things he remembered? If he was the kittens' father, he and Angel must have *some* history. After all, you don't make kittens through the mail!

Angel. Beautiful Angel with eyes the color of mustard and stripes the color of marigolds. The phrase echoed through his mind. *…eyes the color of mustard…*

His heart surged with love. What was so bad about Angel having kittens, anyway? So what if he wasn't their real father. Even if he was their *step-father*, wouldn't that be okay? Five or six little Angels running around calling him *Daddy Black Cat* wouldn't be so bad, would it?

He was willing to forgive and forget. She'd wronged him, but he would be the bigger cat and welcome her back with open paws. She didn't even need to apologize for lying—sort of lying. Maybe all females were like that, all persnickety and shy about private, personal things. Maybe she just wasn't the sharing type. Deal with it.

The warmth of forgiveness swept through his body and tender feelings toward Angel tickled his toes. How magnanimous and generous he would be, considering the extent of Angel's indiscretion. He raced toward the house. He stood against the door and scratched. *Meow!* Wouldn't Angel be thrilled that he had forgiven her? *Let me in. I forgive you, Angel. I'm not mad anymore!*

Cindy opened the door, tears streaming down her face. "Where's my daddy? I want my Daddy!"

What's going on? Tears?

Cindy clutched Black Cat to her chest and collapsed on the sofa, shaking with sobs. She wiped the back of her sleeve across her cheeks. "Oh, Black Cat. Where have you been? I was so scared. I called and called. Mama took Angel away. I thought she took you, too. She's taking Angel to the pound!"

Chapter Ten

ound? Angel? The words rattled around in his head like marbles in a teacup. Black Cat's head swam, worse than when he woke from the accident. It didn't make sense. He gazed into Cindy's tear-streaked face. She lay curled in a ball, tears trickling down her cheeks. The room swayed, all blurry and out of focus. His head hurt. He needed Angel. Where was she? The last time he saw her, he was sitting at the door…

Kittens! His head cleared. He remembered now. The mama said Angel was going to have kittens and he'd gone away mad. He stared at the cabin door. A chill traveled across the back of his neck and paraded up and down his spine. *What did Cindy say about the pound? The mama took Angel…?* Impossible! Cats don't come back from the pound. Never!

How could it be true? This kind of thing only happened in movies or books. Penny novel drivel, not in real life, like now.

He raced from the couch to the door and clawed the handle. How could he have treated his precious love that way? Thinking she had betrayed *him*! If he'd known the mama would take Angel away, he would never have been so rude. He was going to forgive her! Now she was gone. How would she ever forgive him for not being there when she needed him? It was well over an hour since the mama drove away. If only he'd known Angel was in the car, he would have… What could he have done?

When will I learn to treasure each moment? It could be your last. Now, it's too late.

Black Cat slunk back to the sofa. *It's my fault.* If he'd stayed in the cabin, maybe he could have done something. He snuggled next to Cindy's side and laid his head on his paws. He pulled his tail over his face. *Just make the world go away.* Angel was gone and he'd never see her again. How he wished he could cry, like Cindy.

The door opened and John came in, the scent of outdoors, all woodsy and piney, clinging to his red, checkered shirt. He stamped his feet and bits of sawdust tumbled off his boots. "What's the matter, honey?" He sat on the sofa and drew Cindy onto his lap. He pulled a handkerchief from his shirt pocket and wiped her wet cheeks. "What is it? Tell me."

"Mama came." Cindy's head slumped onto his shoulder. "She said Angel was going to have kittens and you couldn't afford to keep them, *a passel*, so she took her to the pound!"

John's jaw tightened. "That blasted, meddling woman. I didn't know she was in town or I wouldn't have left you home alone. I'm so sorry, Cindy." He patted her shoulder. "Remember? We were only going to keep the cats until we found their family. She'll be okay. And, it's not exactly the pound. It's the animal shelter. They'll take good care of her. They'll find her a good home for her and her babies, too. Don't worry." He turned his face away from Cindy. Drops of perspiration sprinkled his forehead. His cheeks reddened.

Black Cat buried his face deeper under his tail. John didn't believe a word he said about what would happen to Angel. He knew that when a pregnant cat ends up at the animal shelter, it's doubtful they'd keep her around long enough for her kittens to be born and then have five or six more mouths to feed and homes to locate.

Cindy's mother, Carolyn, might have thought she was protecting Cindy from feeling bad in the future, but had she considered for one minute that her decision was Angel's death warrant? Maybe she had, and she just didn't care.

"Run and wash your face, Cindy. What's done is done. Your mama thought she was doing the right thing, though I do wish she'd mind her own business."

Cindy sniffed and wiped her nose on her sleeve.

Black Cat followed her to the bathroom and sat on the rug staring up at her reflection in the mirror. She washed her face and then went to her room and closed the door.

John sat in the rocking chair, rubbing his calloused hand over the stubble on his cheeks. His shoulders slumped. He leaned back in his chair and closed his eyes.

Black Cat crossed the room and crouched by the potbelly stove. His head swam in a misty fog. *Eyes the color of mustard.* He might never see those beautiful eyes again. How could he go on without her? Angel was his bridge between the past and present, his lifeline, so to speak. Wasn't Life a cruel master? Just when he realized how much he loved her, she was lost to him. He was going to be a father…maybe… and now he would never know if he had sons or daughters, if they were well, or even alive, for that matter, if the animal shelter decided…

Black Cat closed his eyes, willing his mind to wander back—back into the past. In his mind's eye, the sound of flying hooves thundered by. Like seeing through a giant kaleidoscope, the colors of brown, red, black and tan blurred together. A herd of wild horses raced across the plains beyond stone fences crossing fields of green. A horse ranch! Was it the ranch Angel had mentioned? Maybe that's where they met.

He squinted his eyes tight, forcing his mind to remember. There. A shadow at first, and then he saw a fountain beneath a sprawling oak tree, with water splashing over the edge and…a little orange striped cat half-hidden in the grass. Her eyes flicked from side to side and her ears lay flattened to her head as she eyed the little birds dancing through the spray. Angel!

Was it possible? His chest swelled with overwhelming joy one minute and then crashing despair the next. His memory was coming back! Clearly now, he remembered a house by the lake, and a ranch with horses. And he remembered Angel…now that it was too late and she was…gone. His head dropped to his paws.

Angry voices across the room interrupted his melancholy. He opened his eyes. There stood the hated mama at the front door, shouting at John. *Did she come back to get me, too?* Black Cat dashed under the table and crouched between the chair legs. His fur snapped to attention on the back of his neck. *She took my Angel! Should I kill her now or listen to what she says and kill her later?* He slunk a little closer. *Now's good.* He clenched his teeth. Hate saliva filled his mouth and drooled from his jowls.

The mama stood with her feet apart and her head jutted forward. Her balled fists trembled and her eyes bulged from her sockets. She looked as if she wanted to take John apart with her bare hands. And she looked like she could do it. *Maybe I better hear what she has to say.*

John glared at the mama. A muscle in his cheek twitched. "How could you dare come back here after what you've done?" He jabbed his finger into her chest. "What right do you have taking Cindy's cat to the pound without consulting me?"

A blotch of red crept up her cheeks. She unclenched her fists. "I'm her mother. That's what gives me the right. I don't want my child going hungry so you can feed a mess of stray cats." The mama's voice trembled. Maybe she wasn't as confident as she tried to appear. A strand of blonde hair tumbled across her forehead, over her eyes. She brushed it off her face.

"Let me put your mind at ease, Carolyn. Cindy's not in any danger of going hungry." John's voice softened, almost more frightening than when he was shouting. His mouth twisted into a sneer. "Your sudden concern is touching. Where was all this concern last year when you left us for…that man?"

The mama's cheeks paled. "You know why I left. I couldn't take it anymore. The fire. The debt. Scratching to pay the bills and keep food on the table." She put her hands over her face. "He offered me a way out and I took it." Her chin dropped onto her chest, her eyes downcast. "I was wrong. I know it now. I should never have left Cindy. I'm not proud of myself." She sighed. "I've left Charlie. Go ahead and say *I told you so.* Now, I want my little girl back." She lifted her head and looked into John's eyes.

His face turned bright red. He took a step toward her and raised his hand. "You abandoned her a year ago, and *now* you want her? Well, too bad. The court gave me full custody and I don't plan to give her up now. And, as for my financial problems, don't worry. It's none of your concern."

"John. Let me take her." The mama's voice softened. She laid her hand on his arm. "It's not right, her being alone all day while you're out cutting wood and tending the vineyard. She must be lonely and it's not safe. Something terrible could happen. I'm scared. Let me take her, at least for the rest of the summer until school starts."

John jerked his arm away and turned his back. "I think you better go. You've done enough harm today. You've already broken her heart when you took her cat. You're not getting Cindy this summer or ever!"

He took her arm and propelled her toward the door, reached over and turned the knob.

"You haven't heard the last of this." The mama knotted her hands into fists, again, her voice rose to a screech. "I'll go to court if I have to. I'll see you rot in jail. I'll…" She stepped out onto the front porch, took a deep breath. Her chest heaved. She lowered her head. Her voice was so quiet now, it was hard to hear. "Tell Cindy I didn't mean to hurt her. The cat's not at the pound. When I stopped for gas and opened the door, she got away from me." The mama grabbed the doorknob on her car.

"Which gas station?" John stepped off the porch onto the pine covered pathway.

Cindy's mama slammed the car door. Her car careened down the driveway, pitching gravel as it raced toward the road.

Black Cat's head went up. His bleak world brightened for a moment and then went dark again as the full extent of her words struck home. Angel wasn't at the pound. She'd escaped. She was out there somewhere, lost and alone…hungry and pregnant. He wasn't sure which was worse. Captured at the pound or free and lost. At least at the animal shelter, she would have had food and shelter until…

The mama's engine roared as her car sped away down the country road.

John went to Cindy's bedroom and knocked. "Sweetheart? You can come out now. She's gone. I'm sorry you had to hear all that. It's rotten, isn't it, having your mom and dad quarrel. I know it's hard for you to understand, but we never learned how to disagree without quarreling. Mama wants you to live with her and I want you to live with me. We'll just have to work it out, won't we?"

The bedroom door cracked open. "I don't want to live with Mama and Charlie. He doesn't like me. He's mean."

"I know."

Cindy rushed out and flung her arms around John's waist.

"Your mom said she isn't with Charlie any more. Next time you see her, he won't be there." John pushed the hair off her forehead. "Listen. Did you hear Mama say Angel got away? She's not at the shelter. She's somewhere near a gas station."

Cindy's head reared back. A smile lit up her face.

"I'll call the Chevron station and AM-PM. They're the only two stations between here and town. Maybe someone has seen her. When we go into town tomorrow, we can stop at the gas stations and talk to the fellows. Maybe she's still hanging around."

Cindy gave a little yelp. "Can you call and ask? Now?"

John went to the phone and dialed. "Hey Bruce? John Goldstein here. Was my ex-wife at your station a while ago? Yellow Honda, four-door? She was? Listen. She had a little orange cat in the car with her. She said it jumped out when she opened the door. Would you keep an eye out for the cat? If you see her, try to catch her and give me a call, will you? Thanks. Appreciate it."

John grinned at Cindy. "Let's go right now. We'll stop by the station and look around. Maybe we can find her."

Within fifteen minutes, Cindy and her daddy left to search for Angel.

Black Cat paced the floor for several hours until they returned— without Angel.

Before Cindy went to sleep that night, she knelt by the bed and said her prayers.

"Dear Jesus. Thank You for my daddy and the Emus and for Black Cat and thank You for letting Angel get away from Mama. But, Jesus, now I need to ask a big favor because Angel got lost. You know what she looks like, all gold and sort of stripy and she has a kink in her tail. Please find her and bring her home. I know You can find her because Daddy says You can see everywhere, even through the trees. If You'd do that, Jesus, I'd be ever so good and mind Daddy. Oh, I almost forgot. Bless Mama too, because somebody should love her and I'm mad at her right now, so maybe You can be her friend. Okay? That's all I need. Amen."

Black Cat snuggled by her pillow, and added a few prayers of his own to the Father of all living creatures.

Cindy rubbed Black Cat's head. "You'll see. Everything will be alright now. Jesus will protect Angel and keep her safe. She'll be home soon."

Black Cat stared into her eyes and blinked. *I hope you're right, but how can you be so sure?*

"It's true. I know, because Daddy told me so."

Black Cat turned to look out the window. A blue jay hopped onto the bird feeder hanging on the limb just beyond the window. It pecked at the seeds, then kicked off and disappeared. The empty feeder swayed from side to side.

Was there a chance he'd see Angel again one day? Would the Father of all living creatures care about a little lost cat? Would He hear Cindy's prayers? Black Cat nestled closer. The faith of a child is a beautiful thing.

Chapter Eleven

ohn dialed the animal shelter. Wouldn't hurt to tell them Angel was lost, in case someone picked her up. He turned his back to Cindy's room. Best not let Cindy overhear the call. She was already upset enough.

"Hello? Nevada County Animal Shelter."

"*Um.* Yes. This is John Goldstein. I called before and reported finding a couple of cats? A cream-colored tabby and a black and white tom?"

"Yes, Mr. Goldstein. I've got the report right here. It says you're keeping them at your house in case someone calls? Is everything alright?"

"Well, not exactly." John scratched his head and looked around the cabin.

Black Cat, lying on the back of the sofa, peered out the window. Perhaps he thought Angel would come waltzing home on her own. The house already felt empty without her.

"*Uhh.* Under circumstances that I'd rather not discuss, the tabby female—her name is Angel, by the way. She's…*uh*…lost. Could you give me a call in case she's turned in?" Just what would he do if someone found her and turned her in? He'd already told Cindy they couldn't keep the cats.

"Sure thing, Mr. Goldstein. I'll make a note. We'll be on *Angel-alert* and let you know if we find her."

"She has orange stripes and goldish colored eyes." John lowered his voice and glanced again toward Cindy's bedroom door.

"Yes, I know. You gave us her description yesterday."

"Okay, thanks. Good-bye."

Guess that was all he could do. The guys at the service station might spot Angel, or someone might see the posters Cindy made. They were doing everything possible to bring Angel back. What if Angel's owner saw the posters? But, wasn't that the point; to find her real home? They'd deal with that, if and when… *Do I want the cats or don't I?* It was all so mixed up in his head.

The cats were supposed to cheer up Cindy. Instead, she barely had time to wrap her head around the idea that they could stay for a while, than Carolyn waltzed in to spoil it. Just like two years ago. He'd no sooner come home after eighteen months in Iraq and some careless camper burned down forty acres of timber, including three homes and their vineyard.

Right after the fire, Carolyn announced she needed to *find herself* and took off with the propane delivery man. He had hoped she'd *find herself* in another state and stay there, but here she was again, making trouble.

How many nights had Cindy cried herself to sleep, thinking her mother didn't love her? Hadn't he about gone out of his mind dealing with a grieving child, the divorce, making ends meet, building the Emu enclosure and buying the birds with the last bit of borrowed funds? He was so close now—with the eggs due to hatch in a few weeks. Just a little longer. If he could keep the bank off his back and keep Carolyn off his neck. He was due for a break. Surely someone would spot the little cat and call—

Knock. Knock. Knock.

Lord! Now what?

Black Cat brushed past John's leg and beat him to the door. *Probably thinks it's someone bringing Angel back. Hope he's right, for Cindy's sake…*

He opened the door while Black Cat danced between his feet. "Yes?"

A tall man with a thin mustache and piercing blue eyes stood on the porch. He had a mole just below his lower lip with a hair standing straight up in the middle. *Like on the hill in Iraq where we planted the American flag.* The man grinned and rubbed the side of his nose, his eyes drifting from side to side. He had something on his mind, for sure, but he wasn't bringing Angel back.

"Mr. Goldstein? I'm your neighbor, Chuck Skimmer. I live over yonder." He jerked his thumb over his left shoulder. "Can I talk to you for a minute?"

It was hard not to stare at the mole because the hair swayed when he spoke. John opened the door wider. He gestured toward the sofa. "What can I do for you?"

Mr. Skimmer ambled in, sat and folded his hands on his knee. A few scraggly blond hairs stuck out from his shirt collar above the top button. "I have a cousin who works at the bank down town and…*um*… well, I hope you're not offended, but he sort of mentioned that you're having some financial problems."

Great. Now, I'm the talk of the town. First the bank manager, and now Mr. Scammer…Skimmer.

Mr. Skimmer cleared his throat. "He said…my cousin that is, said the bank has started foreclosure on your property." Mr. Skimmer rubbed the back of his neck.

The vein alongside John's neck throbbed. He drew in a breath and crossed his arms over his chest. "Mr. Skimmer—"

"Now, don't get mad, I'm not trying to embarrass you, Mr. Goldstein." He put up his hand. "I'm actually here to do you a favor. You see, your land touches mine and I thought you might be willing to sell me your property before the bank takes over."

"I don't have any intention of selling my land. I'll figure—"

"Sure! I know you'll do your best, but sometimes things don't work out like we plan. I just wanted you to know that I'm willing to help you out, see. This is what I'm willing to offer." Mr. Skimmer's hands trembled. "You sign a quit-claim. I'll take over your note for the balance you owe the bank and give you…say, $25,000 cash for a grubstake somewhere else. I'll even pay your back taxes—"

"Don't say another word." John stood and shoved his chair up to the table. *Who does he think he is, coming in here, offering to take my land off my hands?* "Get out of here before I bust you in the nose!" John lurched toward the sofa, his fist clenched. "I'd be an idiot to even consider your offer. This ranch is worth several million dollars. You think I'd let you have it for a measly $25,000 and the back taxes?" His cheeks stung. His chest heaved.

Cindy peeked out her bedroom door, and then eased the door shut, with barely a sound.

Mr. Skimmer jumped up from the sofa and backed away. He put up his hands, and bumped into the door. His words rushed out in a jumble. "If the bank forecloses, like they're planning, the sheriff's gonna throw you and the kid off the land and you'll have nothing in your pocket. If you don't go quiet, like, they'll toss you in jail. What happens to your kid then, *huh*?"

Mr. Skimmer raised his fist toward John's face. "You'll come around to my way 'a thinkin' in time." His mouth twisted to one side, a dribble of saliva at the corner caught the light. "Don't wait too long." Mr. Skimmer smirked, all noble-like, as if he'd offered a nickel to a panhandler. "When them papers get filed, it'll be too late. Give me a call when you come to your senses. Here's my number." He shoved a Motel 6 card with his phone number scribbled on the back, into John's hand, then reached back, groping for the doorknob.

"Here! Let me help." John tossed the card onto the floor, reached past Mr. Skimmer, turned the knob and pulled open the door.

Mr. Skimmer kept his gaze locked on John's face as he backed onto the porch.

John slammed the door.

Cindy crept from her room, her cheeks the color of tissue paper.

John turned toward her, his face still stinging. "I…I need a few minutes, sweetheart. I'll be right back." *Gotta get control of myself. Don't want her to see me like this.*

Cindy stood stock-still, her eyes wide, a stricken look on her face. John hurried into the bathroom and closed the door.

Black Cat hunched down and stared at the bathroom door. His head moved back toward Cindy. *Poor thing.* She looked like someone hit her. *Could things get any worse? First Angel disappears, and now this.*

Cindy ran to Black Cat and buried her face in his neck. She carried him to the sofa, her tears soaking his fur. It was going to take a complete *lick-bath* to get all the salt off his fur, but it was a small price to pay if it would comfort her. He set to purring, his rumble shaking his whole body. *Brrummm… Hrrummm… Come on, Cindy. Don't cry. I'm here.* His efforts seemed to work, as Cindy's sobs quieted.

John stepped out of the bathroom, calmer now, and knelt down by the sofa. "There, now, Cindy. Don't let that man upset you. No one's going to take our land. We'll find a way out of this, even if I have to rob a bank—"

Cindy's head jerked up, tears streaking her face. She wiped her cheeks. Her lips trembled. "Oh, Daddy, you wouldn't do that, would you? They'd put you in jail for sure, and I'd be all alone." She flung herself back into his arms, squashing Black Cat between their bodies, her sobs shaking her thin frame as though her heart would break.

"There, there. I was kidding. Don't take on so. Now, run in and wash your face. I'll figure something out." He patted her shoulder, shoved Black Cat onto the floor and sent Cindy to her room. Parents were like that. They'd say most anything to make a kid feel better. What he needed was to pull a rabbit out of his hat. And he didn't own a hat…much less a rabbit.

Things were quiet the rest of the day. John didn't share any of his ideas of how he planned to get out of this fix and Cindy was wise enough not to ask questions. She played with her dolls and read a book. In the afternoon, she plugged in a Disney movie.

Black Cat paced the floor, rushing to the window whenever a truck rumbled by on the road. The problems they faced swam through his head. *Impending foreclosure! Mr. Skimmer! Angel! Cindy!* Black Cat jumped at every noise, as nervous as a cat in a butcher shop on Pork Chop Tuesday. What could he do? His paws were tied.

In the late afternoon, the phone rang. Cindy looked up from the TV, and then clicked the mute button. Actors mouthing soundless words played across the screen.

Black Cat lifted his head and perked up his ears. His heart quickened. Maybe it was someone from the service station, calling about Angel? Or from the animal shelter?

John picked up the phone. *Are your carpets dirty? Too busy to clean? Call Stan, the Carpet Man.* John slammed down the phone. *False alarm.*

John fed the Emus while Cindy played.

The sun crawled across the sky and finally dropped behind the trees.

Time dragged on until 9:00 P.M.

"Run on in and get ready for bed, Cindy. Maybe tomorrow, we'll hear some news about Angel. We'll drive down by the AM-PM in the morning and look around again, okay?"

She nodded. "Don't forget to say your prayers, Daddy. You pray for Angel, too."

"I'll do that, baby girl. Good night."

Cindy kissed him, went to her room, and called from the door. "Good night, Black Cat."

He curled up on the blanket by the stove with a heavy heart. What a terrible day. Mr. Skimmer's visit replayed through his thoughts. The man was a real snake in the grass, trying to take advantage of John's situation. Why did he look so familiar? Could he have been one of the men they overheard down by the river? The rushing water had muffled their voices and the underbrush was too thick to see either of their faces clearly. But showing up today and his ridiculous offer—it was possible.

At last, Black Cat slept…caught up in his dreams… *The prairie. A two-story house with twin gables. Red barns. Horses behind white painted paddocks. Angel, by the fountain. Eyes the color of mustard and stripes the color of marigolds—his Angel.* He shivered. *Angel. Where are you? A bearded man walks across the barn yard. There. An old woman…*

Meow!

I hear her. She's calling me. His front leg twitched. *Fog drifts around the big house. Angel! She needs me. I have to go to her.* His legs jerk. *Dark shadows close overhead. A cold wind whistles across the yard.*

Meow!

I have to help her. Legs won't move.

Meow! Louder now. He stirred, lifted his head. So real. Not like a dream at all. He blinked. Awake now…

Meow!

He shook his head to clear the sleep from his eyes. *That sounds like a cat.* He went to the front door, tilted his head and listened. Could he dare hope?

Meow!

There it was again. *There's definitely a cat out there.* His heart thumped against his chest. He howled and leaped at the doorknob. *John. Come quick. Open the door.*

"What is it, Black Cat?" John pulled earphones from his ears. He clicked off the infomercial on his computer and came to the door. "Do you need to go outside?"

Couldn't he hear it? What was it with *persons*? Deaf as a cement light pole!

John opened the door. "What on earth?"

Chapter Twelve

A damp and dirty figure tumbled through the door and collapsed at John's feet.

"Angel?"

Stickers and mud tangled her matted coat. Her body shook with cold. Her eyes—huge. John picked her up and hurried toward the kitchen. "Cindy. Wake up and come in here!" He grabbed a kitchen towel, wet it in the sink and wiped Angel's face, then wrapped her in Cindy's sweater and laid her on her blanket. He shoved a log into the pot belly stove. The coals licked around the log and soon the fire roared.

Black Cat rushed to the blanket and groomed the top of Angel's head and shoulders, the parts hardest for her to reach. "Oh, Angel! You're back!"

Cindy stumbled out of her bedroom, rubbing her eyes. "What's wrong?"

"Nothing's wrong, sweetheart. For once, something is right. Look who came home."

"Angel?" Cindy gathered her up, sweater and all, and hugged her to her chest, then lay down beside her on the blanket.

Within a few minutes, Angel stopped shaking, started to purr and went to work to scrub the mud off her coat.

Maybe God had heard Cindy's prayer, after all. If He could bring Angel back, maybe John's other problems would work out, too "Tell me everything. What happened?" Black Cat gave Angel's head another lick.

"Give me a few minutes, dear. I just want to lie here and get warm.

I'm so glad to be home."

Home? Wasn't that an interesting choice of words? They weren't anywhere near home. *Home* was still out there. Somewhere. The sooner they got back on the road, the better. Of course, she meant she was glad to be *back* where it was safe and warm.

John ran his hands over Angel's head. "She's almost dry. I'll bet if you warm a little milk and soak some bread in it, she'd really like that. She must be starved."

Black Cat lay close beside Angel while she drank the warmed milk. When the bowl was as clean and dry as if it had been washed and dried with a paper towel, she licked her whiskers and curled up on the blanket.

"You'd best get back to bed, sweetheart." John smiled at Cindy. "You can see Angel in the morning."

Cindy kissed Angel's ears and stroked Black Cat's head. "Good night, Angel. Good night, Black Cat. I love you. I'll see you in the morning." She jumped up and skipped into her room. Now, wasn't that the best thing ever? Her prayers were answered.

But, there was another little girl…the child in his dreams. Maybe she was praying for her lost cats to return, too. His heart lurched. He and Angel should leave before Cindy became even more attached. Look how upset she was when Angel was missing. How sad will she feel when they both moved on? How could they leave now and break her heart? This wasn't turning out the way he'd planned at all.

Before long, Angel's fur felt soft and dry. She folded her front feet under her breast, closed her eyes and turned up her nose in the strange little way he had come to love.

"Are you ready to talk about what happened?"

She stirred and then turned toward him. She blinked. The light glinted off her golden eyes. "Well, you know part of it." She gazed into his eyes.

He shivered with joy. *She loves me. She truly does. I can see it in her eyes.*

"The mama grabbed me and tossed me in the back of the car. I stood on the seat, but all the windows were rolled up tight. She used her cell phone and got directions to the animal shelter. On the way, she stopped for gas. I pretended to be asleep. When she opened the door, I jumped out and took off running. No way was she going to catch me." Angel's whiskers curved back across her cheeks. Cindy would have called it a smile, but cats can't smile. It was more like a demonstration of the pure wickedness seeping out as she told her story.

Black Cat twitched his whiskers and dropped his head. *You go, girl!*

Knowing Angel's temperament, even with as little time as they'd spent together, somehow it didn't surprise him that she'd managed to outwit the mama. "Go on. Then what happened? How did you find your way back to the ranch?"

"I headed down the road, the way we'd come, until dark. I passed a house where there was a shed with the door open. I figured it would be safer to sleep inside. When I woke up, someone had closed the door and I was trapped inside all day and last night. This morning, a man opened the door.

"As I ran out of the yard, their big dog barreled out of the garage and took off after me. I tried to climb a tree, but he grabbed me by the neck and shook me like a chew toy. I thought my brains would fall out my ears. I thought, 'This is it!'"

"Angel! You could have been killed." Black Cat's heart thumped. *I should've been there. I'd have saved you.*

"I thought I'd never see you again. I kicked and squirmed and my claws caught the side of the dog's face. The man by the shed hollered and the dog dropped me." She took a deep breath, sighed, and laid her head down on the blanket. Maybe she was too tired to finish her story.

"I jumped over the fence and walked the rest of the day. Once, a car almost hit me. That's when I jumped off the road and fell in the mud. I walked and walked. Then I heard an Emu off in the distance and I followed the sound. That's about it. Here I am."

"I'm so glad you're…back." He swallowed a lump in his throat. Words couldn't express what was in his heart. Even his ears tingled with the sheer joy of her safe return. He licked her shoulder and dampened it with kitty kisses. "I…I'm so sorry I walked out on you, when the mama said you were…expecting. I'm so ashamed. Are you okay?"

"I'm fine. The…*um*…they're fine too. I should have told you. I was waiting for the right time." She dropped her head. "I'd rather not talk about it right now, if you don't mind." She closed her eyes and lay still for a moment. "What's new here since I've been gone? Has John decided what to do with us?"

"John and Cindy put up posters, but no one's called. Carolyn, the mama, came back. She and John quarreled. I doubt she'll be back for a while. Oh, yes. The guy from next door heard about John's trouble. He offered John peanuts for the ranch. John threw him out!"

"Not surprised." Angel stood, turned in a circle and flopped on her opposite side.

"John wants to hold on to the ranch, but he might not have a choice. He could go to jail if they come to repossess and he won't leave. I don't know how we can help, short of waving a magic wand."

Angel put her head on the blanket. "I'm afraid I'm flat out of magic wands. Good night, my dear. Sweet dreams."

"Oh, I didn't tell you…"

Too late. She was asleep. He wanted to tell her that he had dreamed about the ranch and he remembered her. A chill chased up and down his spine. Should he wake her and tell her, or let her sleep? If he'd learned anything over the past few days, it was not to put off important things until tomorrow. *Who knows how many tomorrows we have?*

Chapter Thirteen

For several days after bringing Kimberlee home from the hospital, Brett kept busy doing the laundry, cooking, and taking care of Amanda. He came to understand why gals complained of dishpan hands. Even with a dishwasher, he felt as if he'd scrubbed enough pots and pans and crystal glasses to put permanent wrinkles in his fingers.

He scraped the bottom of another blackened pot—the result of getting distracted by his e-mail when he should have been watching the pot. Brett leaned over the sink and peered through the kitchen window. Across the lawn, a red plastic Frisbee with a dog attached whizzed past the glass. The dog flopped to the grass, golden tail waving, then raced back to Jack's side and dropped the Frisbee at his feet.

Jack stroked his pet, picked up the Frisbee and gave it another heave toward the dock.

Chance barreled across the lawn, levitated and snatched the Frisbee before it hit the ground.

Brett grinned. *Dogs!* They were good at chasing Frisbees, but not so good at finding lost cats. His mouth pulled down. *That's not fair to the dogs.* Sam had found his share of lost boy scouts and Chance was still a pup learning her trade.

"Brett, honey? Is there any iced tea left?"

Kimberlee.

"Yes, dear, in a minute. I'm almost finished with this—*mumble mumble*—kettle." He gave the pot a final scratch with the scrubber and filled it with water. *Maybe it would help if it soaks for a month or two.*

Brett filled two glasses with iced tea and carried them to the porch. "Here you are, sweetheart. Do you need anything else?"

"Not right now. Thanks. Can you sit with me a while?" Kimberlee set her glass on the table and scooted back against the pillows in the lawn swing.

Brett sat beside her and made wet circles with this glass on the arm of the swing. He gazed intently at the sailboats drifting past the dock.

"I've been thinking," she said, reaching for her glass. "Maybe you and Jack should go back down to the levee road and put up some *Lost Cat* signs. We'll never find Thumper if we don't let the community know where they were lost."

"I've left messages with the animal shelters in Cloverdale and Healdsburg. They'll let us know if someone turns them in."

"Someone could be feeding them and they wouldn't know where they belonged. You know how cats are. They'll linger wherever there's food. Maybe we should put some ads in the local papers, as well."

"I can do that. Do you have a picture of Thumper? I'll run off some posters and pin them up on the telephone poles along that levee road. It might work." His smile looked positive, but his heart—not so much. If Sam couldn't find the cats, he had doubts they were going to be found.

Kimberlee tucked a stray curl behind her ear. "If they're alive, they're probably together. I wish I had a picture of Noe-Noe." Tears sprang to her eyes. She turned and put her arms around Brett's neck. "Why did this happen? Thumper…" The tears trickled down her cheeks.

Brett's jaw tightened. "I'm sure they're alive, honey. Only question is, where are they?" *As if I haven't beaten myself up about this enough already.* "It's my fault. I was so worried about you and Amanda, I didn't even notice they were gone. I've kicked myself a hundred times."

Kimberlee jerked back, her eyes wide. "Oh, no, honey. No one's blaming you. You were hurt too. I shouldn't have said that. I'm sorry."

Brett sighed. "I'm surprised Amanda is taking it so well. I thought she'd be heartbroken. Jack's even more upset, poor guy. He was so sure Sam and Chance could find them. He really cares about Thumper."

"It's no surprise. Thumper was his cat until last year when I…

well…shall we say…appropriated him. I hope they found a home where someone will love them as much as we did…do."

Brett nodded. "Thumper's easy to love, no doubt about that. You call the newspapers. I'll put together some posters. Amanda and I can drive down tomorrow and tack them up along the levee road." It was worth a try. It would make Kimberlee happy and Amanda would feel like she was doing something. "We'll keep looking. Something might turn up."

Chapter Fourteen

Several weeks later, just as the sun peeked over the pine trees, John sat on the front porch swing, sipping coffee and paying bills. The faintest scent of apple trees blended with the spicy scent of pines. Just yesterday, he'd noted little green apples had replaced the blossoms on the trees down by the vineyard. Summer was waning and fall was in the air.

John signed the last check, thanks to a loan from Barney, his friend from Sacramento. Enough to catch up two mortgage payments and the overdue phone bill. He peeled off stamps and pounded them onto the envelopes. A frown crossed his face. The unpaid tax bill still languished in the pile. *Before I can say Nelly's Ghost, it'll be time for next month's mortgage payment.* With Barney's loan he could beat the wolf from the door, but he could almost hear the beast howling in the distance.

It was Barney's idea to raise the Emus in the first place. He suggested they would tide him over until the first grape harvest. 'Only eighteen months until they'll reproduce,' he'd said. So part of the bank loan went to purchase the first twelve chicks. The ticking time clock was almost upon them.

Angel tippy-toed across the porch and reached her foot up his leg. *Meow!*

"Hey, kiddo. How's it going?" He reached down to stroke her pudgy belly. Over the past weeks, the cats had quickly become part of the family. So much so that, like Cindy, he'd almost begun to hope no one would see the posters and call.

John gazed across the yard toward the Emu enclosure. He checked the date on his calendar watch. Not long until the chicks were due to hatch. Maybe the firewood sales would pick up soon and maybe the chicks would hatch and get shipped out in the first week and maybe he *could* keep the bank off his back. Maybe. Maybe. Maybe. A drowning man will clutch at any straw of hope floating by.

It was just about time to fix Cindy's breakfast and then he'd have to get after that stand of trees he'd heard about. The price was right. Free for the taking. *All I have to do is cut those suckers down, buck them up and haul them home.* Should yield at least a couple cords of wood. Enough to put several hundred dollars in his pocket when they sold. A nip in the air promised that, before long, folks would be firing up their woodstoves more often.

What should he do about Carolyn? Hopefully, she had given up her plan to take Cindy. More likely, she'd met another man who kept her busy enough that she didn't want to be bothered with her daughter, but how long would that last? John shook his head.

Carolyn had never understood why the vineyard meant so much to him. She knew things would be tough after the fire. But, he had to take out the loan to save the ranch. How could he walk away from his heritage? Carolyn jumped ship at the first opportunity and left him and Cindy to fight the battle alone. More likely, she took up with Charlie even before he got home from Iraq.

Eighteen months had passed since she left, and what did he have to show for it? An immature vineyard, a huge monthly loan payment he couldn't meet, a child to raise alone and his whole life hanging on some green eggs that might or might not hatch over the next few days. When it came right down to it, nothing in life was really worth having if he wasn't willing to take a risk. Succeed or fail. Live or die. Hold on to the ranch, or walk away? Never!

Angel rubbed against his leg. He gave her head another pat. Best get after that stand of trees. They wouldn't chop themselves down. He'd take Cindy with him since the job would take three or four hours. She could bring a book or her dolls and sit in the truck.

He hoisted his body from the porch swing and trudged into the house. "Come on, Cindy. Let's go. Daddy's got to cut down some trees today. You're coming with me." He pulled the bread and peanut butter from the cupboard, flopped a couple slices of bread on the counter and removed a knife from the drawer.

"What about Angel? Will she be alright home alone?"

"Don't worry about Angel, she'll be fine. Even if her kittens come while we're gone, she'll know what to do. Cats have had kittens without any help since time began. Get your dolls. I've just about got some lunch ready."

Black Cat followed John to the front door. *Don't worry, John. I'll take care of things while you're gone.*

John patted his head.

Black Cat wandered back to the stove and flopped onto Angel's blanket. Logs crackled in the potbelly, snapping in the dying embers. Angel gave an occasional little snort as she slept.

John and Cindy were gone about an hour when Black Cat awoke. That itch right behind his ear again! Wait. Something or someone was outside in the yard. Had John come back already? He got up from the blanket and slunk across the rug to the window. Best not wake Angel.

By sitting on the back of the sofa and peering between the curtains, he could just see into the Emu enclosure. Just there! At the edge of the clearing. A man crouched behind a bush. *What's he up to?* The man darted between the trees, headed for the Emu enclosure. *The Emus!*

Black Cat's hair rose on the back of his neck. *Rrooww!* He pawed at the curtains. No way out.

Angel lifted her head. "What is it, dear? Is something wrong?"

"Someone's out there. He's over by the Emu enclosure now." Black Cat scratched on the window pane. "We need a cat door." *Hopeless!*

The man crept to the Emu's gate, unlatched the hook and opened the door. He looked back toward the house. Then he slunk back into the trees and disappeared.

Black Cat hopped on the floor and then back onto the sofa. "He opened the door but he didn't go in and disturb the nests."

"He was probably afraid to, with those six foot tall papas on guard," Angel said.

The Emu hens wandered around the enclosure, eyeing the open gate for several minutes before they stepped through the gate. How different it must have looked, outside the enclosure. They pecked at bugs close to the gate and gradually wandered across the yard and down the long driveway.

Oh, John. Come home. Your hens are getting away. Black Cat ran from the kitchen window to the living room window, keeping the birds in sight until four of the hens wandered beyond his view. Several disappeared down the road, others turned back toward the vineyard.

Two hens clunked across the front porch. Angel crouched on her blanket as the mama Emu pecked at the window glass, and then disappeared behind the house.

Black Cat hopped from the floor to the couch. *Trapped like a rat. There's nothing I can do.*

The dedicated papas may have wanted to follow the hens, but stayed at their post, standing on occasion to turn the eggs, and then hunkering down on their nests. What a tempting situation. Black Cat admired their devotion. What they must be thinking. *Eh? Open gate… hens gone…bugs…grass…must sit on eggs! Open gate…freedom… bugs…duty? Hard, lumpy eggs… Hungry…bugs outside open gate… tempting…must turn over eggs (big sigh)… Fatherhood… Darn eggs… darn hens…darn duty…*

Black Cat kept vigil at the front window through the long afternoon, hoping against hope that the hens would return. What else could he do?

Towards late afternoon, John's pick-up truck chugged up the driveway and sputtered to a stop. As soon as he pulled into the driveway, he jumped from the truck. His face was nearly purple. He raced to the enclosure and slammed the gate shut.

John's muffled voice came through the window as he ran back toward the house. "Cindy. Run up there and stand by the gate. Get ready to open it if I can find the hens and drive them back. Eight of them are missing!"

Missing eggs, now missing hens! Angel was right about a human causing the trouble. John must have come to the same conclusion. These were not accidents.

An Emu squawked. Myrtle ran across the yard with John close behind. She rushed into the enclosure and Cindy slammed the gate behind her. *One down, seven to go.*

John motioned Cindy to come back to the house. "Keep watch through the front window. If I find another hen, I'll give a shout and you run out and open the gate." John took off running toward the vineyard.

Cindy hurried into the house.

Black Cat scuttled between her legs before she could close the door. If he could find the hens, maybe he could help. He did a quick loop around the yard and the nearby fields and tried to pick up their scent. They certainly smelled bad enough.

The aroma of pine needles drowned out any remnant of the giant gross-ugly stupid birds and despite a thorough search, none of the missing hens could be found. Even if he could locate them, not having an ounce of sheepdog in him, how could he drive them home? For that matter, he didn't have any kind of *dog* in him.

John put the last screw into the new lock on the gate. That should take care of it. No one would get in there now without a bolt cutter. But, would it be enough?

John returned to the house, flopped onto the sofa and picked up the newspaper. He stared at it without understanding one word. His head was in such a jumble, the paper might as well be written in Chinese. He threw it down.

Cindy stood at the kitchen sink, putting dishes in the drainer. She hadn't mentioned the missing Emus, but surely she knew what had happened. The hens didn't open their own gate. The first night the eggs went missing, he hadn't the heart to tell her what he really thought.

Cindy must know that someone opened the gate on purpose to make trouble. She must know that if the hens weren't found, there'd be no more chicks and without the chicks, there was no chance they'd save the ranch. She was only ten, but it didn't take a Ph.D. to put two and two together.

John walked to the kitchen and picked up the frying pan. "Here, honey. Run on now, I'll finish up." He leaned over the sink and ran a paper towel around the grease in the frying pan, then held it under the faucet.

Not that his *Emu Project* was going all that well to begin with. Why hadn't he put a lock on the gate the first day when the trouble started? Three of the hens had come back during the night, thank God, but four of them still wandered the countryside. No telling what might happen to them. They could be hit by a car or eaten by a mountain lion or end up on a neighbor's barbecue—the thought made his stomach churn.

Someone wanted him off the ranch even before the bank got their hooks into him. Mr. Skimmer? *Wouldn't put it past the old coot.* He'd already tried to steal the land right out from under his nose. Doubt he'd hesitate to pull something like this.

If the bank foreclosed, where would they go? How could he take care of Cindy? He dried his hands on the kitchen towel. How much more was a man meant to take?

Black Cat licked up the last slurp of fried egg from Cindy's plate. He would have left the piece of bacon for Angel, but her taste went exclusively to Friskies and warm milk. She had no interest in people food. *Too bad. Her loss.*

Just yesterday, he'd left a nice greasy slice of bacon on his dish. Angel sniffed at it and backed away. "No, thanks. I don't eat meat. I'm a vegetarian."

"What do you mean you're a vegetarian?" Black Cat shook his head. Apparently this was something else she'd never mentioned. "You eat cat food, don't you?" He flicked his whiskers.

Angel reared back, her eyes wide, her ears tipped back over her head. "You mean there's meat in cans of cat food? How come no one ever told me? *Yuck!* I'll never eat cat food again!"

"Then what are you going to eat? Salad? You're a cat!"

"I'll become a…a…Friskie-tarian. I'll just eat Friskies."

"Angel. Sweetheart." Black Cat sighed. "You can eat all the Friskies you want, but there's a certain amount of animal product in Friskies too."

"There is not. It's just crunchy stuff. It comes in a bag."

"They put some meat *in* the crunchy stuff."

"Then I'll just eat the pieces that don't have any meat in them." Her bright eyes glittered. She swayed a bit, her round belly swaying as she stalked away from the kitchen stove.

"How can you tell the difference? It all looks alike. Oh, never mind!" Black Cat called after her. *Females. No point arguing. She's never going to admit she's wrong.*

John dipped the frying pan into the sink and picked up a scrubber. "I hoped some of the hens would come home during the night. I walked all around the ranch before breakfast, but no luck." He turned to Cindy. "Can you clear the table and put away the butter and—"

Ring! Ring!

John grabbed the telephone. "Hello? Oh, hello…really? That's great… Yes. They are pretty big and funny looking. First house on the right off Quaker Banner Road? Got it. I'll be right over. Thanks for calling."

John's face lit up. He hung up the phone. "A lady saw the sign I posted down at the corner store." He grabbed his coat off the hook by the door. "She's spotted one of the hens on the back of her property. I'm going over and see if I can drive it back. I'll unlock the gate before I leave. You stay here, Cindy, and watch out the window. I'll give a whistle when I get to the end of the drive. Get ready to run and open the gate. If I can get the hen into the yard, I think she'll go back into the enclosure."

Black Cat sat with Cindy near the window watching for the elusive hens.

No sooner had John driven out of sight, than an old man shuffled up the driveway. Almost as if he had been watching from the bushes, and waiting until John left.

The hair on the back of Black Cat's back reared up as the old man staggered toward the house. Drunk! Or something worse?

"Someone's out there. Daddy said…"

The old man glanced toward the front porch. He rubbed his chin where several days' growth of whiskers sprouted. He must have seen Cindy through the window because he grinned, pulled off his rumpled hat and bowed, like a court jester.

"Oh!" Cindy bounced off the sofa and stood, staring out the window as the old man came closer to the house.

The old codger shoved his hat back over his straggly grey hair. A gust of wind rippled open his old coat, two sizes too big. He stepped toward the porch and shuffled up the steps.

Black Cat's hackles rose. *Probably harmless. Or not!* What could he possibly want here? And, Cindy was alone. The itch behind Black Cat's ear raged.

The old man stumbled across the porch and pounded on the door.

Black Cat's heart raced. *I never had much respect for dogs before, but, I sure wish I could bark.* He hurried closer to the door, exchanging glances with Angel.

She cringed beneath the kitchen table. The appearance of the old man had set her fear barometer off, as well.

Black Cat's tail puffed out and his hair stood on end. He growled, for all the good it did. It wasn't likely the old man could hear him through the door. Even if he heard, he wasn't in any condition to notice.

Cindy hurried across the room. *Don't open the door, Cindy!* Couldn't she see by his body language that she shouldn't open the door? *She's going to open it!*

Why hadn't John taught her better? *Don't open the door to strangers.* Her kind heart was about to put her in harm's way.

His heart thumped. At best, the old guy was looking for something to eat or a bit of money. At worst, when he found Cindy home alone, he might push his way into the house and try to rob the place or…

He remembered the voices from the river. 'Convince John to leave, whatever it takes…' Was the old guy following their orders? What better incentive for John to leave than to find his little girl assaulted.

Black Cat hissed and clawed at Cindy's sleeve. She jerked back for a second, then reached past him and put her hand on the knob. *No Cindy. Don't do it.* She flipped the lock on the door and then ran and locked herself in the bathroom.

Black Cat's breath whooshed out in a sigh.

Hopefully, the back door was locked, as well. Better check! He raced through the house toward the back, spotted the latch flipped over, then turned and dashed back to the living room. If the man was bent on mischief, he might look for another way into the house. The doorknob rattled! The pounding on the front door continued.

Black Cat cast another glance toward Angel. *It's okay, my sweet.*

Angel had moved from under the table to their bed by the stove. She had clawed the blanket into a pile. She turned in circles, first in one direction and then the other, lying down, and then standing, her eyes wide. She hunched her back and pulled her ears down. He heard her moan, and then twist her body.

Not now! God have mercy. Could things get any worse? Angel's kittens were coming!

Chapter Fifteen

ncertain whether to stay with Angel or confront the man on the porch, Black Cat ran between the blanket and the door. If the old man got into the house, Angel was helpless…

Not unexpected, the ragged man walked around to the back, jiggled doors and checked all the windows. Thank goodness, everything was locked tight. After what seemed like an eternity, but was probably no more than fifteen minutes, he went away.

Cindy stayed in the bathroom with the door closed.

Black Cat rushed to Angel and hovered by her side. What should a guy do in a situation like this? How long does it take for kittens to come? His heart was beating like a shutter in a wind storm. He wanted to tell her how much he longed to be a good father. To let her know how much she meant to him. For the first time in his life, words failed him. He gulped, swallowing down a ping-pong ball sized lump in his throat. "Angel, I—"

"Leave me alone. Can't you see I'm busy?" Angel's occasional scratching on the blanket was the only sound in the house. Her nervous purrs rasped and shook her body.

Black Cat's heart had just begun to slow when he heard little mewing sounds. He crept closer and peered into the pile of blankets. "They're here already? Three? Is that all?"

The look she gave him could melt ice cubes. "Give me a break. I'm fairly new at this." She licked each kitten dry and pulled them to her tummy. Two of the kittens were the image of Angel, all creamy-gold with light pinstripes. The third had a mottled colored coat, a mixture of black and orange and a cream blaze on her tiny nose.

"Boys?" Black Cat whispered.

Angel sighed. "Three little girls."

"Oh…" His head dropped, one ear drooped to the side.

"You're disappointed, aren't you? I thought you liked girls."

"I do like girls. But, a fellow always wants sons. I'd hoped—"

Angel's head jerked up and she glared into his eyes. "Well, isn't that a shame. Maybe next time, you should have the kittens. Maybe you… Oh! Oh!…*Uumm!*" Her eyes grew big and then she twisted, sending the little girls flying as a black and white kitten with four white feet appeared on the blanket.

"There," Angel panted. "I hope you're happy now. Meet your son."

"My son? Angel!" The kitten was his spitting image. Long black fur, a white collar, four huge white feet and a little white mustache.

Black Cat leaned over the blanket. "One, two, three, four, five, six. Yes! Six toes on his little front foot. That's my boy!" Guess that answered his questions about the paternity of the kittens. "Oh, Angel!"

"Yeah! Yeah! I know. You love me. Now go away and let me sleep. I'm exhausted." Angel licked the black and white kitten from head to tail. Her purr hummed and rattled as she closed her eyes and moved into a zen-like state, her tongue moving up and down as she tumbled each kitten, drying, loving, making their scent her own.

"Yes, my queen." Black Cat tiptoed over to the locked bathroom. *Meow! Cindy? Are you alright?*

Cindy opened the door. "Is it safe to come out now? Has the old man gone?"

Come out and see my beautiful new family.

Black Cat and Cindy hovered over the Madonna and babies.

Angel lifted her head, her little pink tongue still visible between her teeth. She gazed at Cindy. *So, now that they're dry, what do you think?* Her eyes dropped to the kittens, two snuffling around and eating, the other two sleeping. She purred like a miniature Husqvarna tractor.

"Angel! Your babies are beautiful. I'm so proud of you." Cindy stroked her finger over the little tortoiseshell kitten. Nothing like a litter of new kittens to make a little girl forget about the old man who'd tried to break into the house. She caressed Black Cat's head. "You're such a proud papa. If you had buttons on your white vest, they'd pop right off, wouldn't they?" She giggled and rolled on the floor, obviously amused at her joke. She sat up when John's truck crunched up the driveway.

John stomped his way across the front porch, paused, and then tried the handle. Finding it locked, he turned his key in the lock, flung open the door, and stepped inside. His face was as twisted and dark as a thundercloud.

Uh-Oh! That doesn't look good.

"Where did this come from?" John shook a naked, headless baby doll.

Cindy's face paled. She shrugged. "I don't know. It's not mine." She looked toward Black Cat. "Maybe the dirty old man left it?"

"What dirty old man? Who was here?" John threw his sweatshirt on the chair and slammed the door, reached back and flipped the lock. He hurried to the stove and stooped down beside her. He put his hand on her shoulder. "Did someone come while I was gone? You didn't let him in, did you?"

Cindy shook her head. "An old man came on the porch. He was dirty and walked funny. I locked the door and went into the bathroom, like you told me." She leaned over the blanket. "But, Daddy, just look! Angel's kittens are here. Four of them. Aren't they sweet?"

His expression softened a bit when he glanced down at the kittens. "Yes, I see. But, Cindy, listen to me. This doll!" He shook the headless thing. "This doll…" His face paled and his voice faded, as though he had second thoughts about sharing the implications of a headless doll left on the porch when a little girl was home alone.

Even without much memory or experience in an evil world, Black Cat had enough sense to know that things might have been different if Cindy had opened the door.

"You should let Angel rest now. Come on away." John took Cindy's hand and pulled her to her feet.

"I almost forgot. Did you find the Emu?" Cindy ran to the window and peeked out, as if she expected to see the errant hen pecking bugs beside John's truck.

John ran his hand through his hair. He shook his head. "When I got to the house, the woman didn't know what I was talking about. She said she didn't call. It must have been someone playing a trick…" John turned away from Cindy, poked at the fire, his head bowed, hiding his face from her. *What was he thinking?*

The hair on Black Cat's neck paraded down his spine. It wasn't a *prank* any more than when someone stole the eggs or let the hens loose. Someone wanted John out of the house—wanted Cindy vulnerable. The headless doll on the porch was a warning.

If Mr. Skimmer was behind this, how far would he go? Would he hurt Cindy? *Doggone it. How can we protect her? We're just cats, but we've got to find a way!*

Chapter Sixteen

Kimberlee's chair scraped the floor under the dinner table. She sat, bowed her head, took Amanda's hand, and then reached for Brett's hand, making a full circle.

"Thank You for this food," Amanda prayed. "Bless Mama and Daddy Brett and…and…please God, take care of Thumper and Noe-Noe and bring them home safe."

Brett lifted his head, glanced at Kimberlee and frowned. Hadn't he called the Humane Society every week, until the lady at the counter recognized his voice at his first 'hello?' Hadn't he run the Lost Cats ad in the Cloverdale paper for eight weeks straight without results?

Did Amanda have to pray for the cats at every meal and in every bedtime prayer? Sooner or later, she had to understand it was no use, no matter how much she wanted her prayers to be answered. He was almost getting used to the wrench in his heart every time she asked God to bring her kitties home.

Just that afternoon, while Amanda was at kindergarten, he and Kimberlee had discussed that very thing on the patio.

"Maybe we should get another kitten. I don't think there's much hope we'll hear anything now. It's been over two months since the accident. What's the use of keeping up this pretense? They're not coming back." *Isn't it time to let this whole Thumper-watch go?* "I asked her the other day if she wanted another kitten. She said if we got another kitten, Thumper would think she had stopped loving him."

Kimberlee sighed and sipped her coffee. "I don't know what to do. I hate to tell her to stop praying. It's never a waste of time to give thanks for our blessings and ask for help when we're troubled. Just last week, I heard about a cat lost for over a year, and it came home. Maybe—"

"Honey, stop. You're just holding onto false hope. They're gone. They're probably dead. Something probably got them that first day. Maybe a hawk or a fox."

Kimberlee put her hands over her ears. "*La la la…* I'm not listening. I'd rather believe they've found a good home and they're happy somewhere."

Brett shook his head. "If it makes you feel better, believe whatever you like. But, one of these days, we have to deal with Amanda. It's not healthy for her to keep praying and risk having her faith destroyed. Better she should accept reality and get another kitten. Maybe I'll get one from the local SPCA and bring it home. She'll love it as soon as she sees it."

"Not yet. Let's give it a while, please?" Kimberlee touched his arm.

A while, she had said and he had no choice but to agree. Well, he would do some praying of his own, not for the cats—Amanda was taking care of that, but for Amanda—that she would not suffer a lack of faith when her prayers went unanswered.

The phone rang. "If you think that's best." Brett turned. "I'll get it." He pushed back his chair and picked up the receiver. "Hello. Clarke residence."

"Brett?" The old crone's voice jabbed into his brain, just like it had back in Texas, earlier that summer.

Brett glanced at Kimberlee, his face without expression. "Can you hold the line, please?" He put his hand over the phone. "Will you hang this up, honey? I want to take this call in my office." He handed her the phone and headed into the house. "Okay, I've got it," he called as he shoved the door shut. The phone clicked as she hung it up.

"Okay, I can talk now." Brett's stomach did a flip-flop as he sat at his desk. He ran his hand over his face. "How are you, Grandmother? What can I do for you?"

"I want to speak to my granddaughter. Is she there?"

A vein throbbed in Brett's cheek. "She can't talk right now. She's giving Amanda her dinner," he lied. "Haven't you talked to her since we left Texas?" *I thought Kimberlee called her about taking Noe-Noe a long time ago.* His pulse quickened. Perspiration popped out on his forehead.

"No. I haven't heard from Kimberlee. I suppose she's still mad at me over that misunderstanding when you were here." Grandmother's voice raised a notch.

"Misunderstanding? That's a curious way to put it, considering what happened."

"Well, never mind that now. That's not why I called. It's about my cat. Juan said the last time he saw her was the day you folks left. He thought you might have taken her. I couldn't believe you'd do such a thing. I'm not saying you did, mind you. But, if you know something about it, you better tell me. If you have my Noe-Noe, I want her back."

A trail of perspiration trickled down Brett's forehead. Bad enough they had *appropriated* the cat when they left the ranch. They'd figured Grandmother wouldn't miss the cat, or might not care. Or, considering the grief she had caused Kimberlee during their visit, she might leave well enough alone. *Probably wistful thinking.*

Well, that ship had sailed. Grandmother wanted her cat back. That would be the cat they lost, over two months ago. The cat left behind on the levee road with Thumper the day of the accident. The cat that disappeared from the face of the earth, in spite of posters and newspaper ads and a child's constant prayers. Now, how was he supposed to fix this?

Why hadn't Kimberlee called and straightened this out? How could he tell Grandmother at this late date, that her cat was not only missing, but probably dead?

"Well, Grandmother, I don't know how to say this. We can't give her back because—"

"What do you mean, you can't give her back? So you admit you *stole* my cat? I invited you here for a wonderful vacation and this is how you repay me?"

Brett gulped, and took a breath. *Wonderful vacation? What a laugh.* "If things had been different, Grandmother, we *would* have told—"

"I was near death in the hospital, and you stole my cat? What kind of people are you?"

"We *should* have called you in the hospital before we left but—"

"What an ungrateful child! And to think I almost left my entire estate to Kimberlee."

Now wasn't that the biggest joke of all? Despite their current problems with Grandmother, she was right. They should never have taken Noe-Noe without permission. Well, it was too late now to think about *shoulda, coulda, woulda.*

"Listen, Grandmother, it was all rather sudden. Believe me. We didn't plan it. We were on our way home. Noe-Noe just sort of…well, found her way into Thumper's cage…*um*…by mistake."

That's not quite true but it's always easier to ask forgiveness instead of asking permission. No point in going into details about the cats' disappearance.

"Some mistake. I suppose she opened the wire door and sneaked into the cage when you weren't looking? *Humph!* You knew what you were doing. You *stole* her to get even with me because Kimberlee was mad."

What? "Look, I'm sorry. We thought, considering your convalescence, the cat would be better off with us. We thought—"

"Hogwash. I'm calling the sheriff and filing charges. Cat-napping, that's what it is. Downright, malicious, *pre-medicated* cat-napping."

"Go ahead and call the sheriff. While we're at it, let's put him in touch with the Los Angeles detective you hired and the plans you had for Amanda." Brett slammed the phone down. Even if he wanted to give the cat back, what could he do about it, anyway? The cat was gone. Brett's hand lingered on the phone. Now, what was he supposed to say to Kimberlee?

Maybe it would be better not to even mention Grandmother's call. Considering her role in the Texas fiasco, he doubted she would ever have the nerve to press the issue.*

*See *Black Cat and the Lethal Lawyer* for events that took place in Texas with Thumper, Noe-Noe, Kimberlee, Grandmother, and Amanda.

Chapter Seventeen

"indy is going with John again today." Black Cat's fur rippled down his back as John pulled the door shut and headed for his truck. "He's going to cut down some trees."

Angel pulled her ears back "When does he plan to sleep? He's been up half the night patrolling the yard. He's starting to look like a raccoon and he hasn't shaved his whiskers for three days."

"He says he has to make sure none of those two-legged skunks that hanker for a man's land is skulking around. And, it gives us some alone time with the babies." Black Cat jumped sideways and gave the tiny tortoiseshell kitten a playful swat.

"More time to act goofy in front of the kiddies without giving up your *macho persona* in front of John, is what you mean." Angel yawned and rolled onto her back, her four feet in the air. "At least the house is quiet and I can get some sleep."

Black Cat stared shyly at the eight creamy-pink dots peeking through her white tummy fur, and then averted his gaze. "Angel! You're much too cynical, but still cute as a button."

The next morning, before breakfast, John ran out to the enclosure to check the nests.

Black Cat tagged along, patrolling the fence line, checking for any sign of intruders. Not that he could do much about it if he found any, but it was important that he do his part to protect the family. All the hens were back, safe and sound, thanks to an ad in the local paper and help from the Humane Society when neighbors spotted a six-foot-tall feathered intruder in their back yards.

On the days John took Cindy to the vineyard, Black Cat would tag along. The sun warmed the *Gewürztraminer grapes*, botanically designed to grow at higher elevations and in cooler weather, like the weather in Nevada City, California, just west of the Nevada border. Puffy white clouds hung low in the sky. The apple trees along the field were now heavy with young apples, promising a good harvest.

John pruned the young grape vines while Black Cat and Cindy scampered through the rows and played hide and seek.

Cindy pulled off a piece of vine and dragged it back and forth in front of Black Cat's nose.

He chased the vine from left to right, his imagination running wild. In his mind's eye, Cindy disappeared, and the other little girl with the bouncing brown curls took her place.

He chased the child through the front yard, past the porch covered with purple flowers climbing across the rafters. Sailboats with bright colored sails bobbed beside the dock next door.

Cindy's vine became a snake, like the stick in his memory. Certain hideous death awaits the child unless I prevail. To the left, again to the right, staring into the serpent's evil orange eyes. The hideous intruder—finally within my grasp, the viper lies silent on the grass, a mere shred of its former self.

"Get it, Black Cat! Get it." Cindy's voice pulled him away from the lake house and back into the vineyard.

When he tired of the game, he lay down in the shade beside Cindy. She lay on her back, pointing up at the clouds. "Look, Black Cat," she whispered. "That one looks like an angel. Can you see it?"

He looked up and gave her a polite meow. *I can't see anything except clouds and sky.* Little girls must have more imagination than cats. Or maybe they saw things differently.

"Daddy. Black Cat thinks the cloud looks like an angel, too. He told me so."

"Sure thing, baby."

The mellow afternoon begged for a nap in the shade beneath the vines. It was the kind of day when one could hope that John's problems might work out, after all. Perhaps the sale of firewood could keep the bank off his back for a while longer. The chicks were due to hatch any day and the money from their sale could pay the back taxes. Perhaps one day, he and Angel could even go home…

Another cloud passed overhead. Cindy pointed up. "Look, over there, Daddy. It's a car."

John turned to look and dropped one of his gloves. As he leaned down to pick it up, a blast exploded from the trees. A bullet whistled past his head. He threw himself onto the ground.

Black Cat flattened into the dirt. *Holy cats and little fishes. What was that?*

Cindy sat up. "Daddy. What happened?"

"Stay down!" John crawled between the wires toward Cindy. "That bullet darn near hit me." He lay on the ground for a minute. "Stay right here. Don't get up. Will you do that? I'm going to see who's shooting. Maybe it was a stray bullet."

He ran his hands over Cindy's flyaway hair.

Her eyes were wide, her cheeks pale.

Black Cat hunkered beside her. That was a tad too close for comfort.

"Don't be afraid, honey. I'm sure it was an accident. You stay here with Black Cat. I'll be right back."

Cindy clutched Black Cat to her chest as they lay in the dirt between the vines. Her heart thumped against his chest in a half-time beat, matched by the beating of his own heart.

What must John be thinking as he crept through the vineyard toward someone with a rifle aimed at his head? He had to leave his child alone in the middle of the field with only a cat to protect her. It's bad enough to find a headless doll on the porch. It's quite another when someone tries to shoot you in your own vineyard. Poor John! Poor Cindy! *Poor me!*

If the shooter would try to take out a man and his little girl, he wouldn't think twice about killing his cat. How might the lead story on tomorrow's nightly newscast go?

The bodies of a man, his daughter and their heroic cat were found today in a local vineyard, shot to death by an unknown assailant. Drops of blood found on the brave cat's feet bore witness to his courageous effort to save the lives of his master and child.

Most grievously missed, and unfortunately dead, the lion-hearted cat will be posthumously awarded a medal of valor for his herculean efforts to thwart the foul murderer. DNA examination of the blood found on the gallant cat's feet will no doubt identify the killer. The noble efforts of Nevada City's departed feline hero will not soon be forgotten. A statue in his honor will be erected in the center of town…

Oh, good grief, Black Cat. Get a grip. This was no laughing matter. Somewhere in the trees next to the vineyard, a killer lurked with a rifle, and he was the only thing between the madman and Cindy.

Chapter Eighteen

here is that sucker? Black Cat lifted his head and peeked through the vines. Nowhere in sight.

John waved from the end of the row, pointed toward the house, and then pushed his hand down again and again. Then, he put his hand to his ear like he was talking on the phone.

"Daddy wants us to stay low and go back to the house and call for help." Cindy was a bright child. She started crawling down the row toward the house.

Black Cat scampered along beside her. *I'm already low, by virtue of being only fifteen inches tall from the ground to the top of my head.* When they got to the end of the row, Cindy stood and they raced across the yard, stomped onto the porch and into the house. Cindy grabbed the phone and dialed.

"911. What is your emergency?"

"Someone is shooting at my daddy. He told me to call for help." Cindy pulled the curtain away from the window and peered out toward the vineyard. "I'm Cindy Goldstein. Please hurry. I'm scared… Yes, all right… I'm ten… Yes, I'm in my house and I've locked the door… Just my cats…two…Angel and Black Cat… They were lost and we found them in our truck…"

Black Cat hurried over to the blanket by the stove.

Angel's eyes looked like two black ball bearings. "What is she babbling about? She said our names." Angel pulled her babies close to her side.

"The dispatcher is keeping her on the line until the sheriff can get here. Don't worry. The gunman's not near the house."

Her hair bristled. "Gunman? You mean a man with a gun? He better not come in here."

"He doesn't have any intention of coming inside. Anyone who hides and shoots at a man with a child is a coward. He wouldn't dare confront someone face-to-face."

The shooter was wise to avoid the house. If Angel thought he meant to harm her babies, he'd likely go away missing some part of his anatomy—any part she could reach.

Before long, the sheriff's unit skidded to a stop in the driveway.

Cindy unlocked the door. A man and a lady officer rushed into the house. "Okay, honey. Everything's alright now." The lady officer's gun holster creaked as she knelt down and placed her hand on Cindy's shoulder. "Where's your daddy?" Her light brown hair was pulled back in a ponytail. Freckles on her nose wiggled when she smiled.

Cindy pointed toward the window. "He's down there at the end of the vineyard. That's where the bad man shot at us."

The second officer opened the front door. "You stay with the girl. I'll go on down and check it out."

Black Cat raced to the door. The officer pulled it closed before he could sneak through.

The lady officer stepped forward and snapped the lock. She returned to the potbelly stove blanket where Cindy sat beside the kittens. "My name is Nina. I'll stay with you until your daddy comes back. What's your name?"

"I'm Cindy and this is Black Cat." She gestured toward Black Cat, "and this is Angel and her babies." Her face beamed with pride. "The babies are just opening their eyes."

The officer knelt beside Angel's blanket.

Angel hissed, laying the ground rules right from the start. Until she had established *who was who*, anyone with a gun should approach her family with caution.

"Don't worry, Angel." Black Cat gave her head a lick. "Officer Nina's alright. She's here to help."

Angel scrubbed the kittens, flipping them from side to side. Any sort of unusual situation or case of nerves on her part seemed to affect the kittens' hygiene adversely, requiring at least a partial if not a full body bath. *Guess it's a female thing.*

Officer Nina reached to pet the black and white kitten, and the little fellow, all of four inches tall, peeked through his half-opened eyes, bristled and hissed a tiny little *"zzhit!"*

That's my boy!

Cindy laughed.

Nina picked up the cream-colored kitten; the one Cindy called Muffins, because she had big feet with extra toes, just like her old man.

"Oh, isn't he just the sweetest little thing?" She rubbed the kitten against her cheek.

"He's a she. Her name is Muffins. Do you like cats?" Cindy's eyes grew bright.

I can almost see the wheels turning in her little head. You go, girl.

Nina sighed. "I lost my cat last year and I haven't had the heart to get another." She stroked Muffins' head with one finger.

Muffins started to purr, a tiny little hum at first that swelled in volume until it replicated a Lilliputian jet liner warming up on the runway.

That clever baby must have paid attention the day Angel taught the kittens their first Life Lessons. Angel had likely started with *Purring 101*… "Humans haven't figured out quite how it's done and we won't go into the exact process at this point. Suffice it to say, it comes from deep within your personal survival arsenal, memories from the ancestors, and without which, many more of us would be homeless… Now pay attention… *Humm… Humm…* Now you try it."

Once they had the knack of purring, she moved into *How to Take Over a Human.* "First you let loose with a purr, grabbing hold of a human's heart. Then you wind your toes in and out a few times…that's it, use all your toes. The prospect sees this as a commentary on their sparkling personality. By this time, they should be rubbing you against their cheek, which is a pretty good sign you've got them. Then, you look directly into their eyes and blink.

"If you haven't quite sealed the deal, open your mouth as if you're going to meow, but don't make a sound. That's called the *silent meow*. It's a powerful tool few can resist."

Angel had finished the lesson by stating, "It would take a hardened San Quentin serial killer to leave you behind following this performance."

Muffins laid it on thick and not unexpectedly, Officer Nina was mumbling kitten gibberish and grinning like a fool within about a minute. She raked the rumbling kitten across her cheek again. "Would you—"

"Would you like to have her for your very own?" Cindy was almost as quick on her feet as Muffins, and knowing the kittens would all need good homes, lost no time bringing this potential sucker, rather, customer, to the table.

Officer Nina smiled and held Muffins at arm's length, turned her from side to side and rained kisses on her head. The littlest Sarah Bernhard of the Cat World purred and wound her giant feet and blinked on cue. She *brought it home* with an impeccable silent meow.

I couldn't have done it better myself. It was a perfect Oscar winning performance. Within less than a minute, she'd wheedled her way into this woman's pocket book…I mean, her heart, for the rest of her natural life.

"I believe I would." Officer Nina handed Cindy her business card. "You call me when they're ready to leave their mother." She gave Muffins a kiss.

Black Cat gave Angel a quick glance. She was as pleased with Muffins' performance as he was.

One down and three to go.

John unlocked the front door. He and the officer stamped in, knocking pine needles from their feet. He took one look at Cindy's face. She must be scared to death. *How can I spin this so I don't scare her even more?*

Cindy threw her arms around his waist. "Are you okay?"

John nodded. "I'm fine. Don't worry."

Cindy loosened her grip and came back to the blanket by the stove. She knelt beside the cats. "Officer Nina wants to take Muffins when she's old enough."

"That sounds fine."

Good. She doesn't seem overly concerned about the shooting.

"Find anything?" The lady officer handed the kitten back to Cindy.

"No such luck. We found the place where the guy waited. Grass all mashed down." The officer held up a rifle casing. "Found a 30-30 brass casing. Typical hunting rifle. Not much chance of tracing the thing." He opened a clipboard and began filling out his report. "Hard to say if it was an accident. Doesn't seem likely he was shooting at a rabbit or something, what with you folks there in the field, but I suppose it's possible. We'll make out a report, Mr. Goldstein, but I don't think there's much chance of an arrest. Whoever shot at you…" He glanced over toward Cindy and clamped his mouth shut.

"Cindy. Run on into your room. I need to talk to the officers." John nodded toward her bedroom. She didn't need to hear this. She wouldn't understand. No point dumping it all on her at her age.

Cindy got up from the blanket and carried the black and white kitten into her room.

"Do you have any idea who might have fired the shot?" Officer Nina pulled a can of breath mints from her pocket and popped one into her mouth. She held out the can toward John.

John shook his head. "The bank is threatening to foreclose on the ranch and someone has approached me about buying my land." John ran his hand through his hair. "Of course, under the circumstances, he offered to pay pennies on the dollar. We've had several incidents over the past several weeks. Eggs have been stolen from my Emu nests and someone opened the gate and let my birds out. A few days ago, a hobo came up to the house and scared my little girl, now this *accidental shooting*. It doesn't all sound like a coincidence, does it?"

"You say someone wants your land? You got a name?"

"My neighbor, Chuck Skimmer, made me an insulting offer." John's face warmed at the memory. He clenched and unclenched his hand. "Skimmer figures he can pick up the property for a tenth of its value." He looked toward Cindy's room. "…my little girl…" *First the bank, and now this?*

The officer nodded and wrote on his clipboard. "We'll stop by and have a word with Mr. Skimmer. See if he has an alibi for this morning." The Sheriff snapped his clipboard shut. "Call us if you need anything. We'll come right out. In the meantime… Do you own a pistol?"

The lady officer glanced at the sheriff.

John nodded. "I've got my rifle and my dad's service revolver in the closet."

"I don't mean to alarm you. You can do as you like, but if I were you, I'd get the pistol out of the closet and keep it handy. I'd not be doing my duty, though, if I didn't tell you. If the gun's not registered, you should go down and get a permit. You shouldn't have any trouble with this report on file."

John nodded. "I'll do that." Next time the skunk tried something, things would be different.

Officer Nina leaned down and ran her finger over Muffins' little head. "I'll see you soon, Muffins." She turned at the door. "Tell Cindy good-bye for me, will you?"

"Thanks," John called, as they pulled the door closed behind them. He went into his bedroom, came back with the revolver and holster and laid them on the buffet.

"Cindy. Come in here." He opened her bedroom door. "I need to talk to you."

"Yes, Daddy?" She carried the kitten back and laid him on Angel's blanket.

"Officer Nina said to tell you good-bye. She'll see you when she comes back for Muffins. Right now, we've got to talk about something serious." John pulled Cindy down on the couch beside him. *Lord, give me the right words so I don't scare her.*

"We've talked about guns before and you know you're not to touch my rifle. I've brought my pistol in from the bedroom and put it on the buffet. Sometimes when we go out, I'm going to wear it. Other times, I'll leave it right up there." He pointed toward the gun. "Guns aren't toys and they're not meant for children. You'll remember that you're not to touch it, won't you? Promise me?"

"I promise. Did the sheriff find the man who shot at us?"

"No. We think someone must have been target shooting and it came our way by mistake. Don't worry about it." He didn't need her losing any sleep over this. Bad enough he'd be lying awake all night.

"If it was an accident, how come you got out your pistol?"

His child was perceptive beyond her years. Just how was he supposed to keep her dreams full of butterflies and roses? How long could he protect her from the dark side of life when she could already see past the cloak of sunshine?

The vein beside John's mouth throbbed and the wrinkles in his forehead deepened.

"I've got work to do. I'll be out in the bird enclosure. Lock this door and stay inside." He picked up the revolver and holster and strapped it around his waist. "When I come back, I'll fix us some pancakes." He smiled and ruffled Cindy's hair. "Now, you and Angel take care of Cindy, Black Cat. I'm counting on you." He set his jaw as he went out the door. This time he'd be better prepared if the shooter came back.

Black Cat curled on the couch for a nap. Sleep wouldn't come, and John's problems swirled round and round in his head. Pushing them from his mind, he lifted his head and gazed at Angel and the kittens. Weren't they the light of his life? He didn't know his own name, much less how to find his home. He didn't know how John's problems would turn out or if they'd be able to stay with him if the bank foreclosed, but right now, he had John and Cindy and Angel and the kittens and that was enough. The babies could care less of the woes of the world as they nuzzled and kneaded Angel's tummy for a mid-morning snack. Wasn't life just the best? How could it get any better? His heart lurched at the joy of the *now*.

The phone rang, interrupting his reverie.

In that instant a chill rippled from the back of his ears to his tail. He stood and shook his long fur, trying to shake away the sense of foreboding. *I knew it was all too good to be true. Don't answer, Cindy. Let it ring. Please. Make it go away.*

Cindy ran to the phone and lifted the receiver. "Hello? Goldstein residence…yes…*uh huh*… She's gold with stripes and gold eyes… yes…she just had kittens… Alright…" Cindy wrote something on a piece of paper. "I'll have my daddy call you in a little while. Good bye." She hung up the phone and turned toward the stove. Her eyes were bright with tears that threatened to spill at any moment. Her mouth quivered.

Black Cat hung his head. *I knew it. It was about Angel, wasn't it?*

Cindy burst into tears as she hurried to the sofa and buried her face in Black Cat's fur.

No. No. Please God. Not Angel. I don't want to hear.

"Oh, Black Cat! The lady on the phone said Angel is her lost cat. She wants Daddy to call her back. She's going to take Angel away."

Chapter Nineteen

ost and Found posters! Someone had recognized Angel from Cindy's posters. A shiver ran down Black Cat's back. *But, what about me?* They were a pair, weren't they? If the lady was Angel's *person*, why hadn't she mentioned him? Didn't they belong together? Would the caller take Angel and leave him behind? He couldn't let that happen. He wiggled out from under Cindy and ran to tell Angel. They had to leave before John called the lady.

His breath caught in his throat when he saw her asleep on the blanket, one paw thrown over Muffins and the other babies curled in a ball next to her tummy. *My little family.* And, now, they were about to be torn apart.

Angel would never leave the babies and they were much too young to take along on a hike to God knows where. Angel's *person* would probably take her and the babies. If the bank foreclosed, maybe John would bring Black Cat with him, but more likely, he wouldn't be able to have a cat underfoot. *I will be completely alone and homeless. A stray, like Cindy's mother said. Where will I go? What will I do?* The questions pounded through his head.

John opened the door, his face flushed from his work outdoors. He stopped just inside the door when he saw Cindy's tear-streaked face. "Now, what's wrong?" He glanced at Angel and the kittens clustered on the blanket near the potbelly stove. He looked out the window. "Did someone come to the house again?" He crossed the room, sat beside Cindy and pulled her into his lap.

"A lady called," Cindy sobbed. "She said someone sent her the poster. She said Angel is her cat that was stolen a couple months ago.

She wants to come and get her." Cindy buried her face in his shoulder and wept.

"There, there, now." He patted her back. "We knew this might happen. Isn't that why we put up the posters, so we could find their families? Now, you're all upset. This is what your mother feared would happen. That's why she thought it best to give up the cats before you got attached. You see? She wasn't being mean. She wanted to spare you all these tears when we found Angel's family."

"But, Daddy. Nobody called for so long. At first, I wanted to help Angel find her home, but nobody called and now she and Black Cat belong to us. And the babies… I love them so much." She sniffed and wiped her sleeve across her wet cheeks.

Preach it, sister. Black Cat's heart beat in unison to Cindy's lament. Angel belonged to him, too. And the children.

"Angel and Black Cat—they're our cats now." Cindy leaned over and shook her daddy's shoulders. "Don't you see? We can't give them back."

John took her hand off his shoulders. "Cindy. Listen to me. If you lost your pet and someone found it, wouldn't you want them to give it back?"

Her chin dropped. "Yes." Her voice was just a whisper. "I'd want them to call me. But, Daddy!" Her face brightened in a smile. "She didn't ask about Black Cat. So we can keep him, can't we?"

"We'll see." A shaky smile crossed his face. "Perhaps she only mentioned Angel. Surely they came from the same place. He's the kittens' father."

"Maybe they met and fell in love after Angel got lost." Cindy's smile brightened and her tears stopped. She wiggled out of John's arms and ran to Angel's blanket.

Black Cat's head swirled. Could that be the explanation? Surely he was the kittens' father. It was so obvious. Just look at them. The black and white kitten, newly christened Rambo, looked just like him, and they all had six toes on each foot. How was it possible that he and Angel didn't belong to the same family? He glanced over at Angel sitting all prim and proper on the blanket, pretending she couldn't understand any of this conversation and having the nerve to look not the least bit concerned.

"Angel? Is she right? Did we live with the same *person*? Don't we belong together?"

Angel put up her nose and turned her head.

She knew. Why wouldn't she tell?

John dialed the lady's phone number. He spoke to her for a minute, and then went into his bedroom.

Black Cat tried to follow, but John closed the door before he could wiggle through. He danced on pins and needles, trying to hear through the door. No luck. It was as quiet as a mortuary. What was he saying in there? Did they belong to the lady caller or not?

The door finally squeaked open. John's face looked pale. He wasn't happy.

Black Cat's heart sank.

"What did she say, Daddy?" Cindy hopped on one foot and then the other.

"She's convinced that Angel is her lost cat, but Black Cat doesn't belong to her. Apparently her cat has been gone for several months, long enough for Angel to meet Black Cat and find their way here. She wants to come and get Angel."

Black Cat's heart pounded in his ears, almost preventing the words from penetrating his head. They didn't belong together. The woman only wanted to take Angel?

"When is she coming?" Cindy's eyes sparkled with tears. She clutched Angel to her chest.

"Tomorrow morning."

"Then we have the rest of today and tonight." Cindy rubbed Angel's head with her chin.

"Are you going to be okay? I wouldn't want you to be naughty about this and make a scene. If you'd rather not be here when she comes, Cindy, you can spend a few hours with Mrs. Ramsey at the little store."

"I'll be good… What's Angel's real name? Did she tell you?"

"Yes." John laughed, but it came out more like a snort. "Her name is Miss Boopkins. Now, isn't that the stupidest name you've ever heard? I'd run away too, if my name was Miss Boopkins." John's chest shook with a chuckle.

Black Cat shuddered. How could he have fallen in love with a *Miss Boopkins*? On the other hand, it wasn't Angel's fault she'd been given a ridiculous name. For all he knew, his real name might be *Clyde* or *Throckmorton* or something equally idiotic.

Cindy stroked Angel's head, then put her fingers under her chin and tilted her face. "Miss Boopkins? Is that your name?"

Black Cat stalked to the door, reached up and scratched. He couldn't bear to watch Angel recognize that absurd name. His stomach did back flips. *I have to get out of here.*

He stepped off the porch and headed across the yard. With each step, a mixture of woodsy scents like moss and pine and the faint odor of Manzanita and wild flowers drifted up from the pine needles. Every time he came out the door, the pleasure of being in the woods was as exhilarating as the first day he woke up in John's pick-up truck.

I'm not going with her. Now, I have to face life without Angel… He'd never come into the yard again without remembering their walks through the woods and the vineyard and down by the stream where they first saw the men messing with the dirt in the riverbank. Over yonder lay the woodpile where he'd pouted when he first heard about the kittens. Bile rose in his throat, just thinking about that day. *I need to chew grass. I think I'm going to be sick.*

Across the yard, the Emus prowled around their enclosure, thrumming their odd calls and picking at bugs in the fresh straw John spread several days ago. Just beyond the enclosure, stood a stack of soiled straw John raked from the yard. Steam rose from the hay as it dried in the sun.

One of the papa Emus rose from his nest and flapped his stubby wings. *Yark! Yark!* His long neck lunged forward and back.

Several hens scuttled closer to investigate. *What's going on in there?*

Something had upset the papas. Had someone put something in the enclosure that could harm the birds? Better check it out. With Cindy so upset, John wasn't likely to come out again for a while.

Black Cat's fur puffed out. He walked stiff-legged toward the enclosure.

Chapter Twenty

Black Cat crept closer to the fence and sniffed. What was going on? Was there a snake in the water pan? He shuddered. *Hope not. Hate snakes.*

A hen rushed toward the fence, tipped her head and planted one huge eye to the wire.

Black Cat stood on his back legs. *Well, will you look at that?* Three of the Emu chicks had hatched! The three spotted chicks struggled to stand amidst broken shells scattered in the nearest nest. Another chick lay on its side, still damp, its body curled, moving its head and stretching its little wings. Several other eggs showed cracks where the babies struggled to break free of their oval prisons.

John! Gotta get John! Black Cat raced back to the house, scratched at the door and howled.

Cindy opened the door. "What's the matter, Black Cat? Are you hungry?"

He ran to John and pawed at his leg and then ran back to the door. *Aren't humans supposed to be the most intelligent animals on earth?* Black Cat ran back and pawed John's leg, then raced to the door again. *Why is he so totally clueless when I need to communicate something important? The chicks are hatching!*

John stood and sauntered to the door. "I think he wants me to go outside with him."

Duh! Do ya' think?

"What's happening?" Angel left her babies on the blanket and ambled toward Black Cat.

"The chicks are hatching. I'm trying to get John to come and see."

Black Cat reached up toward the doorknob. "He's as slow as moss growing on the north side of a rock."

Once outside, with Black Cat in the lead, John picked up the pace and jogged toward the bird enclosure. "Is something wrong at the enclosure?"

Angel trotted along with Cindy close behind. Angel sat beside Black Cat while John unlocked the gate and hurried to inspect the newborn chicks. "Oh, yeah!"

The papa bird stepped aside and allowed John to approach the nests.

The chicks stood about ten inches tall, with spotted heads and covered with striped light *down.*

Black Cat twitched his whiskers, imagining the papa's walnut-sized brain assessing the situation. *Eh? ...red shirt man...good man... Eh? Eggs broken...chicks...leave nest...hungry...leave nest...eat... eat...hurry...must get back to chicks...*

The papa bird pecked his way across the yard like he hadn't eaten for weeks—which he hadn't!

"Angel. Cindy said the papa sits on the nest the whole eight weeks while the eggs incubate. He doesn't eat and rarely leaves the nest, drinking only the morning dew he can reach with his long neck. He survives on body fat, built up prior to incubating the eggs. Can you imagine going that long without food?"

"Bet you're glad you didn't have to work that hard to be a papa. And, it's obvious that you haven't missed any meals either, while I did all the work. At least now, the papa can get back to his life." Angel craned her neck toward the chicks.

"I'm not fat. I'm portly. There wasn't exactly a way I could help you carry kittens, was there? As for the papa Emu, according to Cindy, now he has to raise the chicks. They'll follow him around. That's how they'll learn how to eat." *These guys sure aren't doing a lot for my 'father' image.*

"*Huh!* I'm practically raising our kittens on my own, thank you very much. A little help with pottying and bathing your youngsters wouldn't kill you, would it?"

Black Cat hung his head. "You never asked—"

"Should I *have* to ask?"

The chicks milled around the nest until the papa returned from his initial forage, and then followed him around the yard like the Pied Piper as he demonstrated how to peck through the straw at insects and grain.

Angel looked over at the mama Emus, standing clustered in a corner, looking as if they were engaged in a gossip session. "What about the mamas? Don't they do *anything* to help? What am I missing here?"

"*Umm.* It's even worse than you think. The mama may have already taken up with another fellow and laid another clutch of eggs…" Black Cat turned away, not wanting to risk meeting Angel's eyes.

"Oh, good grief! I can't listen to this heresy of motherhood another minute." Angel spun on her heels and turned her back on Black Cat.

Cindy hopped up and down, clutching the wire.

"The other chicks should hatch over the next several days," John said. He turned on the hose to fill their water containers. "Now, if enough of them hatch, I'll contact my buyers and we can get the eleven I've pre-sold shipped off before the end of the week!" His smile lit up his face. Probably mentally paying bills with the proceeds.

"You have to ship them so soon? Won't they miss their mamas?" Cindy picked up a stray Emu feather and ran it back and forth across the wire.

John shook his head. "Best to ship them when they're three to five days old and they can grow up with their new owners. They grow so fast, if I wait more than a few weeks, the airlines won't take them."

Angel looked back over her shoulder. "They are kind of cute, aren't they?" She leaned against Black Cat's shoulder as the chicks followed their papa around the yard, darting left and right to keep up with him. "I'm not really mad at you, dear."

Black Cat nodded. "Better look quick. They may be cute now, but within six months, they'll be five feet tall."

"Don't think I'd want to meet up with one of them in the dark!" Angel shivered.

"Angel. Come walk with me," Black Cat jerked his head toward the vineyard, lifted his hind leg and scratched at his left shoulder. "We need to talk. You've been so busy with the kittens, you haven't had much time for me."

"I really should get back. Besides, I—" She looked over her shoulder toward the house.

"The kittens are fine. You need the exercise. You've hardly left them since they were born. Come on. We'll go down to the creek."

"What do you mean, exercise? Are you saying I've lost my figure since the kittens were born?"

"Of course not. I love every stripe on your pudgy back… Oh, you know what I mean. But Angel, we have to talk. Tomorrow, that woman is coming…"

They left John and Cindy cooing over the chicks and jogged toward the vineyard. Black Cat's heart beat double time. He had something on his mind and he didn't have much time. Angel wouldn't want to stay out long. Her *person* was coming tomorrow. He had to tell her how much he had come to love her and it wasn't the easiest thing to say.

They walked in silence between the rows in the vineyard. The plants and wires curled high over their heads. Next year, if John's luck held and he could avoid bankruptcy, the vines would hang heavy with clumps of fruit, growing fat and purple in the afternoon sun, but today, only small bunches of grapes the size of little green raisins dotted the immature vines.

"You don't look very happy." Angel turned to him, her eyes sparkling.

He stopped in his tracks. *Happy?* How could she ask such a thing? Happy that she was leaving tomorrow? Was she so besotted with motherhood, that it blotted everything else from her mind? She certainly didn't have leaving on *her* mind. But, then, her babies would go with her.

He wouldn't.

"How can I possibly be happy when I'm losing you?" His heart wrenched. The pressure in his chest was almost more than he could bear.

She glanced around the vineyard and up at the sky. "How can you not be happy? We're safe in a nice home. Our four babies are healthy and Muffins already has found a good home. John's chicks have hatched and he'll ship them soon. Maybe he can pay some bills and stall the foreclosure. Things are working out beautifully. What more could you want?"

Black Cat pulled his whiskers down and laid back his ears. "You failed to mention one teeny, tiny thing. You're leaving tomorrow."

"Am I?" She looked up at the puffy clouds floating by. "Oh, look, that one looks like…what do they call them? Mushrooms?" She took off at a trot toward the river.

Black Cat ran to catch up. "Angel. How can you be so unfeeling? Don't you even care if that woman takes you and the babies away and leaves me behind? I thought you loved me."

He stopped. The ache in his heart stole his breath away. How could she be so…so…happy? Apparently, she didn't give a spit and a whistle about him. Perhaps he only imagined they had a relationship. Oh, she'd needed him in the beginning, alright, a healthy stud to contribute to her magnificent offspring, but now that she was going home, it was over. *Maybe that's just the way it is with lady cats.*

The distance between them grew as she trotted on. Was it symbolic? The distance between them had grown every day since the birth of the kittens, and he hadn't even noticed.

Chapter Twenty-One

Awash with sadness, Black Cat turned back toward the house and trudged down the path.

"Aren't you coming?" Her melodic voice stopped him in his tracks.

He turned.

She sat in a square of sunlight surrounded by dancing shadows filtering through the trees. She looked like an Egyptian statue with her striped toes tucked beneath her curled tail. The sun glinted off her golden head, as though Heaven itself had reached down and declared her an angel. *My Angel.* A lump formed in his throat. He would remember her like this forever, whether he lived for twenty years or only one more day. Wait! *What did she say? Am I coming?*

She tilted her head to the side, one ear tipping forward. "Well?"

He raced to her side. "Are you sure? You still want me to come with you?"

"Of course. I said so, didn't I?" She rubbed against his shoulder and licked his head.

Black Cat's heart swelled almost to bursting, his breath coming in short gasps. Wonder of wonders. *She loves me!* He drew a breath. "I'll be here for as long as you want me. For as long as I'm able. For a lifetime."

She ducked her head and then raised her eyes to his. "A lifetime is not measured by minutes or hours, but by the quality of its moments, however long it lasts," she whispered.

What an odd thing to say. A shiver raced down his spine.

He snuggled against her in the soft grass. His purrs hummed through the pine trees. Black Cat gave Angel's ear a lick, a declaration of his love and commitment. Oh, if only it *could* last forever, not just until tomorrow morning. "Aren't you going to miss me even a little when you're gone?"

Angel tipped up her head in her odd little way, her eyes closed. She looked so peaceful, lying in the grass, as though tomorrow would never come. "What makes you think I'll be going anywhere tomorrow?"

That peculiar remark, again. What about this situation doesn't she understand? I don't belong to Angel's person. She doesn't want me. She said so on the phone.

He pulled his ears back. "Have you forgotten already? Because, tomorrow your *person* is coming to take you away from me, forever." He gulped. Was that a bit too sarcastic? Probably!

"Really? I don't think so. But, don't ask me how I know, dear."

"What is that supposed to mean? You're saying that just to make me feel better."

"Trust me, I know."

He opened his mouth to ask more questions, when voices down by the river caught his attention. "Who's that?"

She shrugged, stood and started running toward the river. Clearly, there shouldn't be anyone down there. John and Cindy were both still ogling the chicks.

Black Cat pushed past Angel before they came within sight of the river, creeping through the bushes, as soundlessly as possible. Mr. Skimmer and another man stood in the river with metal pans. They filled the pans with dirt from the embankment and swished them around, spilling water out with each rotation until the pans were empty. Then, they dropped in another couple of handfuls of soil from the riverbank.

Angel's hackles rose. "What are they doing?"

As Black Cat watched the men in the river, the scene faded and another river took its place…another time. As though in a dream, he saw the beautiful lady and the tall blond man.

The man stands in the river wearing long rubber boots, holding a metal pan. The little girl with bouncing curls sits on the riverbank nearby, playing with a black and white cat. The lady takes sandwiches from a basket. The man swishes the metal pan around and around, spilling out the water. When the pan is empty, leaving only grains of sand, he pulls out a tiny rock. 'Hey, look! It's a gold nugget. That's what I'm talking about. This one alone is worth $300.'

The figures in his mind disappeared and the voices in his dream became the water rushing down the stream.

Angel's voice… "Are you okay? You had the strangest look on your face."

"I was remembering. I saw myself with a little girl and her parents. Her daddy found gold in the dirt." Black Cat looked back toward the men in the water. "Angel. There's gold in John's creek. That's why Mr. Skimmer wants John's property! He knows about the gold."

Angel's mouth twitched up on the corner. "*Ah!* It's all beginning to make sense now."

"If John knew, he could pan the gold and save his ranch."

She shrugged. "That's going to be a fine trick. How are we supposed to tell him? Come on, let's get back. The babies will be awake and hungry." She scampered along the path toward the house.

Black Cat turned and looked back at the two figures, stealing gold from John's creek. Had the greed for gold made Mr. Skimmer do unspeakable things? Even try to kill a man and his child?

A shiver traveled down his spine. He followed Angel back to the babies, waiting for their mother, back to John, who didn't know the answer to his prayers lay scattered in the river, and back to the last few hours he would spend with Angel.

The kittens waddled around the room that afternoon, playing with a wadded-up aluminum ball. They stumbled around the blanket, knocking the shiny toy around and falling over every fourth or fifth step.

Cindy pulled a feather in front of the yet-to-be-named tortoiseshell sister. The kitten chased it, knocking it left and right. She'd be a mighty hunter one day, like her old man.

John showed Cindy how to shove the kittens' noses into a bowl of milk. They sputtered and stepped in the bowl, and then the ancestors' memories kicked in and they knew to lap the milk. They were so cute, their faces smeared with milk mustaches and milk up to their knees. They'd lap the milk and sneeze, and the sneeze would knock them off their feet. Then the little darlings would sit and lick the milk off each other's faces. Before long, they were licking a front foot and drawing it across their own faces. How quickly the ancestor's lessons became part of their own rituals.

God bless those ancestors who shared their memories with kittens so they recall the process of bathing before they're even a month old.

Angel finished up their baths and in no time, with tummies round and hard, the kittens were all fast asleep. *Maybe I should have helped with the baths?*

Muffins lay with her feet in the air with Rambo's head resting on her belly.

Black Cat's heart ached as he stared at his family and soaked up every moment of the happy afternoon. It was the last day they'd spend together and these memories had to last a lifetime.

He lay awake on the couch that night, watching his family sleep. He could only remember the littlest bit of his former life. What happy days had come and gone, without leaving an imprint on his mind? The image of his family burned into his brain. He could never forget these happy quiet moments.

The moon passed overhead, casting long shadows across the yard and the bird enclosure. All too soon, the sky brightened and turned pink as the sun rose in the east, casting patches of sunshine down through the pine trees and warming the air around the little house in the woods. *Why can't it stay dark just a little longer?*

"Mrs. Stubblefield is due around noon." John looked at his watch. "We should straighten up the living room a bit."

Cindy hung her head and carried her doll and her sweater to her room. She'd promised not to raise a fuss, but she wasn't going to be happy about Angel leaving, in spite of her promise to John.

Black Cat sat in the windowsill, staring at the driveway. Mrs. Stubblefield wasn't going to take him. No point hoping. She wanted Angel, but she wasn't interested in a stray black and white tomcat. *I'm glad Angel has found her family. Really, I am. Will I ever go home again?*

All too soon, the crunch of tires in the driveway announced the arrival of Angel's *person.*

John went out to meet her in the yard, opened her car door and shook hands.

Mrs. Stubblefield had grey frizzy hair and wore a pink tee shirt with *Miss Boopkins* scrawled across the front. She handed John a pink cat carrier with lace around the door and a big red bow tied on top. *Miss Boopkins* was emblazoned across the side in script matching the lettering across her pendulous breasts.

Cindy knelt on the blanket and pulled Angel and the babies into her lap. Her lip quivered as she waited for the inevitable.

Black Cat hovered beside her and growled, fighting the urge to tackle the woman when she came through the door. He wanted to fight for his family until his dying breath…but he knew he couldn't. He had to put on a cheerful face for Angel and Cindy's sake. A bloody cat fight to the death wouldn't change anything. And, it wouldn't make Angel's departure any easier for anyone.

His heart seized as the front door squeaked open.

Black Cat froze, facing the moment he dreaded, his heart pounding like a pile driver.

John followed Mrs. Stubblefield inside and set the huge pink cat carrier on the floor.

Mrs. Stubblefield strode across the room, her face wreathed in smiles. She leaned over the blanket.

The old witch! How dare she look so happy, when his heart was breaking?

Angel looked up into Mrs. Stubblefield's face. Their eyes met.

Mrs. Stubblefield scrunched up her face and burst into tears. Tears of joy?

It was too much. Black Cat tried to be brave; he tried to hold it together. *I can't watch. If I stay another minute, I'm apt to bite her.*

He sprinted out the door and over to the woodpile, where he'd gone the day he heard about the kittens. He'd thought on that day, there couldn't be a more miserable cat in the entire state of California. He was wrong. The pain of that day couldn't compare to the agony today. Suicidal thoughts one minute, and homicidal thoughts the next, raged within his breast. *I can't go on living if I lose her. I'll kill the old battle-axe before I let her take Angel. No. I'll kill myself. No…her…*

Cindy shrieked.

His head jerked. So much for Cindy's promise not to throw a fit.

The door opened and Cindy dashed out onto the porch. "Black Cat. Come quick. Here kitty, kitty. Come back. I have something to tell you."

Yeah, right. As if he needed a lecture on etiquette and civility while he watched Mrs. Stubblefield pop Angel into that trumped up Gypsy wagon she called a cat carrier. He flew off the woodpile, out past the Emu enclosure and skidded to a stop at the edge of the vineyard. He couldn't do this.

Didn't I learn my lesson that day when the mama took Angel away? I can't let her and the babies go like this. No matter how much it hurts, I have to say good-bye and wish them a happy life. I have to tell her one more time how much I love her.

He slunk back across the yard, a broken defeated soul. His belly dragged through the yard gathering pine needles that clung to his fur and dropped off as he crossed the porch.

He skulked through the front door, his head hanging.

Mrs. Stubblefield sat on the blanket with Cindy, cooing over the second unnamed cream-colored kitten.

John smiled from across the room.

What's going on here? How dare they look so happy? Way too much jocularity in my moment of misery.

"Oh, there you are, Black Cat." Cindy's face lit up like the light at the railroad crossing. "Come and meet Mrs. Stubblefield. Angel isn't her cat after all, but she wants to take the little cream sister home with her. Isn't that wonderful?" A beam of sunshine shimmered through the window, casting a spear of light across Angel's smug face. *Not her cat? Do I hear a choir of angels singing? Hallelujah! Hallelujah!*

Angel turned toward Black Cat. She dipped her head and blinked, as if to say, "I told you so…"

Mrs. Stubblefield stroked the cream baby across her cheek. "I think I'll call you…Miss Bubblekins… Yes, dats dust what I'll call you."

Black Cat shuddered. A whisker twitched. Who would think that I would welcome the day a daughter of mine should go through life with the name of Miss Bubblekins…but the kitten wound her toes in and out and mouthed an appreciative silent meow. She liked it!

And Mrs. Stubblefield? Any woman who would wear a tee shirt with her cat's name spread across her boobs couldn't be all bad. It looked as if…Miss Bubblekins…had bewitched an unsuspecting victim…*er*…prospective doting owner, which, after all, is the hope of any mother and father cat.

"Can I take her today? I promise to make sure she gets enough to eat." Mrs. Stubblefield had no intention of letting the kitten go.

"I don't know." John shook his head. "She only started to drink from a bowl yesterday. She hasn't had her shots."

"If I have to, I'll get up every two hours and feed her with an eyedropper. Please! And I'll take her to the vet tomorrow and get all her shots. I promise."

"Okay. Cindy, come and say good-bye. Miss Bubblekins is going home with Mrs. Stubblefield."

They all kissed the baby good-bye and wished her well.

Within minutes, Mrs. Stubblefield's car shot down the driveway before John could change his mind, the pink carrier shoved in the back seat and Miss Bubblekins cuddled in her lap.

That afternoon, John took Cindy to the vineyard.

Black Cat snuggled with Angel on the blanket with Rambo, Muffins and the yet-to-be-named tortoiseshell kitten.

"I know she's going to a good home, but I'm a little sad to see her go so young." Angel's eyes sparkled. "I thought I'd have more time to get her on the right track."

"I have to agree." Black Cat patted her foot with his paw. "But, this is the way it's meant to be. It's our job to give them life, teach them right from wrong, make sure they pay attention to their ancestors' wisdom, and kiss them good-bye. That's what we do. You don't have any regrets, do you?"

Angel sighed, her whiskers twitching. "I guess not. Though, I do regret her name is *Miss Bubblekins*."

Black Cat rolled over, four feet in the air, showing off his magnificent white tummy. He chuckled. "I do regret calling her cat carrier a trumped up Gypsy wagon."

Angel glared at him. "You didn't!"

"I did, but I have to admit, she was kind of cute, sitting in the carrier with all the lace and the red ribbons around the door."

"She looked awfully little in there."

Angel looked through the window into the now empty yard where only a few moments before, Mrs. Stubblefield's car had zoomed down the driveway, carrying her baby away forever. She dragged the other kittens closer to her heart.

Are those tears in my Angel's eyes? Cats aren't supposed to cry. Or am I looking through my own tears. It's hard to say.

John rose early the next morning, fixed a pot of coffee and carried a cup to the porch to watch the sunrise. The early morning sky glowed pink and gray.

Got a few minutes before I need to fix Cindy's breakfast. The porch swing squeaked as he settled into the cushions. A bit of quiet might help him sort through the jumble in his mind.

How did the old bum know that Cindy was alone? What exactly was the reason for leaving the headless doll on the porch? What was that supposed to mean?

Maybe he was wrong to ask for sole custody of Cindy. If Carolyn really left her worthless boyfriend, maybe she was ready to make a home for Cindy. *It's so hard to know what's best for her.* Was it in her best interests to keep her with him, or had he made that decision just to spite his ex-wife?

He closed his eyes and listened to the stillness. A hummingbird barreled passed, paused at a flower by the porch, sipped and as quickly as it appeared, flitted off into the trees overhead. Nearby, in the bird enclosure, the papa Emus gurgled and cooed over their charges. The sitting papas shifted position and scratched at their unhatched eggs, fluffed their feathers and settled down on their nests.

John lifted his heart in an unspoken prayer. *I have faith that You can hear me. Help me, Lord. Help me make the right decisions for Cindy. Send me a sign that You're in charge and everything—*

"Daddy?" The screen door squeaked. Cindy stepped onto the porch.

"Good-morning, sweetheart. You're up early."

"Black Cat woke me. He jumped on the bed. Is it time for breakfast?" She yawned.

"It's early. Do you want to go back to sleep for a while or sit and watch the sunrise with me? It's so peaceful this time of day."

Cindy curled up next to him and shoved her feet, swaying the swing. "I'll sit here with you." She pulled her bathrobe tighter around her body.

"Cold?" John draped his arm around her shoulders and pulled her against his warm chest.

She shook her head and snuggled closer. The swing creaked.

"Daddy? I've been trying to think of a name for the tortoiseshell kitten and I just can't decide. Pansy? Missy?"

John smiled. How *did* pets get their names? They named Angel because she held her head a certain way that looked like she was praying. Black Cat got his name because…because they couldn't think of anything better. The Emus got elegant names like Gilbert and Myrtle because they were elegant. But, what do you call a striped mixed-up colored black and orange little kitten? Nothing came to mind.

"I guess you can name her Pansy or Missy. Whatever you want, honey." He squeezed her arm.

"I named Muffins and Mrs. Stubblefield named Miss Bubblekins. You name this one, Daddy. I want you to. We've been calling her *Kitten* long enough. She needs her own name."

"I've been thinking about faith this morning. Faith is a pretty name. What do you think of that?"

Cindy's forehead wrinkled. She put her finger on her lip and nodded. "I like it. I'll go and tell Faith she has a new name." She jumped off the swing. "Thanks, Daddy." The screen door slammed as she dashed into the house.

John rocked, sipped his coffee and looked across the bird enclosure to the vineyard, just visible in the early morning light. Twenty minutes ago, it was bathed in shadow. Now, the sun just glinted off the tops of the wires. The vineyard and the Emus were his future.

Faith. Good name for the kitten. Good thing to have. He shook his head. Faith wasn't really his problem. He had faith that his chicks would sell, faith that the vineyard would produce again. Now that he thought about it, he even had faith that he'd made the right decision about Cindy. She was better off with him. He wasn't going to let Carolyn take her.

No. faith wasn't the problem. What he really needed was time. If only he could hold off the bank long enough for the rest of the eggs to hatch and the vines to produce next year, he'd be home free.

He smiled. Faith *was* a good name for the kitten. She'd remind him daily that he needed to believe that things would work out. If things didn't work out and they had to lose the ranch, then they would need the grace to accept God's will. Faith. Hope. Grace. That's what they needed, all three. If they had another couple of kittens, he'd call them Hope and Grace.

They already had Faith.

Chapter Twenty-Two

"'d much rather sit here in the sun with you girls, but according to my agent," Brett forced his gaze away from his watch, "I should be working on my manuscript today." He winked at Kimberlee, threw back his head and closed his eyes against the sun streaming onto the patio.

"And, I should be down at the bookstore, helping Mrs. Wilson stock the last batch of summer reading books. My excuse is that Dorian came to visit. What's yours?" Kimberlee sipped her tea.

"Just lazy. I'm tired of working on my manuscript."

Dorian huffed. "Are you really going to call your latest novel *Guilty as Charged and Unrepentant?* Could that be any shallower?" She grimaced.

"I've been trying to convince Brett to write another fiction novel. He's such a good writer. I don't know why he's gone back to writing true-crime." Kimberlee leaned over and punched Brett's shoulder.

"Hey! My true-crime books pay the bills. I'm just following my agent's advice. I'll write another fiction novel one of these days. I'm waiting for the right inspiration." Brett put on his sun glasses, tipped his face toward the sun and leaned back in his chair.

"How about making your protagonist a buxom blonde detective?" Dorian patted her hair. "I could give you plenty of plot ideas. In fact, I've been thinking of bleaching my hair from honey-blonde to Marilyn Monroe gold. What do you think?" She shook her flaxen ponytail.

"Talk about shallow…" Kimberlee giggled.

"Which reminds me. Have you heard anything more from Grandmother? Did she ever call back about Noe-Noe?" Dorian reached down to pat Sam. He lifted his head and gave her a doggy grin.

"No. Or if she did, Brett didn't tell me." Kimberlee glared at Brett. "He didn't tell me about her first call for several weeks. I guess he figured I had enough to worry about. My headaches were still bothering me every day, right after…you know."

"Better now?" Dorian added sugar and stirred her tea.

"Guess so." Kimberlee put her hand to her forehead. "I've always had headaches. But they were worse after the accident. Now, only about once a week."

"What did you decide to do about Grandmother's cat?" Dorian shook her head. "I told you the day we left Texas, I didn't think it was a good idea to take her."

Brett set his glass on the table. "I don't think we have to worry. Grandmother was just spouting off. She isn't going to file charges against us. She's just being ridiculous. What good would it do her, anyway? The cat's gone. What *can* we do about it? Get her another cat?"

Kimberlee touched Dorian's arm. "How serious is it to steal a cat?" She lowered her head.

Dorian laughed and gazed across the lodge. A brown leaf dropped from the tree overhead and landed on the patio table. She brushed it away from her glass. "I don't exactly know the penalty for cat-napping…" She grinned. "I'm sure it's a crime, but, I don't think you have too much to worry about."

Amanda wandered through the kitchen door, crooning to the black and white stuffed cat Dorian had bought her. Not that it would ever take Thumper's place. "Now, Thumper, don't cry. Are you hungry?" Amanda rocked the toy in her arms as she crossed the patio, then lifted it to her shoulder and patted its back. "You stay here with Dorian. Mommy will be right back." She laid the stuffed cat on Dorian's lap. "Will you take care of the baby for me, Aunt Dorian? I'm going to get Thumper a snack."

"Sure, honey. I'll…"

Amanda skipped across the cobblestones and into the house.

Brett reached across the table and took the toy from Dorian, slowly shaking his head.

"Do you see?" Tears sprang to Kimberlee's eyes. "Some days I don't even think about losing the cats, until I put Amanda to bed. She prays for them every night and that brings it all back fresh in my mind. Every night! I hate knowing how much she's hurting. She won't even talk about getting another cat. She's so sure…"

"Maybe she's just developed a habit, like, *now I lay me down to sleep, please bring home my cats.*" Brett leaned over and picked up Sam's ball and gave it a heave across the lawn. "It would make things a lot easier if she'd let us get another kitten. It's not like we'd ever forget Thumper, but it would be nice not to be reminded of the accident every single night."

Sam took off in a golden streak, after the ball.

"Maybe you should get another kitten even if she says she doesn't want one." Dorian leaned back and closed her eyes. "Maybe she'd stop thinking about Thumper and *what's-her-name.*"

"It's hard to say." Brett shook his head. "It might be worth a try. The lost cat ads have lapsed and I haven't called the Humane Society for several weeks. Wouldn't they call if something turned up?"

"You should call them again this afternoon, just to be sure." Kimberlee ran her fingers over his hand. "I got a book in the store last week." Kimberlee gestured toward the house where Amanda had disappeared. "It's about helping a child deal with the loss of a pet. The experts are divided on whether you should get another pet right away or wait. I don't know why they bothered to write the stupid book when they don't have any solution to the problem. So, we're back to square one. I don't know what to do."

"Afraid I can't help. I don't have a kid. You'll have to figure this one out yourself. Now, if you want to know anything about dogs, that's another matter. Is there any more tea?" Dorian held up her glass.

"Thanks. You're a big help." Kimberlee poured Dorian another glass.

Many miles away, Black Cat lay half-dozing on the rumpled Indian blanket on the back of the sofa. He shifted away from an uncomfortable lump just beneath his left shoulder. *What is that?* A button sticking up from the sofa? *Oh good grief. Now I'm awake. The darn thing has ruined my nap.* He stood and arched his back, stretched his front legs and curled his toes.

Tires crunched outside in the yard. Black Cat opened one eye, and then sprang to his feet. *Not her again.* "Cindy's mother is back!"

He bounded off the sofa and streaked across the room. "Grab Muffins! I'll take Rambo and come back for Faith. We need to hide. The mama's coming. Hurry! If she finds you, she might try to drag you and the kittens out the door before John and Cindy get back from the vineyard."

Black Cat snatched Rambo by the scruff of the neck and waddled into Cindy's room. Rambo's fat little body swung from side to side.

Angel followed with Muffins and dragged her under Cindy's bed.

Black Cat ran back for Faith. "Now, you kids keep quiet!"

The fur on Black Cat's back bristled. Not this time. Never again! No more *pussy-footin'* around. If the mama tried something again, this time he would fight.

The front door opened and closed. Cupboard doors squeaked and slammed. Cups rattled. Water from the faucet hissed and the coffee grinder growled. Several minutes passed and the coffee pot began to gurgle. The mama settled in like she owned the place. *Who does she think she is?*

Rambo mewed and Angel pressed her paw on top of his head. "*Shh.*" She pulled him over to her tummy and he began to nurse.

The television clicked on. Black Cat breathed a sigh of relief. The

TV would drown out any sounds from the babies. He stretched out alongside Angel. *Might as well finish my nap.* The kittens were safe under the bed, as long as the mama didn't know they were there.

John's voice cut into Black Cat's nap. "Carolyn. What are you doing here? I asked you to call before you came. Put out that cigarette."

"I have a right to see my daughter. Come here, Cindy, and give me a hug."

The front door slammed.

"Where's Angel and Black Cat? What have you done with my kitties?" Cindy's wails grew to hysterical shrieks. "Daddy, she's taken my kitties again."

Poor kid. I should let her know we're okay. He almost felt sorry enough to go back into the living room…almost, but not quite.

"Oh, stop! I haven't touched your stupid cats," the mama snapped. Chairs scraped across the floor. "I didn't see any cats when I came in. So, the cat found her way back? I thought maybe you'd come to your senses and gotten rid of them."

John's voice took on a quieter tone. "Don't cry, honey. They're around here somewhere. Angel's probably moved her babies. Cats do that sometimes. Go look in your bedroom."

Cindy hurried to her room.

Black Cat stepped out from under the bed. *We're here, Cindy. Don't worry. Angel's under the bed with the kids.*

Cindy knelt and lifted the coverlet.

Angel and the babies huddled against the far corner.

Cindy put her finger to her lips. "Good. Stay there until she leaves and be still."

Carolyn's voice rose again. "I heard about someone running off your hens. What are you thinking, John? Our child shouldn't be left out here alone. Whatever you're mixed up in is going to get someone hurt. Why are you putting Cindy in the middle of this?"

"Cindy is just fine. Remember? She's my concern, not yours. You gave up that right long ago. Just stay out of it."

"That's easy for you to say. Cindy's not safe here and you know it! Someone's trying to run you off the ranch. I heard somebody took a shot at you in the vineyard. Sounds to me like you're involved in something illegal. Are you growing marijuana? Is that it?"

John snorted. "Don't be ridiculous. Of course not! Just where do you get all this information? Nobody knows about the shooting incident except the sheriff. I haven't told anyone—"

"I…I…guess I heard it somewhere."

Black Cat pulled his ears down. The shooting incident would be particularly worrisome to a mother…even a bad one. How would she feel if she knew about the old man and the headless doll on the porch?

John mumbled something and closed Cindy's door.

"Don't worry, Black Cat." Cindy leaned over and peeked under the bed again. "Daddy won't let Mama take Angel or the babies. You're safe."

Angel scooted further toward the head of the bed.

"You stay right there, sweetheart," Black Cat hissed. "Better safe than sorry. I'll sit with Cindy." He sprang onto the bed.

Cindy opened a book and propped a pillow behind her head. She patted the bedspread beside her.

Black Cat flopped against her hip. Before long, his head drooped and he fell into a semi-doze, the kind where his mind wandered and thoughts rushed around inside his head, flitting from one topic to another, willy-nilly, without much direction.

He tried again to force some kind of memory of his former life. He concentrated on the scattered images he had remembered. The little girl with the bouncing curls and the horse ranch. Then another memory played out in living color.

A black and white streak raced across the lawn beside the lake. A golden puppy raced behind in hot pursuit, yapping and barking. The cat headed for the nearest tree and in one leap, scrambled up the trunk and onto the safety of the lowest branch, spitting and hissing at the exuberant puppy. Black and white fur puffed up, until the cat was three times his normal size.

Black Cat sat up and stared across the room. *That was me. I'm the black and white cat!* The lake…the lodge next door…the house with the purple flowers across the porch! I remember! He jumped down and crawled under the bed. "Angel. Wait until you hear. I remember my family. Our home is at the lake."

She blinked. Her eyes opened wide. She trembled.

"Why, what's the matter? John won't let Mama come and take you. Don't worry."

"It's not that. I'm not worried about the mama. It's just…your memory. You're beginning to remember…"

She gazed at Rambo, Faith and Muffins, curled up in little furry balls. "The babies are born and old enough to find homes…and now, you're getting your memory back. I…I thought I'd have more time…" She stood, turned her back to him, and lay down again.

"Why, what difference does it make if I…what's this all about? I thought you wanted me to get my memory back." The more he learned about Angel, the less he understood. *More time? More time for what?*

She tipped her head slightly toward him. "It's not that. It's a good thing…your memory. But, I thought… I can't explain." She whipped her head around. "Do you remember *me*?"

He ducked his head. If he were human, he would have blushed, but having only black fur on his face, with a smudge of white over his mouth…

"I have a memory of you beside a water fountain, but I don't think it's at the house by the lake. I really don't remember how we met or… how you came to be my soul-mate."

He licked her shoulder. "But, I'm glad you are. I'm sure of that. I love you and our children. My hope for them is to find good homes where they'll be loved. And, I want us to find our real home."

"What about Cindy and John? Don't you care about them?"

"I…I…do love them, but I think I love my *persons*, too. And, I want to be with you. Oh, Angel, I'm all mixed up. What are we going to do?"

"Some things are within our control and some things aren't. You can't go back to your *persons* at the lake unless someone takes you there… You don't even know where *there* is. So, in the meantime, I guess you'll have to stay with Cindy and John and…with me."

"I'm happy to be with you for as long as I live."

Angel half-closed her eyes and turned her head away. "Then, what is the point of this conversation? Learn to appreciate the time we have together and…and…stop worrying about…about the future."

"Angel?" He nudged her shoulder. She buried her face deeper among the kittens. As much as he hated her silence, he tried to understand. She was worried about something. Her feelings were hurt because he still didn't remember her. If it was fate that they would stay with John and Cindy for the rest of their lives, that would be okay, too. A shiver started from the tip of his tail and worked its way up his back, clear to his ears. They did have the rest of their lives to be together… didn't they?

The front door slammed. Cindy jumped off the bed and peeked out her bedroom door. "Mama's gone. You guys can come out now."

It took an hour or so, but eventually, Angel brought the kittens back to the blanket by the stove.

Rain pattered against the window all afternoon and spattered across the roof, a surprise summer storm, gaining in momentum as the wind rose and whipped the branches over the cabin. *Good napping weather, if I do say so myself.*

John poked up the fire in the pot belly stove and put a movie in the VCR to pass the time.

After supper, Rambo discovered the joys of a pipe cleaner. Muffins and Faith each played with an aluminum ball, but Rambo preferred his *snake*.

"Isn't he cute?" Cindy dragged the pipe cleaner under Rambo's nose. He swatted it with both little, white feet. "I wish we could keep him."

"My child and I used to play with a pipe cleaner." Black Cat peered into Angel's eyes. "Her name is Amanda? You remember Amanda…" Was there any sign of recognition? Of course she must remember Amanda.

Angel turned her had away. She didn't answer.

"You better get to bed pretty soon, Cindy. We have to get up early in the morning. I'm taking the chicks to the airport." John stood and tossed his newspaper on the sofa.

Cindy dropped Rambo's pipe cleaner and sat up straight. "Can I come?"

"Not this time, sweetie. The chicks have to be there by noon. I'm just making a quick trip over and back. It wouldn't be any fun for you. I'll be back before you know it. I've asked Gus if you can stay with him down at the little store. I'll bet he'll let you dust the shelves."

Chapter Twenty-Three

Up ahead, the red SUV crept forward in front of John's pick-up. A flagman flipped his sign from SLOW to STOP. John stomped his brakes. The four Emu carriers in the truck bed shifted with a squeak. John glanced at his watch for the third time since he'd left the house. 9:23 A.M.

Eleven Emu chicks in the four carriers were scheduled for a 12:30 P.M. flight to four different states.

What's with this roadwork? Sure didn't expect this. Should have checked road conditions or gone through Auburn instead of taking Hwy 20. *Am I going to make it?* Another road sign. Reno—62 miles. Did that mean sixty-two miles of roadwork? *God help us.*

A rush of adrenaline shot through his chest. Why hadn't he left home sooner? He was no stranger to unexpected delays along the rural mountain highway. Just coming into view, another Caltrans sign. *Expect Delays.* Really? Should have read, *What do you expect? No delays?*

He glanced through the rear view mirror at the Emu carriers in the back. Finally, the ad he ran on the Internet for several months had had results. With the Utah farmer who'd ordered four chicks, the three going to Wyoming and four to Nevada, he had only sixteen chicks from the current hatchlings left to sell. $4,400 for the eleven chicks sold so far. *Thank you, God.* Things were finally coming together.

Now, if only the remaining chicks could sell within the next two weeks… Timing was so crucial. If they didn't sell, he'd deal with it. They'd grow and add to his flock next year. The females would lay eggs and the papas would take care of the rest. God bless papa Emus.

If worse came to worse, there was always the freezer! That is, if he had the heart to butcher them.

If the ads kept running, the next batch might sell even before they hatched; if he could afford to keep paying for the ads. Thanks to his efforts to fend off the bank, keep a roof over Cindy's head and pay for high priced bird food, all he had left in his pockets was lint.

None of that belly-aching. Time to take himself in hand and concentrate on *faith* again.

9:40 A.M. Almost three hours to his deadline. Reno—58 miles. Traffic crept forward. Another flagman! Of all days, why did they have to work on the road today?

A blood vessel throbbed in his forehead. The chicks had to be at the airport an hour before the flight. If not, they'd make him reschedule. The buyers were most likely already on their way to meet the plane on their end. If the chicks missed their flight, what could he say to his buyers? *"So sorry. Yeah! I'm so irresponsible, I missed the flight and, oh, by the way, you'll have to come back again tomorrow."* No surprise if they canceled the sale and bought from another breeder.

He felt like a man on a tightrope. What if? Missed flight? Buyer cancels. No money to feed the birds. Have to cancel the ads. No more potential buyers. Ranch repossessed. Like a row of dominoes, a missed flight could put every bad thing in motion. Everything could tumble, his dreams, his family legacy, custody of Cindy…

Keep it all together. Surely his life wouldn't go down the drain just because they decided to work on the blasted road today. Beads of perspiration dotted his forehead.

John whacked the steering wheel. "Come on, already! Let's go." The effort was so pointless and futile, his face warmed with embarrassment. *Get a grip, John!*

Another logging truck swooshed past, headed the opposite direction, rocking the pick-up truck. At least they were opening the road in the opposite direction. Their side should be moving soon. His truck hit a pothole, jounced and shook the Emu carriers. John checked the rear-view mirror again. *Guess there's a reason for everything, even when we don't understand. I do have faith. Please Lord, I'm counting on You. Show me the way.* He sighed and a smile worked its way across his cheeks. Caltrans had to work on the road sometime. Why not today?

The long line of cars crawled forward. Up ahead, a man trudged along the road, his backpack bumping up and down with each step. Why on earth would someone be walking way out here? They must be thirty miles from a town in either direction.

From time to time, the hiker turned, glanced at the cars passing and turned back as though he wasn't trying to hitch a ride, just checking traffic and enjoying the scenery. What a place to be on foot, miles from Nevada City and further from Truckee up ahead.

Another road worker waved his flag and traffic came to a stop.

Oh, sure.

9:50 A.M. He'd probably miss the flight at this rate. Well, stewing over it wouldn't change anything. Might as well stop worrying and think about how to deal with another trip to Reno tomorrow. Maybe he could book flights for later in the day.

John's truck edged forward and stopped, almost alongside the hiker.

He turned, locked eyes with John and extended his thumb. Guess he was looking for a ride, after all. The young man smiled. A nice smile. A smile that seemed to say, "Life hasn't been so good to me lately. Can you help?"

Like me. Life hasn't exactly done me any favors lately, either. Except for the chicks…

The young man walked toward the passenger door, an eager expression on his face.

He shielded his eyes from the sun and peered through the window.

Great. Now he's going to ask me for a ride. John's cheeks warmed. What could he say? Sure, I'm going your way, at two miles an hour. We're thirty miles from the nearest town and I have an empty seat, but no, you can't ride with me because somebody once told me it wasn't safe to pick up strangers. 'He could be Jack the Ripper.'

His heart did a little two-step. *This is ridiculous.* I'm a big, strong man. What harm could this kid do? *What if he has a gun?*

What if he doesn't?

Maybe the guy just needs a ride into town. Maybe a few bucks. How much money did he have with him? Not much, that's for sure. So, if the kid was bent on robbery, he picked the wrong pick-up truck full of Emus. Murder? That's another story.

A disarming smile crossed the young man's face. He circled his fist in a thumbs-up gesture.

John pushed the button to roll down the passenger window.

The kid leaned into the truck. "Ride, mister?"

John hesitated, and then pushed the unlock button. "Sure. Get in." *What have I got to lose besides my money and my life?* He smiled.

The hiker pulled off his dirty backpack, dropped it on the floor and slid into the truck. He turned and extended his hand. "Thanks a lot. My name is Peter."

John glanced over at him. Kid needed a haircut and a shave. His jacket collar was frayed and dark with perspiration stains.

"I'm John. From the looks of this traffic, you might make better time walking."

They shook hands. *Interesting.* The way he was dressed, Peter looked like a street person, but his hands were smooth, nails trimmed and clean, like he'd never done a lick of work in his life. He reminded John of a man he used to know who played the piano.

The line of cars lurched forward about ten feet and stopped again.

"Where you headed?" John gripped the steering wheel. His knuckles turned white and the muscles in his neck tightened.

"Down the road a piece. Not far. My uncle has a ranch just outside of Reno on the main highway. If you'll drop me there, I'd appreciate it."

John nodded. They sat in silence, as the cars crept forward several more feet.

Peter leaned down and picked up one of John's business cards off the floor. He glanced at the card and shoved it in his pocket.

"I can't believe this." John checked his watch. I've got a load of chicks in back and a plane to catch at 1:00 P.M. If I miss the flight, I'm apt to lose the sales." He whacked the steering wheel again.

"Hey! Don't sweat it. You'll make it." Peter tapped the clock in the dashboard. "You've got plenty of time. Once we're past the roadwork, it's less than an hour to Reno."

John heaved a sigh and shook his head. "You don't understand what's riding on the chicks making that flight today. And, now this." He waved his hand toward the string of stopped cars moving forward at a turtle's pace.

"What does it matter if you make the flight today? You can always ship them tomorrow."

John huffed. "Ever heard of an Emu? They grow to be six feet tall. If they aren't sold before they're two weeks old, the airlines won't take them. I've only got a small window of opportunity. These chicks have to go today. I could lose everything if I…"

Whoa! Hold it. Peter hadn't been in the truck for three minutes and here he was spilling his guts to the guy. The kid would think he was some kind of a nutcase.

John lifted his hands from the wheel and flexed his fingers, then hunched over the steering wheel. "Look. I didn't mean to dump on you. Let's just say, it's important I get the chicks to the airport today and leave it at that. Okay?"

Peter leaned back in the seat and put his hands behind his head. "Fine with me. Just so you know. You're not the only guy in this truck with troubles."

John shrugged. "You got troubles? You're way too young to know anything about troubles."

Peter wiped his hand over his face. "You see a man hiking in the wilderness with nothing but a backpack and you think he don't have troubles? Everything I own is in that pack." He nodded toward his backpack. "I've got the world's trouble on my shoulders, and that's the truth." He crossed his arms, his lips pressed tightly together.

John turned away and peered at the rear end of the SUV in front of his truck. The world's troubles, indeed. Didn't seem as if Peter wanted to talk about his troubles, and it wasn't his place to question the kid. The cars moved a bit faster now. The clock on the dash read 10:22 A.M. He had an hour and a half to get to the airport. Maybe they'd make it, after all.

"Your birds remind me of several verses in Psalms. Do you know your Bible?"

John's cheeks flushed. "I…I…not as well as I ought to, I guess. I've been—"

"It's kind of appropriate, I think, what you said about depending so much on selling your chicks today. It goes like this. …He is my refuge and my fortress: He shall cover thee with His feathers, and under His wings shalt thou trust: His truth shall be thy shield and buckler."

John's fingers loosened their grip on the steering wheel. *Under his wings shalt thou trust…* That sounded pretty good. Maybe he ought to get out the Bible and read up. The way things were going haywire in his life these days, it might not be a bad idea to plug into a Higher Power.

The cars inched forward. A road worker stepped into the road holding up a SLOW sign. John's truck crept past tractors moving dirt off the road.

"There must have been a landslide." John eyed the tractors as they passed. No way could they let a landslide go for another day. The road crew *had* to do the work today. Once past the crew's work site, just as Peter had predicted, the traffic picked up speed.

As the forest thinned, John and Peter became better acquainted. John told Peter about Cindy, the Emus and shared the story of how the cats came to the ranch.

"So you named her Angel? How did that happen?" Peter raised an eyebrow.

"Cindy said she looked like she was praying, the way she held up her nose, so she called her Angel. She just had a litter of kittens."

"How's she doing?" Peter unzipped his jacket and pulled the collar away from his face.

"Who? Cindy?"

"Angel."

John turned toward Peter. *What a strange question.* "Fine, I guess. Why do you ask?"

"No reason." Peter stared out the side window. "Just curious. I love animals, especially cats."

Before long, the road dropped down into the valley. Another sign zipped by. Reno—16 miles.

John checked his wristwatch. 10:49 A.M. He was going to make it!

"Right up there." Peter pointed to the left. "See that red marker on the side of the road? That's my uncle's place. You can let me off right there, if you would." He leaned forward and zipped his jacket.

John stopped the truck at the end of a long driveway that threaded through the meadow. A white two-story house peeked through the trees.

"Here?" John peered down the driveway. "Do you want me to drive up to the house and make sure someone's home?" He turned into the driveway.

"*Nah!* This is fine. I can walk up. I don't want to keep you any longer." He glanced at the clock on the dash. "Remember? You've got a plane to catch."

"*Uh-oh!* What's going on up there?" John peered down the freeway. Taillights flashed on another long line of cars, stopped about a quarter mile ahead. "Looks like there might be an accident. Just when I thought I was in the clear. I just can't catch a break."

Peter opened the door and stepped out. He leaned back into the truck. "See that dirt road just off to the right up ahead? It goes back about a mile and then doubles back to the freeway. It should get you past this slow-down and back on the highway past all that traffic. After that, it's clear sailing into town."

"You sure? I wouldn't want to get lost back there. Maybe I should wait here and take my chances."

"Suit yourself, but I know the area. Spent a few summers here on my uncle's ranch when I was a kid. Anyway, thanks for the ride."

"Thank you for the company." John glanced back toward the road. "Hope things work out for you. Thanks for the encouragement, too. Means a lot..."

"Not a problem. Have a blessed day!" Peter closed the door, waved and started walking up the driveway.

John checked the traffic and pulled onto the road. Just as Peter said, the dirt road veered off the freeway just ahead. He glared at the red taillights strung out down the freeway. The cars hadn't moved an inch for the past five minutes. John swung the pick-up onto the dirt road. *Sure hope Peter knows what he's talking about.*

Peter. What a strange young man. They'd spent almost an hour together and the only thing he knew about him was that he loved kids and animals, especially cats, and that he had *troubles*. Wonder what kind of troubles? He never said a word about them. He glanced across the seat. Wait! There lay Peter's backpack on the floor. How could he have gotten out of the truck and neither of them noticed it? *Now, what am I supposed to do?*

He stopped the pickup and glanced at his wristwatch. 10:55 A.M. He had to be at the airport by noon. Just enough time to get sixteen miles and then across town, if Peter was right and the dirt road connected back to the freeway, beyond the accident. Barring any further delays.

On the other hand, it was about a half a mile back to the driveway where he'd dropped Peter. He said all he had in the world was in that backpack. But, the round trip would take ten to fifteen minutes, and that was cutting his trip mighty close.

It was the right thing to do, to go back. John turned the truck at a wide spot on the road. He stomped the gas. Dust flew up behind the truck as he bumped back down the dirt road to the driveway where he'd left Peter. The red marker was just up ahead. He'd just pull up to the house, honk and toss the backpack out.

He rumbled down the long driveway. What luck! A woman in a blue housedress stood near the front porch, watering flowers. He'd hand the pack off to her and be on his way. The truck slowed and pulled to a stop. He slammed the gears into park, jumped out, and hurried around to the passenger side. "Good morning," he called over his shoulder.

The door squeaked open, and he hefted the backpack onto his shoulder. "I'm in a big hurry, ma'am. Could I just leave this with you? Can you give it to Peter?"

The woman turned off the nozzle on her hose. "Peter?"

"I gave him a ride. He left his backpack in my—"

"I don't know anybody named Peter. Whatever you're selling, I'm not interested." She tossed the hose on the ground and took a step toward her porch.

John stared at the woman, and then glanced toward the highway. "I dropped him at the end of the driveway, not ten minutes ago."

The housewife shook her head. "Nobody's come up my driveway." She backed up the steps.

She must think I'm some kind of religious nut or a mad rapist. "Thanks anyway." John tossed the backpack into his truck and hurried around to the driver's side. "Look, sorry to bother you. I must have taken the wrong driveway." He called over the top of the truck.

John turned around and raced back to the highway. The woman's face reflected in his rear view mirror, still staring after his truck.

At the end of the driveway, he checked the time. 11:05 A.M. Near the end of the driveway, the red marker flapped on the pole by the side of the road. This *was* the right driveway! What's going on? Where did Peter go? *I don't have time for this.*

He grabbed the backpack. Maybe there was an address or something inside. Somebody he could call when he got home. He slid the zipper. Shoes, an undershirt, an energy bar, toothbrush. There…an address book or a small tablet. John flipped through the empty pages. A piece of paper fell from the notebook. He picked it up.

Highway 20—August 31—9:50 A.M.—Red pick-up truck

There shall no evil befall thee, neither shall any plague come nigh thy dwelling. For He shall give His Angels charge over thee, to keep thee in all thy ways.

Chill bumps careened down John's arms and prickled across his neck. What did it mean? Today was August 31. He'd picked Peter up at exactly 9:50 A.M. on Highway 20!

Peter knew I was coming. He was watching for me. But, how?

John slipped the paper into his wallet, the words crashing through his head. *For He shall give His Angels charge over thee…*

Lightning slashed and collided with a roll of thunder somewhere over the hills. Dark clouds blotted out the sun and hung over the foothills. There'd be more rain by nightfall. A sense of peace flowed through John. He checked the clock on the dash. 11:15 A.M.

Thanks to Peter and his knowledge of the dirt road, there was just enough time to get to the airport, just enough time…the chicks would make the flight and maybe he'd get home before the storm hit.

John squeezed into the traffic on the highway and then bumped along the shoulder beside the cars, until he reached the dirt road. He swung onto the dirt road and bounced along until it curved back to the highway—just beyond the accident, as Peter said it would. Off to the left, ambulances and fire trucks lined the highway. A tow truck had pulled a delivery van out of the ditch and back onto the asphalt. He turned right onto the freeway completely ahead of the accident.

A road sign. Reno—13 miles

Later that night, just before bedtime, Cindy asked about his trip to Reno.

"We got to the airport at 11:58 A.M., just before the chicks' deadline. They made their flight."

"I'll bet they're glad to be in their new homes tonight." Cindy crawled into bed.

"Funny thing," John said. "I picked up a nice young man on Highway 20 and gave him a ride. He asked about Angel. It was almost as if he knew her." John laughed.

"Maybe they were friends before she came to us." Cindy laid her teddy bear on her pillow.

"When I dropped him off, he left his backpack in my truck. I tried to take it back to the house where I left him, but he wasn't there. And, in the afternoon, when I came back up the freeway, I couldn't find the driveway with the red marker where I left him."

"You mean he disappeared? Where did he go, Daddy?" Cindy's eyes popped open. She pulled the blanket over her nose.

"Now, isn't that a good question? It is a mystery, isn't it? I guess if he needs his backpack, he'll give me a call. He took my card."

"If he calls back, ask him if he wants one of Angel's kittens."

John grinned. "I'll do that." *This child was a natural salesman if there ever was one.* "You get to sleep, now, you hear? Good night." He tucked the blanket around her and kissed her forehead.

He closed her bedroom door and stood for a moment, thinking about the note in his wallet. A rumble of thunder echoed over the hills.

He took the Bible off the top of the buffet, sat on the sofa and laid it beside him. He pulled out his wallet and opened the slip of paper he'd taken from Peter's notebook. *There shall no evil befall thee, neither shall any plague come nigh thy dwelling. For He shall give His Angels charge over thee, to keep thee in all thy ways.*

John slipped the paper back in his wallet and opened the Bible, flipped to the Concordance, and skimmed the pages. *Anchor… ancient… Ah, there it is. Angels…*

Chapter Twenty-Four

ewdrops of rain clung to the ridge of the porch. Black Cat's gaze fastened on a particular droplet as it oozed into an elongated shape, then separated from the beam and splatted into the dirt. *Plip. Plop.* Another raindrop formed at the edge, then trickled over to follow the first droplet to the ground. Throughout the night, the summer squall had raged down the mountain. But now, with the storm clouds blown away, the morning sun dried the wet earth and was warming the vineyard and the yard.

"Angel. It's so beautiful outside. Leave the kittens sleeping. Come with me. Let's walk down to the stream and see if there's any storm damage."

Angel patted Faith's multi-colored back, gave Muffins' golden head a slurp and rasped her tongue across Rambo's back. She squeezed through the cat door John had cut into the back door for Black Cat's convenience and followed him around the house and out past the Emu enclosure toward the vineyard.

"John is cutting some trees, but we'll be back before they get home." Black Cat hopped over puddles, carefully placing each foot to avoid patches of mud. *Ick…ick…ick. Hate mud between my toes.* Raindrops still clung to the grape vines, like blue and green and amber diamonds, reflecting the sky and autumn leaves. A rumbling sound came from the direction of the stream.

Angel tipped her head to listen. "That can't be the creek, can it?" She scrambled through the brush to the water's edge.

Run off from the storm now sent torrents of rushing water downstream, tearing at the riverbank, uncovering previously buried rocks. Glistening through the water, irregular shaped objects sparkled and rolled from side to side in the bottom of the creek bed.

Angel stepped carefully toward the edge of the embankment. "Look! Can you see it?"

"It's gold! That's what those men were looking for. The run-off from the storm must have washed more of it from the bank. We've got to find a way to tell John!"

"He'll be gone all day. How can we get him down to the river when he gets home?" Angel pulled her ears down.

Communication! It always reared its ugly head when he needed to tell his *person* something important. "This much gold could save John's ranch! We have to think of something."

The cats stood on the riverbank, staring at the gold nuggets shimmering beneath the water.

"I have an idea." Black Cat leaned further over the edge. "I'll dive in and pick up the biggest nugget. We can take it back to the house."

"You can't! It's way too dangerous. The current is too strong. You'll wash away." Angel nervously trod the grass, her tail whipping back and forth.

"Oh, pooh. What's a little water? I can do it." Before the words were out of his mouth, he realized how foolish they sounded. She was right. The water could very well wash a cat down the river. Even if the water didn't send him crashing to his death against the rocks…he hadn't even thought of that…how could he grab hold of a little nugget in his teeth without swallowing the whole darn river?

He gulped down the bile in his throat, his stomach twisting. *Leave it to me. I always have to play the big hero.* Too late now. He was committed. After such a bragger's claim, Angel would think he was a scaredy-cat if he didn't follow through.

He eyeballed the nugget, gathered his feet together and jumped in. The cold water took his breath away. He headed straight for the nugget, but the force of the water pushed him sideways. He couldn't even see the object, much less pick it up with his teeth. Angel was right.

It was hopeless.

Okay, forget the nugget. I've got to get out of here. Survival instinct took over. He turned back toward the bank, choking and coughing as his head broke water. He thrashed toward the water's edge, scrabbled at the bank, trying to get a purchase on a root or something solid, but the rushing water dragged him back, toppling him upside down. Struggling to raise his head above water, he thrashed and gasped for air. As he tumbled down the river, crashing into branches and rocks, a flash of gold caught his eye. *Angel!* He heard her faint and garbled voice.

"Black Cat! What shall I do? Oh, Black Cat!"

Panic gripped his heart. *Angel! The babies!* Why had he been so stupid? *Is this the way it ends?* His head broke the surface. He gulped a breath of air and swallowed water. The bushes blurred as he passed. The sky grew dark. Water swirling…choking…*Angel!* Which way was up? A rock loomed ahead and everything turned black.

"Black Cat!" *Numm numm* (lick, lick). "Wake up. Oh, please don't die." *Numm, mmm.* "Won't you please speak to me?" *Mmm mmm…* (lick, lick).

The roar of the river still filled his head, muddling her voice. Something wet and rough rasped across his face, the coarse texture ever so gently caressing his cheeks, his forehead, pulling him back from the darkness, pulling him back…

Black Cat opened his eyes. His face reflected back from Angel's eyes. He shivered. *Cold…so cold.*

Water dripped off Angel's nose onto his face as she licked his mouth and eyes. He lifted his head, coughed and gulped in a breath of air. "I'm…okay…I'm…" He rolled to the side, coughed and water spewed through his nose and mouth.

"Oh, oh. You're alive. Thank goodness. You've got to stop doing this. That's twice. How many times can I bring you back from the dead?"

"*Ah-choo!*" He took a deep breath. "And, how many times am I going to come back from the dead? How did I get out of the river?"

"You washed downstream. The water wasn't so deep down here. I...I pulled you out."

He lifted his head, his eyes wide. "Angel! You shouldn't have. You could have been washed away, too."

"No. It's alright. You don't understand. I can't die. It's the only reason why I'm here. I knew I could save you. I had to save you—"

"What do you mean...you had to save me?" He sat up and stared at her wet, mud-caked face. Water puddled on the ground beneath his body. "What are you talking about?" A tremor went through his body. But, it wasn't from the water soaking his fur. It was something more. Something big and scary. Something he couldn't put into words.

Angel closed her eyes and sighed. "I haven't been honest with you, but, now, I have to tell. The day of the accident. I...I died when the truck hit our car and our carrier was thrown out. I died, Black Cat. I died and went to Heaven."

Black Cat gasped. *She what? Died?* His eyes burned.

"St. Peter met me at the gate. I begged him to let me come back, not to take me yet. You were so badly hurt and you needed me. I told him about the babies. I pleaded with him to let me come back and stay with you, just for a little while."

Black Cat closed his eyes. "I can't listen to this." Her words made his blood run cold.

"You must. I have to tell."

"No. No. Please, don't say anymore." The darkness threatened to consume him again.

"You must listen. You have to understand. At last, St. Peter relented. He agreed to let me come back until the babies were born and settled, until your memory came back, until you didn't need me anymore. He promised I could stay...but, only as long as you needed me."

"No...No!"

"You see? That's how I knew I could pull you from the river, because all the babies don't have homes yet. They still need me. You still need me. You haven't completely gotten your memory back.

John still needs to save his ranch. I knew I could save you. Don't you understand? My mission… My assignment. I'm not done yet." She dropped her head.

Black Cat laid his head on his paws and closed his eyes. *Maybe if I don't move, time will stand still. Maybe this is all a nightmare. Maybe when I open my eyes, I'll be home with my real family, whoever they are.*

One of his eyes peeked open. A ray of light bounced off the nugget at Angel's feet and danced across her face. He lifted his head. "What have you done?"

She shrugged. "When I got you out of the water, I went back into the river to get the nugget, so we can take it to John. I told you. Nothing can hurt me. Not until you have your memory back and Rambo and Faith have homes…because he promised."

"Angel." Black Cat gulped down the lump in his throat. His memory was coming back. Two of the babies already had homes. Faith and Rambo would soon be settled. With the gold in the river, John could save his ranch… If her story was true, she was running out of time. It must be true because she'd risked her life and pulled him from the water, went back for the nugget and lived to tell the tale. The river couldn't take her…because *he promised.*

But, Angel! How could he lose her now after all they'd been through? Black Cat shook the water from his coat.

She crouched on the ground, her eyes closed, water dripping off her little nose, like she couldn't even feel the cold. She opened her eyes. "If you're ready, we should get back. The babies will be frightened if they wake and we're gone. We're both soaking wet."

Black Cat stood and gave his body another shake and his chest a cursory lick. He'd finish the job back at the house. "I'm as ready as I'm going to be."

Angel picked up the nugget. She led the way back through the vineyard and slipped through the cat door. She put the nugget on the couch where John would see it as soon as he came home.

Black Cat lay on the blanket beside the warm stove while they groomed each other's coats. His thoughts were muddled. Her confession left him speechless. How could it be true? People don't come back to earth after they die, and even though they say cats have nine lives, it didn't mean… It was all too confusing. He curled up, determined to sleep on it. Maybe things would be clearer when he awoke.

By the time John and Cindy returned from cutting wood, the warmth from the stove had almost dried Angel's short fur, but Black Cat's long coat was still damp and clung to his back.

He opened his eyes when John opened the front door. How long would it take before he noticed the nugget?

John laid his jacket across the couch. "Good Lord! Where did this come from?" He held the shiny nugget up to the light, his eyebrows jacked a half inch higher than usual. He turned it back and forth. "It's a gold nugget." He glanced around the room. Maybe he expected to see that leprechaun with a pot of gold jump out from under the table.

"Cindy. Do you know…? Where did it come from?"

She shook her head and shrugged. "Is it real gold?"

John turned toward the cats. He must have guessed the answer and then dismissed the idea as quickly as it came to his mind. He shook his head. "Impossible."

Black Cat waddled over to the couch and rubbed against John's ankle.

John ran his hand down Black Cat's back. "Why, he's soaked to the skin. You don't think… No. It…couldn't be…could it?"

"What, Daddy? What couldn't be?"

"This is real gold, honey." He held up the nugget. "It's worth a lot of money. Black Cat must have found the nugget in the river and brought it back…but it's too much to think… Why would he do that?"

John grabbed his jacket. "Come with me. Let's go check it out." He hurried out the door with Cindy running behind.

"That was easier than I thought." Black Cat started toward the door. "Should I go with them? Maybe they won't find the right place where we—"

"Come on back. They'll find the right place. Don't worry about it. I know…" She closed her eyes and tilted up her chin, like she was praying. She knew.

Black Cat turned back. "If you say so…" He went right back to sleep beside the warm fire filled with assurance. John would find the right place at the creek. He would salvage the gold and he would save his ranch. Angel said it was all part of St. Peter's plan.

Black Cat shivered. Maybe St. Peter's plan would save John's ranch, but it brought the day that much closer when he would call Angel home…

Chapter Twenty-Five

Rumblings from John's pick-up truck brought Black Cat to the living room window. He nosed the curtains aside, just as John turned onto the country road headed for the assayer's office in Nevada City. They'd be gone for a while. *It's up to me to take care of things until he returns.*

Black Cat scanned the yard. It was a golden fall day. The oak trees had dusted the lawn with curled leaves. His head jerked up. *What a scathing idea! Wait until Angel hears!*

Black Cat jumped down from the windowsill and sauntered over to the blanket were the kittens swatted each other's tails.

Angel kept guard nearby, her face alight with mother's love. *Oh, how I love her.*

"I have a wonderful idea." Black Cat danced on his two front feet. "It's a perfect day. Let's take the babies outside. It's time they learned about the outdoors!"

"Are you sure it's warm enough? They're only seven weeks old. What if they catch a chill?" Angel scooped Faith closer to her side. "This little punkin' sneezed yesterday."

"Don't be such a mother hen. Of course it's warm enough. Faith probably got one of Rambo's hairs up her nose."

"If you think it's alright, but you have to promise to stay close and help me watch them. You know how they are. You can't wander off on some wild squirrel hunt." Angel gave Faith a motherly slurp across her back, knocking the baby off her feet. She tumbled and rolled.

Muffins jumped onto Faith's head and a mock battle ensued, ears lowered, tail a-swish, and a stance assumed such as might be expected if the assailant were a buffalo, not a four-inch tall sister.

Rambo waddled over to Angel's side. "We won't wun away, Mama. We be good."

"You see? They're fine. They'll love it outside. Come along, children. Papa is taking you for an adventure."

What fun. The old man's taking the kiddies for a walk. With his head held high and a bounce in his backside, Black Cat traipsed out the cat door. The kittens trailed behind and Angel brought up the rear, grumbling. The kittens stopped short, bumping into each other when they reached the wooden planks on the small back porch.

"Oohh! Papa. What is that?" Rambo arched his back, his fur at half-mast.

"That's a tree, son. Nothing to worry about. See? There are trees all around. Now, follow me around the house into the front yard. I'm going to show you something even more amazing. It's called *grass.* You'll like it." He twitched a whisker, amused by his joke.

The kittens tumbled off the steps and trailed Black Cat down the sidewalk. He ambled along the side of the house, looking back every other step. The kittens spread out behind him and Angel took up the end, like a long and unwieldy parade. With each twig or leaf or rock, the babies had to stop to pat and sniff.

Black Cat's eyes danced between the curious kittens. "See! I told you it was fun outside."

In the front yard, the kittens stepped cautiously onto the tiny lawn, shaking each foot when it touched the grass. It didn't take long before Rambo and Muffins were frolicking across the lawn. *Look at them. What fun they're having, running and falling down.*

Faith hung back by the corner of the front porch.

"Come on over," Rambo called to his shy sister. "We're *pwaying* tag. You can be *it.* We'll *wun* and you catch us." He leaped at Muffins, but she evaded his attack and ran toward Angel.

Faith took one step onto the grass then turned and scrambled back to the front porch steps. "*Nuh-uh!* I don't *wike* it squishing 'tween my toes." She hunkered on the bottom step, her eyes wary, as she watched her more courageous siblings.

"Leave her be, Rambo. She'll come and play when she's ready." Black Cat moseyed to the edge of the lawn, turned in a circle and lay down in a patch of sun. He meant to keep a careful eye on the kittens, but the sun warmed his back and soothed him into a melancholy mood. His eyes grew heavy.

Rambo and Muffins cavorted across the lawn.

A shadow crossed Black Cat's head, rousing his half-slumber. He looked up. High above the house, a hawk hung suspended in the air current, silhouetted against the sky, circling, drifting. Black Cat closed his eyes. *Ahh. Such a beautiful day. Life is good.*

Angel's shriek sent shock waves through his head. "Black Cat. Get Faith! Children! Run."

Black Cat's eyes flew open as his sense of security disappeared like a snowflake in a campfire. The hawk, no longer circling, was rocketing down toward the lawn, its talons outstretched!

Hearing their mother's warning, Rambo and Muffins flattened themselves on the grass. Danger! Then the ancestors' memories must have blazed into their consciousness. Run! Not even knowing why, or what danger might be present, the two kittens sprinted across the lawn and plunged into the bushes beside the porch. Safe! But, Faith froze and crouched, her eyes wide, her front legs spread.

Black Cat leaped to his feet as the hawk hurtled toward Baby Faith. He streaked across the lawn, his legs churning, his heart pounding. *Baby Faith! I can't make it!*

He was supposed to be watching, protecting her. Angel said as much and he'd agreed. Then he lay down and went to sleep. Now, Faith would pay for his mistake. His heart wrenched as each bound brought him closer toward the killer. *Got…to…save her. Almost there… Not enough time! Can't…make…it…*

Black Cat leaped, just as the hawk gouged its talons into Faith's back. He struck the hawk's massive breast, knocking him sideways.

Momentarily off balance, one set of the hawk's talons slipped and missed its grip in Faith's back.

Black Cat screamed and clawed at the bird. The hawk fell again, dragging Faith backwards with one hideous foot. Its huge wings beat against Black Cat, slamming him to the ground, fur and feathers flying.

Black Cat lurched to his feet as the hawk regained its balance and lifted off the ground, hovered in the air, then flapped across the driveway, clutching the thrashing kitten with the talons on only one foot.

Angel leaped toward the hawk, now five feet off the ground. She missed the mark and fell back to the grass.

The bird struck out across the yard toward the Emu enclosure, dangling Faith's body beneath him.

Faith howled, her writhing and twisting preventing the giant bird from sinking his other talons into her body.

Fight, Faith. Fight! You might still have a chance.

Black Cat and Angel raced below, keeping pace with the hawk, now nearly fifteen feet up. *It's too late. Too late…*

Angel screamed. "Faith, darling, mother's coming!"

Oh, Angel. You know it's hopeless. Black Cat sprinted beneath the bird, keeping even with his squalling daughter. With every stroke of the massive wings, Black Cat's hope for a miracle dimmed. The hawk rose higher and Faith's cries began to fade.

Angel stopped near the Emu enclosure and collapsed, panting, trembling.

Black Cat raced on, his gaze locked on the hawk. Angel would never forgive him. *My fault! My fault!*

Faith's fading shrieks stilled the Emus as the hawk flew across the top of their enclosure.

My darling Faith. My baby! Black Cat's lungs ached. His head throbbed. He ran on, so wanting to stop and throw himself on the ground… Block out the horrible sight, but he had to go on. Little Faith might look down and take some momentary comfort seeing him beneath her. He wouldn't stop until either the bird disappeared over the trees or he collapsed. His gaze never left his darling as each flap of the hawk's wings carried her to her death. *My fault, my fault!*

Faith fought on, twisting, struggling to escape her tormentor. How could she know that death was inevitable, even if she succeeded in freeing herself?

And, then her body plummeted down, down, jerking and twisting as she hurtled toward the ground on the far side of the bird enclosure. Her shrieks echoed through the afternoon sky and then grew silent.

Black Cat skidded to a stop next to the Emu's gate, panting, unable to move. The stillness around him was almost palpable. Even the wind ceased to move through the trees. Somewhere beyond the Emu enclosure, near the vineyard, laid the crumbled body of his baby. He had to go to her. He had to bring her home. He glanced back toward the house where Angel lay huddled on the ground, still unable to move.

He turned back and steeled his heart for the ghastly task ahead. He had to find Faith's body and bring her home. He wouldn't leave her. The hawk might circle back to reclaim his kill. Or, she'd be prey to the tiny scavengers that scurried through the night.

Black Cat forced his weary body to take one step and then another, plodding around the enclosure. The Emus clustered next to the wire, their long necks thrust forward, fascinated by the unexpected drama of death playing out in front of their ugly eyes.

Clouds gathered in a blue sky overhead. The afternoon sun shone down on the young vines where John had trundled the soiled straw from the Emu enclosure to spread beneath the vines, to warm the roots and nourish the ground. Nearby, the scent of the pine trees filled the air and now that all was quiet again, the birds took up their songs.

Black Cat paid little attention to the sights and sounds as he trudged along, looking left and right, his heart as heavy as a thundercloud. How could he face Angel? What would Cindy say when she came home and found Faith's body, torn and bleeding?

There! On top of John's haystack, next to the burned-out stumps; a patch of gold and black. Faith's body lay motionless, half covered with filthy straw.

Frantic to reach her, Black Cat clawed his way to the top of the haystack. His stomach turned at the stench of the excrement mixed with straw baking in the sun.

She lay with one leg outstretched, her chin resting on her paw. *She looks so peaceful, almost like a sleeping princess.* A smear of blood and feces matted her fur where the hawk's talons had seized her by the ribs. *Oh, Faith. How I've failed you.* How he wished he could cry.

Black Cat drew in his breath and licked the blood from her side. Self-reproach washed over him, almost choking his breath away. *I'll have to go away now. Away from the ranch.* Angel would never forgive him. He would never forgive himself.

Angel had asked one thing of him, only one thing—to help her watch the children—to protect his family. His heart ached with shame. Better get on with it. He'd take her body home to her mother and then, tonight, when everyone was sleeping, he'd go. He couldn't look Angel in the eyes ever again, knowing he was responsible for the death of their darling. *I'll go before…*

What was that? The barest movement in the straw. *Faith?*

Her body trembled. She gasped and drew a breath. She moved her head.

"Faith! How…? You're alive?" Oh, great Father of all creatures, thank-you!

"I fighted him, Papa. I fighted until he letted go." Her voice a bare whisper. Her little head rocked. She struggled to hold it upright.

"You did. My little hero." He licked her face, her eyes, her mouth, cleaning off the muck and soothing her fear. "Are you alright? Is anything broken?"

"I want my mama."

"She's back at the house with Muffins and Rambo. I'll take you home."

A shadow passed overhead. Black Cat looked up. The hawk circled and dropped lower over the haystack. Had he returned to claim his dinner? *Oh, no you don't. Not this time.* Black Cat straddled Faith and fluffed up his fur, twice his size. From the bottom of his lungs, he brought forth the most hideous shriek he could muster. His heart thundered in his chest. Even his ears tingled from the sound. *If we fight again, this time, hawk, one of us is going to die.*

The hawk passed over Black Cat and turned into the wind. Perhaps the tiny kitten wasn't worth the battle. That small morsel of food would hardly be a snack for his squawking brood. The hunter struck off across the vineyard, perhaps to explain to his scowling wife why today's hunt had been a total bust and he had returned empty-clawed. He disappeared over the treetops.

Black Cat grasped Faith by the nape of the neck, hopped down from the pile of hay and set her on the ground. "Can you walk, my darling?"

"My tummy hurts, Papa."

"Then I'll carry you." He picked her up again, waddled back around the end of the Emu enclosure, down the path and onto the lawn. He laid Faith on the grass and searched the yard. "Angel?"

She was gone. The kittens were nowhere in sight.

His heart churned back into the danger zone.

"Angel! Where are you?" Black Cat sniffed the place where he'd last seen her, then scampered across the grass to check the bushes where the kittens had run. Had the hawk returned and carried off Angel and both kittens when he wasn't looking? *Don't be an idiot. It couldn't carry off all three. Angel has taken the kittens back into the house.*

"Come, Faith." He picked her up and carried her into the kitchen and set her on the floor. "Now, you wait right here beside the door. We'll surprise Mama. I'll bring her back."

He found Angel lying on her blanket, scouring the smell of the yard off Rambo's back until the kitten wailed from the grief she poured into each desperate lick.

"She's alive, Angel. She got away. The fall knocked the breath from her, but she landed in the straw behind the enclosure. She's going to be alright. She's waiting for you in the kitchen. Run and fetch her."

Black Cat trod the floor with his front feet, so pleased was he to bring such good news.

Angel's tongue stopped in mid-slurp over Rambo's back.

The love-drenched kitten took advantage of her momentary lapse to scamper away and hide behind the kitchen table.

"She's alive?" Angel jumped to her feet. "I should have known she'd be alright. *He* promised!

The tingle started at his ears and wiggled down Black Cat's back. So, everything Angel said was true. St. Peter had planned it all in advance. *Nothing I do will change a thing.* The kittens were safe. His memory was coming back. The gold nugget would save John's ranch. And, then…what?

Chapter Twenty-Six

"Nevada City County Clerk. This is it." John read the sign on the building, wiped his sweaty hands on his pants, cranked the wheel and backed the pick-up into a parking space in front of the Nevada City County Clerk's office. He'd lain awake half the night wondering if he owned the mineral rights on his property. Without the mineral rights, the prior owner could swoop in and claim all the gold in the stream. Without the gold, Black Cat's discovery wouldn't change anything and the means for saving the ranch would disappear. "Come on, Cindy. Let's get this over with before I have a heart attack." He wiped the perspiration off his brow and stepped down from the cab. *Here goes nothing!*

Inside, he smiled at the young woman at the counter. "Good morning."

She twiddled a pencil and laid it on the counter. "May I help you?"

"I've found gold on my property. I have my father's deed here." He unfolded an old document and laid it on the counter. John's stomach wrenched. "Does my deed include mineral rights? I…I don't know how to read it."

The clerk glanced at Cindy and smiled.

A tingle crept up John's neck and into his face. He glanced around the office. Rows of shelves were lined with large dusty binders bearing stick-on dates peeling off the spines. The blinds were drawn against the morning sun, casting a shadowy *don't expect a miracle* mood throughout the office. A vase of shriveled roses sat on the counter. Could God be so cruel as to show him the gold and take it away in a heartbeat? He closed his eyes. *Oh, Lord, help me now.* He opened his eyes. "Please. Can you please look it up?"

The clerk picked up John's deed. "1952. That's not going to be on the computer. I'll have to check the old records." She glanced over the binders and pulled one off the shelf. "This looks right. 1949—1953." She placed the large binder on the counter and began to flip through the pages listing recorded deeds. "*Ah*. Here it is." She picked up the pencil and tapped the page. "John Goldstein, Sr. Filed in August, 1952. Let me see… Mineral rights… *Humm…*"

John's heart pattered in his chest. His good fortune hung on the clerk's answer. He held his breath.

The clerk ran her finger down the page, adjusted her glasses and peered at the faded page. "Here it is. The mineral estate of the land includes all organic and inorganic substances that form a part of the soil. It is the right of John Goldstein, Sr. to exploit, mine, and, or produce any or all minerals lying below the surface of the property. Congratulations, Mr. Goldstein. You can claim anything found on your property."

"Yes!" John thrust his fist in the air and danced a little jig. "Oh! Excuse me." His cheeks warmed.

The clerk grinned. "I understand. Now, there are some forms you'll need to complete. Let's get to this paperwork."

Within thirty minutes, the paperwork was completed. John took Cindy's hand. "Now that that's done, let's walk down to the General Store. It's only a block. I'll need some gold pans, hip boots and…and a gold scale! Hope there's enough left on my credit card to…" Enough said. No need to go there with Cindy.

John and Cindy swung their hands as she skipped down the sidewalk. If he were ten years younger, he'd join her and skip alongside. He contented himself with letting his heart do the skipping.

John pushed open the door of the General Store. A bell tinkled overhead. He gazed around the store. Every time he came through that door, the sense of stepping back in time hit him again. Shopping at the General Store was almost as much fun as going to a museum.

Shelves on both sides of the room rose to the ceiling, piled high with boxes of merchandise. Work gloves, hammers, lengths of chain, oil lamp wicks—the very items one might find in a turn of the century hardware store. John glanced up at the wooden ladder attached to a rail near the ceiling, allowing the clerk to slide back and forth, to retrieve items from the high shelves. Years of wear on the original hardwood floor planking felt smooth underfoot. *How long has this store been in business, anyway?*

A sign on the wall stated the 1863 store was as much of a *must see* to visitors as the stained glass windows in the church down the street.

John ran his fingers over the words *National Cash Register* carved into the back of an antique brass cash register sitting on the counter. It was polished to a golden luster and carved in high relief with leaves, ribbons and fleur-de-lis.

John tapped his fingers on the glass counter. "Hello. Anybody here?" He looked around the empty store. His gaze rested on a stack of iron skillets displayed near the door.

Strange. Where's the clerk?

Cindy pointed to a large glass jar of peppermint sticks. "Look at the candy, Daddy."

"Doesn't it look yummy?" John walked to the end of the counter and stared down the aisle. "Hello?"

A curtain parted near the back of the store and a young man stepped out. "Sorry. Sorry. I was counting bolts in the back room. Didn't hear the… Well, hello. John, isn't it?" He strolled down the aisle, his hand outstretched, a smile crinkling his eyes.

John's mouth dropped open. "Peter! What on earth? I thought you were an…*um.*" *Whoa. Don't even go there.* He had tucked the paper indicating the date and the time they met, and the Bible verse in his wallet. After all, Peter *had* disappeared on the Reno highway. Anyone would think… He shook Peter's hand.

"And yet…here I am!" Peter moved behind the counter. He smiled down at Cindy. "Hello, Cindy."

Cindy nodded and looked away.

John stared at Peter. How rude he must look with his mouth hanging open. "I…I… You left your backpack in my truck. I came back, and you weren't there. Where did you go?"

Just exactly how *had* he disappeared within ten minutes? The woman at the ranch house said… John raised an eyebrow.

Peter placed his hands flat on the glass counter and leaned forward. "You know what happened? You no sooner drove away, when I realized my mistake. It's been years since I was on the ranch. We stopped at the wrong driveway. I must have been around the corner when you came back. Hey, I'm sorry. I can see why you'd wonder. Now, what can I do for you?" Peter reached across the counter, opened the jar of candy and pulled out a peppermint stick. "Do you like peppermint?" He handed it to Cindy.

She took the candy. "Thank you."

John gazed around the store. "So, two days ago, you were in Reno, and now you're working here? How did that happen?" *Am I still just a wee bit skeptical? You bet I am.*

"When I learned that I was needed here, I left the ranch and here I am. That's about it, end of story. Now, what can I do for you? If we don't have it, you don't need it." Peter chuckled.

Cindy sucked on the peppermint stick and wandered over toward the humming bird feeders.

John shoved his thumbs in the top of his jeans and rocked back on his heels. "We have a small stream on the back of our property. I thought I'd show Cindy how to pan for gold. Who knows? We might get lucky." John gazed up toward the ceiling and then looked down. His face warmed. *No need to spill my guts to this guy.*

Cindy whirled around. "Daddy! Black Cat and Angel already found a gold nugget. I thought we were looking for *more* gold."

John ran his hand over his mouth. He turned from Peter and glanced around the store. "We need to get some hip boots and gold pans and—"

Peter came around the end of the counter and touched Cindy's shoulder. "Did you say Angel found a gold nugget?"

"Daddy said they must have jumped in the river and pulled it out because Black Cat and Angel were still wet when we came home. The nugget was on the couch."

"Isn't that interesting—"

"Well, now, let's not bore Peter with all that." John pulled Cindy away and pointed toward the back of the store. "Sweetie. Why don't you look around for a bit while I finish shopping? Peter's busy and we mustn't keep him from his work." He gave her a gentle nudge toward the back of the store and turned back to Peter. "If you'll just point me toward the hip boots and the gold pans, please."

"Right over here, John. By the way, I'd like to get my backpack, if you don't mind. I was meaning to contact you about it this weekend."

"Sure. You've still got my card?"

Peter nodded.

"I could drop it by in a couple days, next time we're in town."

"That's a thought. I don't have transportation. Here's the gold panning equipment. Everything you need should be right here. I'll just let you look around. If you have any questions, give me a yell. Those nuts and bolts are waiting."

John's gaze followed Peter into the back room. *Wish Cindy hadn't said anything. Though I can't imagine what difference it makes. Who's he going to tell?*

Chapter Twenty-Seven

The aroma of barbecued Emu steaks hung in a tantalizing cloud, drifting across the front porch where Black Cat lounged in a spot of sunshine. He lifted his head and sniffed.

"How disgusting! They're not eating one of the baby chicks, are they?" Angel shuddered and nodded toward the barbecue pit. John's friend, Barney and his wife, Millie, sat nearby with John at the patio table.

Black Cat shrugged. "Barney bought it at a Specialty Store and brought it from town. They wanted to know what they taste like. From what I understand, humans raise Emus for their meat. John sells the chicks to other farmers, but some of them sell the meat to stores that specialize in exotic food, like Emu and buffalo. Barbecued Emu is supposed to be very tasty."

"Where, pray tell, did you learn so much about Emus?" Angel flicked her tail, shaking a fly off her back.

"I heard John talking on the phone the night he borrowed money from Barney. They were discussing why Emu's were a good investment."

"I still don't understand how *persons* can raise them and then eat their pets." Angel tipped her head and glared at John. "How can he sleep at night?"

"I guess it's because *humans* have inferior brains. It's not something cats would do. I mean, can you imagine? Raising mice for the sole purpose of eating them? *Yuck!*"

"Or selling their itty bitty hides to make Lilliputian mouse fur coats?" Her whiskers twitched.

"Let's get at it, Barney. That gold won't pan itself!" John picked up his gold pan, hip boots and little cloth sack with tie strings. He hadn't been so excited since he was in the sixth grade, just let out of school for the summer. He shoved the last bite of chocolate brownie in his mouth, stood and strode down the path with his hand on Barney's shoulder. *Is this really happening? My gold. Right here in my river!*

Millie and Cindy finished packing up the lunch and arrived at the stream a short time later with a bag full of sodas, snacks and hot coffee, and carrying two lawn chairs. "Set your chair here, honey. If we're lucky, maybe one of them will fall in the river." Millie giggled.

"You're just jealous 'cause you don't have hip boots." John lifted one rubber-covered leg part way out of the water. "You know you're dying to get in here and look for gold. Admit it." He dipped his pan into the water and gathered up a bit of sand from the bottom. He swished the water around and with each swish, a bit more sand and water spilled over the side.

"Hey!" Barney yelled. "I think I see some color." After a few tries, he got the hang of the process and several pans later, a bit of gold dust or a tiny nugget sparkled in the bottom of his pan.

Wouldn't you know, Barney would find the first gold?

John looked out across the vineyard into the hills beyond. "I feel like I've gone back in time—a hundred years ago—like a miner who stepped into a stream and hoped to come out a millionaire. Not that I expect to become a millionaire—"

"Not that many came out any richer than when they went in." Barney dipped his pan back into the water.

Millie pulled the thermos bottle from her goody-bag. "Thousands of fortune hunters came to California when they heard the word *gold*. Some of the women got rich off the miners and opened saloons, and restaurants, and…and…things." Millie's cheeks pinked up. She leaned back and sipped her soda. "Cindy, do you know how Nevada City got started?"

Cindy shook her head.

"When the gold ran out, most of the miners drifted away, but many saw the beauty of the land, planted crops and sent for their wives and children. They built churches and schools and before you know it, Nevada City was here to stay." Millie swept her hand out across the vineyard. "And, other towns too, all over the Sierra Mountains."

"Now, don't forget that, Cindy. You might study California's history next year." John laid his gold pan on the bank and wiped his arm across his forehead.

From time to time, Barney would whoop and climb out of the stream to show Millie a small nugget he'd found. His little sack of gold began to fill. "John should have enough to make his back payments pretty soon."

"You'll have to keep some, too." John picked a tiny nugget out of his pan and dropped it into his sack. Thank God for true friends like Barney and Millie. One of the few couples who'd stuck around and actually supported him, emotionally and financially, after Carolyn left.

"*Nah.*" Barney hefted his gold pan. "I'm just here for the fun of it. You keep all of it, John. You'll need it to get through the winter, until you can harvest your grapes." Barney shot Millie a grin.

She nodded.

"That's awfully nice of you. But, if you find a pretty little nugget, you keep it and make a necklace for Millie. I want you to."

"Alright. If you insist. Hey, Millie, what do you think?"

"I'd rather have two little ones for earrings, babe!" Millie laughed.

"Can you make me a necklace, too, Daddy?" Cindy bounced out of her chair and walked to the edge of the stream.

My little girl is growing up. I should have thought of it myself. "I can, sweetheart. I've seen pretty little bottles with gold dust in them. That would be just right for you." He waded toward the bank. "How about some of that coffee, Millie."

Millie screwed the cap off the thermos. "I'll pour you a cup."

John followed Barney out of the water, drying his hands on the tail of his shirt. They stood on the riverbank, sipping coffee from plastic mugs and taking turns bragging about their little bags of gold.

Meow!

John turned as Black Cat meandered through the brush. He paced back and forth, and then ran toward the house, turned and hurried back a few steps.

Meow!

"I've seen him do this before." John set his cup on the ground. "He wants me to follow him. Something's up." A tug of anxiety crunched through John's chest. What could be wrong, now, just when things were starting to go right? Could someone be after the Emus again? His heart did a two-step. "Cindy, stay with Millie. I'll run back to the house and see what's going on."

Not stopping to pull off his waders, he slogged behind Black Cat, back through the vineyard. Just past the Emu enclosure, where the house came into view, he stopped short. "What the heck? Who are all those people?"

Chapter Twenty-Eight

ho are you?" John hurried toward the house. "What's going on here?

A number of men with clipboards surrounded a yellow television crew van sitting in the middle of the driveway. A woman applied make-up to a man seated in a folding chair. Several others scurried across the lawn stringing cables and carrying cameras and lighting. A refreshment table complete with soft drinks and coffeepot was set up near the front porch. No wonder Black Cat was upset. Who were these people? What right did they have…?

The man in the folding chair stood as the make-up lady gave his face a final pat with the powder puff. He pulled the paper bib from his collar, tossed it on the ground and strode across the driveway, a Cheshire-cat grin lighting up his *Max Factor Strawberry Frost* cheeks.

Must be the ringmaster of this circus.

"Hi. I'm Chet Andrews." He stretched out his hand. "We're from KTLZ news. Hope you don't mind all the confusion. We got a tip about your cats finding gold in your creek. Thought we'd do a human-interest story for the evening news. You wouldn't mind giving us an interview, right?" He grabbed and pumped John's hand.

John's jaw tightened. His stomach wrenched. *Television trucks? TV show. I'm not so sure about this.* He yanked his hand from Chet's grip. "I don't know." He shifted from one foot to the other, his gaze moving across the yard from the refreshment table by the front porch to the make-up girl, now waiting patiently, powder puff in hand. Did he really want his gold strike to be the lead story on the six o'clock news? How about being interviewed wearing baggie rubber britches that stretched from his feet to his mid-chest. Not that the rubber pants were the most disturbing part of this scenario. Announcing his gold strike on television might put the thought in some crazed gold seekers' heads to come and help themselves.

"I'm not so sure I want… Wait a minute." John put up his hand. "Who told you about the gold in the first place?"

"Well, *er…um…* I guess it was the guy at the hardware store. He called us. Said your little girl told him about the gold. He got your name and address from your check. *Heh…heh.* Is it a problem? We don't mean any harm. Just thought it was a great human interest story. You know, the way the cats found the gold nugget—"

"I can't have my name and address broadcast all over the country." John's cheeks warmed. He pulled at his shirt collar, grating against his neck.

"Oh, right. I get it." Chet glanced over toward the man holding the camera. "We could just tell how the cats found the gold. Our listeners would be interested in that angle. Maybe we could just give your first name, no address, and show the cats…that sort of thing? What do you think?"

John turned and gazed back toward the vineyard where Barney, Millie and Cindy were trudging up the path, carrying the folding chairs. *Where had Barney put the sacks of gold? Out of sight, I hope.* As Barney passed the Emu enclosure, the birds rushed to the fence, greeting the walkers. *Yark! Yark!*

What had possessed Peter to give John's name and address to the TV station? Peter had no right, blabbing his personal business. In fact, there was real potential for harm if the information fell into the wrong hands. Just having the television crew know the location was risky, but that ship had sailed. It pretty much shot down his theory about Peter being an…well, a *whatever.* If that were true, he would never do anything that might harm John's family.

What next? Would he have to put up a barbed-wire fence? Maybe get a pit bull to scare off gold seekers? Black Cat and Angel wouldn't like that. On the other hand, it *was* an interesting story. Maybe they *could* just talk about the cats. He sighed. "I guess it's okay if you keep my name and address out of it."

"How 'bout we show the folks the Emus later on. We could—"

"No!"

"No?" Chet stepped back and raised an eyebrow. He glanced nervously back over his shoulder.

"How many Emu ranches do you think are near Nevada City? Anyone could just look me up in the phone book. That's entirely too much identifying information. I can't sit up nights with a shotgun warding off gold hunters." *Maybe this isn't such a good idea.*

"Good point. I should have thought of that. Sorry. No last name, no location and no Emus. Got it." Chet nodded and wiped the sweat off his forehead. "Make-up!"

The make-up girl rushed over and dabbed his sweaty face with a tissue and patted concealer under Chet's eyes. She turned a sloe-eyed glance toward John. "Do you want any make-up, Mr. Goldstein?"

John shook his head. "Let's just get on with it. Wait. Let me get rid of these britches." He unsnapped the buckles and pulled the waders down over his hips and stepped out of the unwieldy garment. He tossed the rubber pants off to the side, tucked in his shirt and adjusted the top button on his collar. He stood barefooted on the grass "Okay. I guess I'm ready."

The television crew set up the cameras aimed toward Chet and John.

The producer clicked his chalkboard in front of Chet. "Quiet! And…action!"

Chet held up his microphone and plastered a television grin toward the camera. "We're broadcasting from a small ranch near Nevada City where an extraordinary event recently took place. We have John, here with us to give us the details." He turned. The camera panned to John's face. "So tell us, John, how did you happen to find gold in your creek?"

Yikes! Show time! John gulped and took a quick breath. "Actually, our cats, Black Cat and Angel found the gold." John blinked into the camera. "I found a fair-sized nugget lying on my couch and both cats were damp. I figured they took it from the river and brought the nugget home. It's anybody's guess what possessed them to do that. I'm just glad they did, because the sale of the gold will come in real handy."

"So, tell us about your cats. How old are they? What are their names again?"

How much should he tell? He didn't want a passel of gold hungry folks prowling the hillsides looking for his property. Viewers from all over the county might be watching. John's chest itched. Perspiration trickled under his arms. It was all he could do to keep from scratching.

"Angel and Black Cat stowed away in my truck about three months ago. We've tried to find their homes, but so far, no luck." John turned toward the house where Black Cat sat on the porch railing gazing at all the *goings-on* in the yard.

"Well, isn't that interesting." The camera panned back to Chet's face. "So, here's the story, folks. We're withholding John's full name and address to ensure his privacy. Apparently, John took in a couple of lost cats and they repaid his kindness by finding gold in his creek. Amazing! Maybe we can get John to introduce us to Black Cat and Angel. Can you bring the cats over here, John? Let's show them to the audience. If their owner is watching tonight, he can contact the TV station and we'll put you in touch with John. That would be alright, wouldn't it, John? We might reunite these amazing cats with their real family."

A cold hand seized John's heart and rippled through his chest. *No. Wait. What have I done?* Did he really want the cats' owners to claim their pets? Of course, he did. Wasn't that the plan all along? To be honest, he didn't want to give them up, now, any more than Cindy. His head shook. But, that's not right. This is an opportunity for them to find their home. Like it or not, he had to do it.

"John?" Chet's smarmy TV voice.

"*Uh*…I guess you're right. Cindy, run and fetch Angel and Black Cat." John jerked his head toward the porch.

Cindy scuffed through the pine needles toward the house, her head down. Perhaps, after the close call with Mrs. Stubblefield, it was all too clear the risk of putting the cats on television. *It is the right thing to do.*

Cindy returned with Angel cradled in her arms, and Black Cat trailing at her feet. She set Angel on the hood of the pick-up truck next to John, and then hurried back to the front porch where she flung herself into Millie's arms.

Black Cat jumped onto the hood beside Angel. Angel hunkered down, her tail tucked under her body, her ears flat to her head. Her body trembled.

John stroked her head. "There, there, Angel. It's alright. Don't be afraid." *Now I feel bad. She hates all this confusion.*

The cameraman moved closer, the lighting man swooped in with lights and the newscaster continued his interview. "Here on this ranch somewhere near Nevada City, John and his daughter befriended two lost cats. Little did they dream that taking in these little lost souls would result in them finding gold in John's creek. Now, we're hoping to reunite the cats with their owners.

"This is Angel, a little gold striped female and her companion Black Cat, a large black and white tom." The camera zoomed in on Angel's wide-eyed, terrified face and then panned over to Black Cat. "If anyone has information about these cats, please contact station KTLZ at 305-555-0167 and we'll put you in touch with John."

Barney shuffled up to the truck, his rubber waders still spotted with water.

"Now, who is this joining us, John?"

"This is Barney. He's been helping me at the creek." John laid his hand on Barney's arm.

"Let's see how Barney feels about all this." Chet aimed a toothy grin at the camera and turned to Barney. "Tell us, Barney, what's it like down there at the stream? Have you found any nuggets?"

"Barney. Keep it simple, okay?" John squeezed Barney's arm. Barney nodded.

As soon as the cameraman turned toward Barney, John hurried over to the porch and sat on the top step.

Millie left Cindy in the porch swing and sat beside him. "So, now you're a TV personality. Were you nervous?"

John reached inside his shirt and scratched his damp underarm. "If I had to stand there even one more minute, I'd have humiliated myself by scratching my armpit in front of God and everybody."

The newscaster and the camera no sooner turned away, than Angel leaped off the truck and streaked around the end of the house. Fame and notoriety were apparently not on her personal bucket list either.

Black Cat hopped off the hood and ambled across the lawn, his tail straight up and his head held high. A yard full of people and a television crew apparently didn't bother him in the least. *I wish I could be so calm in the face of chaos.*

"Are you okay, my sweet? I hope all those men didn't frighten you." Black Cat slurped a kitty-kiss across Angel's head. "They mean well, even if they are misguided attention-seeking fools."

"Well. This is a fine how-do-you-do. You'd think we were heroes home from war. What's next? Our pictures plastered across Time's Square?" Angel flicked her fluffed out tail.

"You've always been my hero." Black Cat moved his caresses to her shoulder. "Or should I say heroine?" His heart swelled with love for this feisty little minx. She liked to sound tough, but underneath, she was just a big softie. His whiskers twitched.

"This heroine is not happy with all those smelly strangers in our yard. I'm taking the children under Cindy's bed." She snatched Muffins by the scruff of the neck and scampered for the bedroom. She stopped at the door and dropped Muffins in a heap.

"Are you going to help, or not? Do I have to do everything myself?" She huffed and grabbed Muffins again and waddled under the bed.

"Yes, my queen." Black Cat grabbed Rambo. His pudgy rear end dragged across the floor. Black Cat dropped him at the bedroom door. "What are you eating these days? You're big enough to walk by yourself. Come on! Your mother wants you."

Chapter Twenty-Nine

E-mail emoticons danced across John's computer screen, but his thoughts weren't on his messages. Cindy had been asleep for hours. *What a day! I thought the news crew would never leave.* Now that everyone was gone and the house was finally quiet, he'd thought he could sleep for a week. Instead, he was so wired, he couldn't close his eyes. *Maybe I'll return Sal's e-mail.*

His college roommate, Sal, had been big on advice as to what John should do during his financial troubles, but he hadn't offered a dime when disaster struck. Once Sal heard about the gold, he apparently spread the word, and old buddies were coming out of the woodwork like roaches when the light flicks on. *I guess if I didn't have fair-weather friends like Sal, I wouldn't have any friends at all—except Barney and Millie, of course.*

"Do you expect to find more gold? You're so clever. I knew you'd figure a way out of your troubles." Sal's latest e-mail erupted with smiley-face emoticons.

John's finger hovered over the delete button. Sal had been so unsupportive. Why had he bothered to tell his fair-weather friend about the cats and the gold in the first place? *Admit it. It's a pride thing. You wanted to crow about your good fortune.* "Don't know how much gold remains in the creek," he typed. "Maybe once the run-off from the rain calms down, there won't be any more, but thanks to Barney's help today, I have enough to get me through the winter. Next year, I'll harvest the grapes and the papa Emus are already sitting on several more clutches of eggs. God bless papa Emus."

John clicked off the computer and fell into bed around 2:00 A.M., his dreams dancing with gold nuggets and newscasters with toothy grins.

The aroma of coffee dragged him back to consciousness. He opened his eyes. Sunlight streamed through the bedroom window. *6:09 A.M. Do I smell coffee? Carolyn wouldn't dare come back again!* John leaped out of bed. Oh, he'd tell her a thing or two this time. If she thought she could just waltz in and out, disrupting their lives, causing Cindy anguish every time… He threw open the bedroom door and stopped dead in his tracks.

"Don't come in, Daddy! I'm making a surprise."

John smiled. "I won't look!" He glanced into the kitchen, making sure Carolyn had not returned, then put his hands over his eyes and stumbled into the bathroom.

Cindy had a plate of scrambled eggs and toast growing cold on the table by the time he showered and dressed.

"What a nice surprise. You should have waited. I'd have fixed breakfast."

"I wanted to surprise you, Daddy. We're celebrating. I even made coffee." She carried the coffee pot to the table and poured him a cup.

"Here! Let me take that. It's heavy." John took the coffee pot from her and replaced it on the coffeemaker. Wrinkles cut deeper into his forehead as he sipped from the cup, and grimaced. John put his hand to his mouth and coughed. "My! It's a little…*um*… How much ground coffee did you put in the pot?" He set the cup back on the table.

"Just a cup full. And six cups of water. Isn't that right?"

"It's just a little too strong." John took his cup to the sink, spilled out some and added hot water. "Next time I make coffee, I'll show you just how much to put in. This is fine, now." He took another sip. "Just right. And you made scrambled eggs? They look delicious."

He sat at the table, sprinkled salt and pepper across his plate and took a bite. "Thank you, sweetheart. You were very thoughtful to cook breakfast. Now you eat, because we have to run back into town this morning. I want to take this gold dust to the County Assayer's Office and see what grade we've got. They'll give us money for it." He laughed. "Won't Mr. Adams be surprised when we show up at the bank and pay the loan payments?"

John carried his dishes to the sink and rinsed them under the faucet. "While we're in town, I want to drop off Peter's backpack at the General Store."

"Now that we're rich, can we afford a hummingbird feeder?"

"We aren't rich, Cindy. With the sale of the chicks and the gold, I can pay a lot of overdue bills. But, we sure have enough to buy you something nice." He reached across the table and squeezed her arm. "We'll even buy Black Cat and Angel a great big catnip mouse." He glanced at Black Cat, dozing on the warm windowsill.

Black Cat lifted his head.

"Why, look at him. He's almost grinning. You don't suppose he understood what I said about the mouse, do you?"

Cindy picked up her dish and took it to the sink. "I told you, Daddy. He understands everything you say. He's a very smart cat."

"You can say that again."

"He's a very smart cat." Cindy slid the butter into the refrigerator.

"I didn't really mean that you should *say*…never mind. Go get dressed. I'll run out and feed the Emus. We'll leave as soon as you're ready." John smiled, picked up Peter's backpack, shook his head and went out the front door.

Within the hour, their truck came off the hill onto Broad Street, into the heart of Nevada City. Miniature flags flapped on the streetlights in commemoration of the upcoming Labor Day holiday. Tourists strolled along the sidewalks, in and out of gift shops, book stores and coffee houses.

The sidewalk in front of the General Store displayed various tables with an assortment of unique household items. Hemp rope, garden hoses, wheelbarrows loaded with small pots of geraniums and marigolds, and odds and ends chosen from *end-of-stock* items displayed red half-off stickers.

"What luck. A parking spot right out front." John checked the traffic on the street and climbed out. "Let's find that hummingbird feeder you wanted."

Cindy hopped out and slammed the door. "Can I put the money in the meter?"

"We won't be here long. A quarter should be enough."

Cindy dropped the coin into the meter and twisted the handle. The hand flipped up to twenty-five minutes.

John grabbed Peter's backpack from the truck bed and pulled open the hardware store door. The bell tinkled as he stepped through the door. He paused and sniffed, once again enjoying the vintage ambience of the store. *Ahh.* The scent of floor wax, spices, and peppermint candy permeated the air.

A middle-aged woman left a customer by the work boots and approached. "Good morning. Can I help you with something? We've got a sale on aluminum dish drainers today. Fifty percent off if you purchase it with a rubber mat." She nodded toward the stack of silver dish drainers stacked on the counter, most likely a result of overbuying and underselling.

John smiled and shook his head. "Thanks, not today." He hefted the backpack. "I'm just here to drop this off for Peter. He left it in my truck a couple days ago when I gave—"

"Who?" The cashier shrugged.

John's stomach tightened. A tingle ran up and down his arm. He thought back to the house outside Reno, where he had questioned the woman with the garden hose. The clerk had the same puzzled look on her face as the woman in the blue housedress.

"Who did you say?" The woman raised her eyebrows.

Déjà vu! All over again! John sighed. *God help me.* "Your clerk, Peter. He just started working here. I spoke to him a couple days ago, right here." John tapped the glass counter. His heart beat quickened. Now, he was getting mad. Peter popped in and out of his life like a Jack-in-the-box. *What's going on?*

The lady shook her head. "Mr. Egerton and I have owned this store for twenty years. I'm quite sure I'd know if we had a clerk named Peter. We've never had anyone by that name, as far as I recall."

"That's impossible. Wait. He just waited on us. Here, I'll show you." John pulled a receipt from his wallet. It would show the purchase of the hip boots, the gold pans and the scales. He slapped the receipt on the counter. "Take a look at this."

Mrs. Egerton picked up the receipt and turned it front to back. "It's our store receipt, #6045, but it's blank. See for yourself." She handed it back to him.

"What?" John flipped the receipt over, checking front and back. Blank! His mouth dropped open. "I…I don't understand."

The clerk pulled a receipt booklet from beside the register and thumbed through the pages. "Here it is. #6045. The original is torn out, but, see here? The carbon is blank. We account for every ticket. It is odd. You say you purchased items here?" She laid the book on the counter.

"Several things. Hip boots, a gold pan and a scale—"

"We don't carry scales. Maybe you're at the wrong store." She grinned and stepped toward the door, pointing down the block. "Could it have been the Yankee Trader Store down the street?"

"Ma'am, I assure you, I was here. I bought hip boots, a gold pan and a scale. This is the receipt." He shook the paper. "I don't know how to explain this, but I'm sure of one thing. I bought items from Peter and he…" John scratched his head and stared around the store, then at the blank receipt. "Actually, I don't know anything for sure right now. Sorry I bothered you. Come on, Cindy."

"What about my hummingbird feeder?"

"We'll go down to Yankee Trader where we didn't go before." John grabbed her hand, shoved open the door and tossed the backpack into the pick-up bed.

He hunched over the wheel, glaring through the windshield as he pulled away from the curb. They drove several blocks to the local park and stopped the truck in the shade of the aspen trees. "You can run over and play on the swings for a while, Cindy. I need to be alone for a few minutes."

"Don't you feel well, Daddy?"

His hand shook as he wiped it across his mouth. "I just need to figure out some things. Run on and play. I'll call you in a little bit, and then we'll take care of the rest of our errands."

John's gaze followed her as she skipped across the grass to the swing set.

What's happening? He dropped his head and rubbed his temples. He'd thought Peter was an angel, the way they met on the road to Reno. Then he turned up at the General Store. Now, Mrs. Egerton said she never heard of Peter. *Did I imagine the whole thing? Maybe I'm losing my mind.*

John reached into his pocket and pulled out the blank General Store receipt. He scratched his head. *My checkbook! I wrote a check for the gold pan and the boots.*

John's hand shook as he retrieved his checkbook from the glove box. The last check should be for eighty-three dollars and change, for the General Store purchases. He flipped through the checkbook to the last check.

$39.62—Where he bought gas at the Seven-Eleven on his way home from Reno. He ran his hand through his hair. *Doesn't make any sense.* No check in the checkbook. A blank receipt from the General Store. It looked as if meeting Peter at the General Store and buying the supplies had never happened.

Wait!

The guy from the television crew yesterday said the clerk from the General Store told them about the cats finding the gold. Said the clerk got his address off his check! That would be the check that doesn't exist?

He had almost convinced himself that he'd imagined the whole thing, but he sure hadn't imagined fourteen guys crawling all over the yard with trucks, lights and cameras…or had he? Was reality slipping away? A trickle of perspiration slithered down his forehead, past his eyebrow.

John leaned out the window. "Cindy! Come here a minute."

Cindy jumped off the swings and ran to the truck. "Is it time to go?"

"No…well, maybe. Get in. I need you to help me with something." He put the checkbook back into the glove box.

Cindy climbed in and closed the door. "What is it?"

John took a deep breath. A warm glow crept up his neck into his hairline. His head itched and the dampness under his arms was certainly real enough. "How many men from the television station came yesterday to talk about Black Cat and Angel?" He gripped the steering wheel and stared straight ahead. What would she say? Was he going to hear that *who* again? The word he'd learned to hate every time he mentioned the name *Peter* to a female?

He closed his eyes and held his breath. Come on Cindy. Don't tell me there wasn't a television crew at the house. Don't tell me I'm losing my mind.

The cushions on the seat squeaked as Cindy squirmed. "*Umm…* Why do you ask? Did somebody call about Angel and Black Cat?"

John's heart did a twist, as though it might beat right out of his mouth and tumble into his lap. Cindy hadn't even tried to pretend he wasn't going *loony-tunes*. She'd changed the subject completely and asked about the cats. *Poor kid must not want me to feel bad about losing my marbles.*

"The cats aren't important. They—"

"Yes, they are important, Daddy. I love Black Cat and Angel. I don't want anyone to take them away." Tears puddled in the corner of her eyes and spilled over the edges.

Now, he had a weeping female to deal with and he still didn't know whether he'd imagined meeting Peter on the road, in the store, or for that matter, if he'd imagined the whole last week. Maybe he never even went to the Reno airport. Maybe he still had seventeen, foot-tall baby Emus stalking around the bird enclosure, eating him out of house and home.

The specter of foreclosure and disgrace loomed its ugly head. Again! Now he'd not only be homeless and broke, he was mentally ill as well. It wouldn't take long for the authorities to learn of his insanity. They'd take the ranch. They'd sell the birds and pay off the light bill or the water bill, whichever came first. He'd be pushing a grocery cart down the street, loaded high with every stitch he owned.

Carolyn would get Cindy, after all. She'd probably drop out of school and marry a guitar player at sixteen—

"Fourteen!" Cindy rolled down the window and leaned on the ledge.

"Fourteen?" She won't even make it to sixteen? Oh, God help me!

"There were fourteen people in the yard. The man with all the teeth talked about Angel on the TV—"

John threw his arms around her shoulders and shook her from side to side, raining kisses on the top of her head. "Thank you, thank you. You're right. It was fourteen."

Cindy tilted her head and bit her lip. "I might be wrong. There might have only been thirteen. Does it make much difference?"

John patted her cheek and shook his head. "Are you ready to go? I think we should stop for ice cream sundaes and then find that hummingbird feeder before we go to the bank. What do you say?"

Chapter Thirty

uardian of all who dwelt within, Black Cat paced the living room. The full moon cast a warm glow through the windows. He passed Angel's blanket where she lay curled with the children. All was well. As the protector of the household, it was his job to keep intruders at bay. John and Cindy were fast asleep, as he would be in a few minutes. Satisfied that all was well, he yawned and jumped onto the sofa, turned in a circle and flopped on the Indian blanket. He closed his eyes. Confusing thoughts plagued his mind, making sleep impossible.

What quirk of destiny had brought them here to John's ranch, anyway? Or had the car accident been inevitable and God just made the best of it to help the most people? Was finding the gold a coincidence? All profound issues to ponder.

Perhaps everything that had happened *was* part of God's divine plan. He and Angel were sent here to find the gold nuggets. Without the gold, John would lose the ranch either to the bank or whoever was trying to take advantage of his financial troubles.

With the birth of the kittens, Mrs. Stubblefield had found a way to repair her broken heart and Miss Bubblekins would replace her beloved Miss Boopkins.

Little Muffins would brighten Officer Nina's lonely life.

The lives of Nina, Mrs. Stubblefield and John had been enriched as a result of their coming to Nevada City.

With his memory nearly restored and the kittens finding good homes, even Angel had nearly fulfilled her assignment here in Nevada City.

Everyone gains but me. What good had come to him from all this? He was still lost, still with some memory loss, and about to lose his soul-mate when God called her home. *Am I just a cog in a cosmic wheel?* If all this was some kind of great celestial plan, he just didn't get it.

Black Cat closed his eyes. His muscles relaxed. His tail drifted from side to side as he began to dream. He and Angel stood outside the gates of Heaven. A dozen angels hovered overhead. The great gate opened and Saint Peter stepped out. "Welcome home, Angel. It's time. Come on in." She walked through the gate.

Black Cat hurried after her, but the door slammed with a clang before he could enter. He clawed at the latch. "Angel, Angel! Let me in!" There was no answer. She was gone.

Clang! Clang!

With the sound of Heaven's gate clanging in his ears, he awoke, his heart pummeling his chest. The house reverberated and shook at the sound of the blast. He leaped to his feet. *That's not a dream.* The blast had come from outside, near the Emu enclosure.

John rushed from his bedroom, barefooted, still zipping up his jeans. He strapped on his holster. He glanced toward Cindy's bedroom and then bolted out the door, leaving it ajar.

Angel hunkered on the blanket, pulling her kittens close to her body. "Black Cat! What was that?"

Black Cat raced to the door and turned. "Stay here, Angel!" He stopped and gazed back. A rectangular streak of moonlight streamed through the window onto her face. She was so beautiful. Fear danced in her eyes as she clutched her kittens to her breast. "Don't be frightened, my dear. I'll be right back." He dashed through the door. "I have to help John."

Black Cat caught up with John on the far side of the Emu enclosure, where a thin cloud of dust hovered over the corner fence post. As they turned the corner, he could see a huge hole gaping in the fence wire, clearly visible in the light of the full moon. Several fence posts lay on the ground and one leaned sideways at a precarious angle. The fence wire lay halfway across a large hole in the fence the Emus could have easily marched through. Chunks of the fence wire were scattered as far as ten feet away.

Grunting and cursing, John yanked on the leaning fencepost and set it more or less upright. He tipped up the twisted fencepost and dragged the fence wire back into place to block the gap. "Get back, Black Cat. Don't get in my way. I might step on you."

When the fence seemed stable enough to secure the Emus until morning, John scanned the yard. He shifted his gun holster and trotted toward the vineyard and the creek.

Black Cat followed his gaze. This blast had been set off by a human hand and the perpetrator was still out there, hiding somewhere in the darkness. If it was the same guy who took a shot at John in the vineyard, he had a rifle, and the advantage of night…

He must know that John had found the gold and the means to hold onto his ranch. Why all this exaggerated violence now that his goal of scaring John from the ranch had been thwarted? Had the objective turned from goal-driven to pure hatred?

Or, was it something else entirely? Something they hadn't thought of yet? A shudder skidded down Black Cat's spine. His hair stood up on his head. Maybe it wasn't about the ranch at all. Maybe it had to do with Cindy. What if the explosion was just a ruse to get John away from the house?

Black Cat turned and barreled back toward the house like the devil himself was after him. Even worse, was the devil after Cindy?

He slowed as he approached the house, the itch behind his left ear tingling. The lawn chairs cast jagged shadows across the front porch. His skin crawled as the crash of furniture and shattering glass inside the house assailed his ears. Then a shriek! *Cindy!*

Angel! Rambo! Faith! Muffins!

Thoughts of broken fences and Emus disappeared. He'd guessed right. Cindy was the target. John was somewhere down by the vineyard and the perpetrator was right inside the house!

Black Cat reached the front porch, his claws extended, dread clutching his heart. *What can I do to save her?*

The front door was closed. He raced around the house and burst through the cat door. He scanned the living room. A chair lay overturned beside the table. Broken glass spread across the linoleum in front of the kitchen sink.

A sweatshirt with a red star on the hood lay sprawled across the sofa, thrown in such a manner as to appear like arms clutching the top of the sofa. Just like the one he'd seen down by the river, worn by one of the thieves.

Cindy's mama stood beside the bedroom door, her arms circling Cindy's waist, dragging her toward the front door. *The mama?* Was it possible? Was she behind all this?

"No. No. I don't want to go with you. Where's my Daddy? I want my Daddy!" Cindy reared back, threw her elbow into Carolyn's stomach, breaking her grip. She ran back into her bedroom, slammed the door and flipped the lock.

"You come out here this instant. You don't understand." Carolyn pounded on the bedroom door. "I love you! I want you to live with me. I did it all for you."

Black Cat froze as the mama yanked on the door handle. His gaze followed her hand as she stooped and rubbed her leg where the skin above her ankle looked bruised and broken. A trickle of blood ran into her stocking. Dark fang marks dotted her skin. Angel! Where was Angel? He scanned the room again.

Something moved beneath the sofa. A little black nose poked out and then disappeared. The puff of fur must be Rambo's tail. Faith and Muffins wouldn't be far behind their sibling, but where was Angel?

His muscles felt locked in place. Panic clutched his heart. He willed his legs to move. He had to find her. She wouldn't have left the kittens. She must be here somewhere.

Cindy screamed again. "Why did you do it? She was just trying to protect me." Cindy's voice trailed off into spasms of sobs.

Do what? Protect her from what? Where is Angel? Chill bumps plunged down his back. He forced himself to move across the room, his eyes flashing, searching…searching. Had she run out the door when the mama came? Had she run away and abandoned her babies? Never!

"It's not my fault. The blasted cat bit me. I had to get her off me, didn't I?"

Angel? Bit her? Didn't sound like Angel, but if she thought Cindy or the babies were in danger… Carolyn got off easy. She was lucky she hadn't lost a leg.

"Where's my Daddy? I want my Daddy." Cindy shrieked. A burst of sobbing drowned out her next words, except for one word, "…Angel."

Black Cat frantically searched the room again straining to focus on every detail. There! The red-stained fireplace poker lay next to the bookshelf. Blood pooled from beneath a pile of books. One gold foot stuck out from the jumble.

Chapter Thirty-One

h, no! Not my Angel. Black Cat's brain clouded over. Everything in the room looked hazy. *Denial! Despair!* He shook his head to clear his vision. He ran to her and pawed at the books, pulling them off her body. He licked her face. She didn't move. *Angel! My darling. Don't leave me now.* Her words echoed through his thoughts. *'I don't have much time until He calls me home.'*

Carolyn snarled. "Cindy. Baby. Listen to me! I didn't go to all this trouble just to argue with a ten-year-old. Open this door. You're going with me if I have to burn the house down to get you out of that bedroom. And believe me, if I have to, I'll do it.

"I paid that man good money to make your pig-headed father come to his senses. I don't intend to waste my money." Her face clouded with rage. "But, no, do you think your father cares about you? He'd rather see you shot dead or kidnapped than let you live with me."

The mama! She'd hired the man who left the headless doll by the door! She'd paid someone to shoot at John in the vineyard! Did she know how close the bullet had come to John's head? From the sound of it, she didn't care.

Then the mama's voice got all sickening sweet. "Now, Cindy, sweetheart. Be reasonable. Mama *wove's* her *widdo'* Cindy. Come out and give Mama a kiss. Mama will buy you another kitty." She moved to the kitchen and began pulling open drawers, digging through the silverware. She picked up an icepick.

"Go away. I want my Daddy. I want Angel!"

Black Cat's eyes glazed. His Angel was dead. He'd never hear her silly complaints again. He'd never see the little tilt of her nose. Life had no meaning without her. The blood in his veins ran cold. *Revenge! Murder!* He couldn't help Angel now, but, he could keep the black-hearted witch from taking Cindy and oh, what a terrible vengeance he would exact in the process.

He turned toward the hideous woman as she poked an icepick into Cindy's doorknob. Carolyn's body looked hazy and blurred. A murderous snarl gurgled in his throat. *Eh! Eh! Eh!* He slunk toward Carolyn, belly to the floor. He acquired a new admiration for the killer, *Jack the Ripper.* Murder throbbed in his heart. *She'll pay, my darling*!

He couched, aimed for the back of her neck and zeroed in on her spinal cord. Every muscle tense, ready to leap… One quick snap of his jaws and never again would this woman spread her evil.

Carolyn twisted the icepick. The lock on Cindy's door clicked. Carolyn reached for the doorknob as the front door flung open and crashed against the wall.

"You! What's going on in here?"

John!

Black Cat froze, saliva dripping, heart aching with despair. His skin tingled with unrequited rage. Would John stand in his way?

John's gaze moved from Black Cat to Carolyn. Her hand stood poised on the doorknob. The ice pick was still clutched in her other hand.

Cindy's wails ricocheted out of her room.

John stomped toward her door. "Cindy, honey, it's Daddy. What's wrong?"

Cindy opened the door and flung herself into his arms. "Mama said she paid a man to make trouble. She said you didn't care if I got shot." She turned and pointed toward Angel. "She hit Angel with the fireplace poker. She…she's…dead!"

Cindy pushed away from John and ran to Angel, lying motionless beside the bookshelf.

Exacting revenge on the black-hearted witch would have to wait. Black Cat stumbled across the room and stood first on one paw and then the other as Cindy gathered Angel in her arms and wept into her still body.

"Carolyn." John grabbed her shoulder. "Is it true? Are you behind all this…this…monstrous behavior?"

The mama turned her nose in the air. The icepick clattered to the floor. "So what if I am? Nobody got hurt. You wouldn't listen to reason. I had to do something to get your attention." Her mouth twisted in a spiteful smile. "I only wanted to take my daughter." She crossed her arms and thrust up her head. "I have a right to my child, don't I?"

"Are you behind the shooting down in the vineyard? Do you realize your daughter could have been killed?" John's face turned red. He clenched his fists. "Are you responsible for setting the explosion out there?" John's hand trembled as he waved in the general direction of the bird enclosure. "Now, you've killed Cindy's cat?"

Carolyn shook her head. Her face paled. Had she finally realized the extent of her despicable decisions? How her actions had risked her daughter's life? Her voice was soft but unconvincing. "But, I love her… I just wanted…" She hung her head.

She *loved* her? Was that her excuse? Was the woman crazy?

Carolyn hunched forward, and then she flung back her shoulders. Her head shot up. "It was just some chemicals I read about on the Internet. It was only supposed to make a small explosion. Something that would get you out of the house long enough for me to take Cindy. I didn't think it would cause such a large…" She put out her hands in a helpless gesture. "I didn't mean to…" She gestured toward Angel. "The cat bit me…" Her face crumpled and her cheeks flushed as she glared at John.

Black Cat stood beside Cindy, licking her hand and then Angel's head.

John took a step toward Cindy. "Put Angel on the sofa and call 911. Tell them to send the sheriff out here. I'll be filing charges, Carolyn, for harassment, reckless endangerment to a child, for attempted murder, animal cruelty and any other charge we can think of."

"Animal… Attempted murder? Wait. Wait. I said I was sorry. I never meant to hurt… John, you can't do this." She grabbed John's shirt. "I'll go away. I'll move out of state. I'll never bother you again, I promise. I won't come back."

John turned away. "Cindy, honey, do as I say." He stalked across the room to the front door and glanced at his watch. "You have exactly thirty seconds to get out of my house. I'm filing a restraining order first thing in the morning. If I so much as see your shadow anywhere near Cindy, I'll file attempted murder charges. Now, get out before I change my mind.

"Cindy, tell your mother good-bye. You won't be seeing her for a very long time." He glanced back at his watch. "Twenty seconds…"

"Cindy? Honey?" Carolyn reached out her hand.

Cindy huddled on the floor, stroking Angel's fur. She didn't look up when her mother huffed and slammed out the front door. Carolyn's car engine revved. Tires spun in the gravel driveway. Her vehicle roared down the road, until the sound died away and the night ached with silence.

Wasn't Carolyn lucky that John came in when he did, or she'd be discussing long-term housing with the devil about now? Black Cat ducked his head. *But, Angel…*

John knelt beside Cindy. She clasped Angel to her chest, tears soaking her golden fur. Cindy didn't seem to notice that Angel's blood had stained her nightgown crimson.

Black Cat's heart throbbed so hard, his head hurt. He must accept St. Peter's decision, he must! But how could he live without her?

"Here, let me see." John took Angel from Cindy and put his finger on the side of her throat.

Black Cat stared into John's face, hoping against hope that he would smile and say, "Everything's going to be all right," but in his heart, he knew it wasn't so. It couldn't be. Angel's time had come. St. Peter had called her home.

Cindy blinked back her tears. Her eyes lifted to John's face. "Is she dead?"

Chapter Thirty-Two

ick-tock. Tick-tock. The room was deathly quiet except for the clock over the potbelly stove. Black Cat closed his eyes, not wanting to hear the words aloud.

John didn't answer.

Black Cat listened for the rustle of angel wings. His memory was coming back. John's gold would save the ranch. Angel had rescued Black Cat…not once, but twice. Muffins and Miss Bubblekins had found forever homes. Angel had even saved Cindy from being kidnapped. She had accomplished everything asked of her…and more. Now, with her assignments complete, time had run out. St. Peter had come for her.

He held his breath. *I can't bear to hear John say she's gone.* His head began to swim. He had to breathe…

"One, two, three," John's voice was barely a whisper.

Black Cat's eyes flew open. He let out his breath and placed his feet on John's knees.

What was he doing? Wasn't it too late to save her?

John blew in Angel's mouth and then pressed her chest. "One, two, three," then blew in her mouth again.

"What are you doing, Daddy?"

"*Shh.* Just wait."

Angel twitched her foot and gasped. Her chest moved. She was breathing on her own!

Black Cat sucked in his breath. A wave of joy washed over him. *Was it true? She's alive?*

John stroked Angel's chest. "Bring me a wash cloth and a pan of hot water. We have to stop the bleeding."

Cindy hurried back with the requested items.

John sponged the gash across Angel's head and staunched the blood with a cloth until it slowed to a trickle.

"Okay, now wrap her up in a big bath towel. Hold this cloth on her head real tight." John picked up the phone. "I'll call and let the vet know we're on our way. It's late, but hopefully, someone can meet us there."

Cindy cradled Angel while John made arrangements.

Black Cat licked Angel's shoulder, each stroke spreading life-restoring love. At last, her eyes opened and she looked around. *She's going to live? Had St. Peter changed his mind? How could it be? We were so sure her time had come.*

Cindy and John whisked her away. Their truck hurtled down the driveway and turned onto the country road.

Can't you drive any faster? Angel could bleed to death before you get to the vet!

The sound of the truck faded into the distance. "You children can come over here, now." Black Cat called from the blanket. "John has taken Mama Angel to the doctor. Everything's going to be alright. We have to have faith."

"I'm here, Papa." Faith danced across the rug and flopped onto her side on the blanket.

"Yes, of course you are, my darling. Papa means a different kind of faith. The kind where you believe that mother will get well and come home to us soon."

Rambo and Muffins bounded out from under the sofa and curled around their father's legs. He licked them down from head to toe and soon, they were asleep beside baby Faith. *There now, I've put them to bed every bit as well as Angel could.*

Why hadn't Peter used this opportunity to call her home? Angel was so sure she was on borrowed time. Why was she still alive? St. Peter said she could only stay until the kittens were settled and as long as he needed her! Those were his very words.

For as long as I need her? Black Cat's eyes flew open. He jumped off the blanket in a bound that took him half-way across the room, his heart pounding against his chest. Could it be that simple? Why, that clever old St. Peter. *...for as long as I need her?* When would there ever be a day he didn't *need* her? He needed her now. He'd need her every day for as long as he lived!

Black Cat paced the floor, mulling over his new-found truth. At last, he stretched out beside the babies and closed his eyes. He'd sleep now. Angel was in good hands. She'd be home soon. He couldn't wait to explain how she had misunderstood St. Peter's message.

His blood ran cold when he thought how often Angel had risked her life, pulling him from the river, retrieving the gold nugget and saving Cindy from her mama. All this time, thinking she was under divine protection until her assignment was complete.

The truth of the matter was, St. Peter didn't send her back just to accomplish a specific mission. He'd given her back her life.

Chapter Thirty-Three

Vet calls first thing in the morning were always risky. John's heart surged when the phone rang. Was it bad news? *I can't bear to break Cindy's heart again.*

"We'll do the best we can, Mr. Goldstein," Dr. Pettigrew had said last night when he examined Angel. "With head injuries, you can't ever be sure. We can stitch up the wound, but we can't tell if there's any brain damage until the swelling goes down somewhat."

John grabbed the phone, crossed his fingers and closed his eyes. "Hello?"

Cindy grabbed the corner of his shirt. Her cheeks were pale with dark shadows under her eyes from crying.

John patted her arm.

"Hello. Doctor Schneider here. Angel's surgery went well and she had a good night. She's awake. I think you can take her home this afternoon, though you'll want to watch her closely for a few days."

"Thanks so much. We'll be in about 4:30 P.M." John hung up the phone and squeezed Cindy's shoulder. "She's okay. We can pick her up this afternoon."

Cindy threw her arms around his waist.

John lifted her, gave her a good hug and set her back down. He poured a cup of coffee and sat on the sofa. A warm feeling spread through his chest and he couldn't keep the smile off his face. Things were finally starting to turn around for the better. His ranch was saved with the sale of the gold nuggets and though last night's events with Carolyn were terrifying, hopefully, she was gone for a while.

Cindy's pale cheeks had pinked with the news of Angel's recovery.

She hurried to share the news with Black Cat and the kittens. The room rang with her squeals of delight as the babies scampered around the living room, stalked each other, attacked and wrestled until they fell exhausted into a heap. Their young lives were not affected by their mother's injuries.

John laughed at their antics until tears filled his eyes. Watching two kittens at play was exponentially more than twice the fun of watching one. And watching three at play was hysterical. "Those kittens would make the most hardened curmudgeon smile."

The phone rang again. Was the vet calling back? Had something happened? The wave of pleasure he'd enjoyed watching the kittens at play, melted away, leaving a shadow of fear.

John answered. "Hello?" His voice cracked. He cleared his throat. "Hello?"

"Hello? This is Officer Nina."

He breathed a sigh. "Nice to hear from you. What's up?"

"I have some information regarding the shooting, but I'd rather speak to you in person. Could I come over this afternoon?"

"Of course. I'm home all afternoon." Maybe they'd made an arrest. Maybe it was just an excuse to see him again. *A man can always hope.* He stood a little straighter, his shoulders thrown back. He had thought about her often since the day of the shooting and his thoughts weren't always about the incident.

"Is Muffins ready to come home yet? As long as I'm coming over, I thought I might as well pick up my kitten." He could hear her breathing into the phone.

"*Uh…* Good idea." His lips pressed together. So, she wasn't coming to see him. She just wanted to pick up Muffins. He glanced toward Cindy, sitting on the blanket with the kittens. They all had to go sooner or later, but saying good-bye was always hard, especially on the heels of what she'd been through last night. "That would be fine. I'll see you later this afternoon." He ran his hands through his unruly hair. How long would it take to get a haircut?

"See you about 2:00 P.M."

He glanced at his watch. *I need more time than that.* "Can you make it 2:30 P.M.?" Thank God for credit cards.

Officer Nina arrived with a carrier and a cute cream-colored cat toy that resembled Muffins.

John opened the door before she stepped onto the porch and grinned a welcome. "Come on in. Have a seat." He scooted Black Cat off the sofa.

Nina set the carrier on the floor. "Hi, Cindy. I was downtown and saw this kitty in the window. It reminded me of Muffins. Since she'll be living with me now, I thought you'd like to keep this one to remind you of her."

Cindy took the cat and gave Nina a weak smile, but still a smile. "Thank you." She hugged the toy and then carried it to the blanket where she danced it in front of the kittens.

John nodded toward her room. "Cindy? Can you take the kittens in your room and say good-bye to Muffins there? Officer Nina and I need to have some grown-up talk for a bit."

Cindy carried the squirming kittens and her new toy to her room.

Black Cat hopped back onto the sofa and curled up alongside Nina's hip.

She took a deep breath and stroked his head while he licked the back of her hand.

"This is totally off the record, but I thought you had a right to know what we've learned so far...

"Mr. Skimmer was stopped last night for speeding. He appeared under the influence of either drugs or alcohol, which prompted a search of his car. The officers found a rifle in his trunk. They arrested him for drunk driving and carrying an unlicensed firearm. We've been looking at him in connection to the vineyard shooting, but up until now, we didn't have anything to go on."

John scooted forward on the sofa. "Mr. Skimmer, from next door? You're kidding. I knew he wanted my ranch, but I never thought—"

"The casings we found by the creek match his weapon. After questioning, he confessed to the shooting, but he claimed he was only trying to scare you. He was anxious to make a deal to lessen the charges."

John's mouth dropped open. Mr. Skimmer was behind all the trouble? Not Carolyn? Last night, he'd accused her of all the trouble. It didn't make sense. He wiped his hand across his face. "I thought my wife was behind…well…never mind…"

Nina shook her head. "I'm afraid there's more. When Mr. Skimmer realized he could be charged with attempted murder, he spilled the whole story in exchange for reducing the charges. Here's where it gets *hinky*."

How much *hinkier* could things get? Was that even a word? So, obviously, Nina hadn't come to see him. She came for her kitten and to report news of the case. *Guess I didn't need to waste my money on a haircut, after all.*

Nina stroked Black Cat's head. "I'm real sorry to tell you this. Here's the *hinky* part." She glanced toward Cindy's bedroom and lowered her voice. Her cheeks glowed pink. "Mr. Skimmer claims your ex-wife hired him to run you off the property. We're still looking into his story, but a $3000 deposit in his bank account matches a withdrawal from your wife's account."

John's breath caught in his throat. His hands suddenly felt cold and clammy. His cheeks tingled with a chill that crept up into his forehead. *Oh, God, what else? And, I was worried about impressing the lady?* "Go on."

Nina nervously smoothed a wrinkle in her slacks. "Mr. Skimmer saw the foreclosure notice in the paper. The sooner you left the property, the sooner the bank could foreclose and he might pick up your ranch at a reduced price. He says he met your ex-wife in a bar downtown. She told him she wanted to cause you enough grief, you'd be inclined to give up Cindy. She offered him money to get you off the property. The District Attorney is considering what charges to bring against them. We've posted an APB on Carolyn for questioning. You don't happen to know where she is, do you." Nina raised an eyebrow.

John lowered his eyes. He couldn't bear it if he saw pity in her eyes. He squirmed and shrugged his shoulders. "I…I…expect she's in another state by now. We sort of had…well, a parting of the ways last night, so to speak. She said she was trying to get custody of Cindy and…things got out of hand. She admitted knowing about the shooting, but I never thought…"

Nina reached toward John and brushed fine hairs from his collar.

He looked over toward Cindy's bedroom.

"With Mr. Skimmer's confession and our evidence… I don't know how a jury would see it, but we're pretty sure we can get a conviction on both of them. I'm so sorry, Mr. Goldstein." She patted his arm.

"John. Please call me John. I'd like to keep this as quiet as possible. I don't want Cindy hurt any worse than she already is. It's bad enough, Carolyn set off an explosion by the Emu enclosure last night and attacked Angel with a fireplace poker." John ran his hand over his face.

Nina gasped and jerked her head. "She did what?"

"Last night. She tried to take Cindy by force and Angel got in the way. Carolyn split her head open with a fireplace poker. Angel's at the vet's now."

Nina shook her head. "I can't believe it. How could any mother… Is Angel going to be okay?" She stroked Black Cat's head so hard his ears were pressed flat.

John stood and crossed the room to the buffet. He lifted the picture of his family, and then set it down. He turned. "They stitched up Angel's head last night. We're going to pick her up this afternoon." He moved back to the sofa. "With Mr. Skimmer in custody we can put all this behind us. As far as I know, Carolyn left town."

Nina nodded. She sat for a minute, gazing at Black Cat. "So, I heard you found gold on your property. That's good news, at least."

"How'd you hear that?" Had Peter been up to his tricks again?

"It was on the evening news. They called the cats Black Cat and Angel. How many Black Cat and Angels are there in Nevada City?" She grinned. "I'm a detective, remember? Wasn't hard to figure out."

"Yeah, well," John's smile wobbled. "The creek is giving up some nuggets and dust. I've got an expert coming out to advise me where to go from here. In the meantime, I've already panned enough to pay some bills and get the bank off my back. I'm grateful for that, even if the gold peters out."

"Look, I shouldn't take up anymore of your time." She stood and reached for the carrier. "If you think Cindy's had enough time to say good-bye, I should take Muffins and let you get about your afternoon. Sure hope Angel will be okay."

"I'll get Cindy." He tapped on her bedroom door. "Bring Muffins out now, honey. Officer Nina is ready to go." *Can't think of any reason for her to stay. Maybe I should have offered her coffee?*

Cindy came out, clutching Muffins to her chest, blinking hard. Tears sparkled in her eyes. She sat on the sofa beside Black Cat. He gave Muffins a good lick across her head.

"Isn't that sweet? Black Cat is saying good-bye to his baby." Nina reached in her purse and pulled out her keys. "I should have brought my camera. I'll take some pictures as she grows up, okay, Cindy?" She put Muffins in the carrier. "There, she'll be nice and safe on the way home. Now, you and your daddy can come by any time and visit us, alright?" She ran her hand down Cindy's cheek and stepped out the front door.

Cindy gulped. Her face squinched up like she was determined not to cry. "When can we come?"

"Any time." Nina set the carrier on the porch and pulled her card from her wallet. She turned and handed it to John. "Here's my phone number. Call me any—"

"Wait!" John followed her onto the porch. "Officer Nina…*umm*… can I call you Nina? I'll walk you out." He picked up Muffins' carrier and walked beside her down the steps toward her car. "*Um*… I don't suppose you'd be interested in having dinner with me some time, would you? Or coffee…or…wait a minute. I should ask first." He stopped on the bottom step. "Maybe you're…involved with someone?"

Nina paused. Then she shook her head. "No. No one. I'd love to have coffee with you…John. Any time."

Her eyes went all soft and her mouth twitched in a smile. "Or, if you need anything at all…just give me a whistle."

"*Ah.* Sounds like you're an old movies buff."

"Love em'…"

Cindy ran down the steps and grabbed Nina around the waist. "Good-bye. Take care of Muffins. I'll bring Daddy over and visit real soon." She gave her face a swipe with the back of her sleeve and smiled.

There's my brave girl.

"You do that!" Nina opened her car door.

John slid Muffins' carrier in the back seat and then she and John leaned against the car. They talked beside the car for the next half-hour before she said good-bye.

Black Cat sat on the back of the couch, waiting, peering out the window. John and Cindy were bringing Angel home any minute now! One thing he knew how to do well was wait. It was in his DNA. For centuries, cats have sat patiently next to gopher holes, waiting for the little buggers to come out, and then *wham*! Lights out! If faded memory served, he'd even caught a few himself. He drifted into a nap, thinking of Angel.

The phone jangled. He jumped, then listened as it went to answer mode. First, John's recorded voice. "*This is the Goldstein residence…*"

The phone buzzed and a woman began to speak. Black Cat's heart fluttered like a bird caught in a net. He rushed to the telephone and sniffed. *Could it be?*

"Hello. My name is Kimberlee Clarke. I saw a television newscast on our local station about the cats that found gold on your property? I'm sure they're our cats, Thumper and Noe-Noe. We lost them near Cloverdale several months ago. The television station gave me your number. Please call me as soon as you can. My number is 707-555-1134."

I know that voice! Kimberlee! The line clicked off. Black Cat's hair jiggled. Images flashed through his mind.

A lake…with boats and colored sails.

A lodge next door…a dog on the lawn.

An old house with purple wisteria vines climbing across the porch.

Kimberlee. Amanda. Brett. My family, and…my name is… Thumper! Thumper? What an odd name for a cat. Sounds like a rabbit. At least it isn't Throckmorton.

He pawed at the answering machine. *Meow! Kimberlee has found us. And she said she recognized Noe-Noe.* That's right. The family was vacationing in Texas. That's where he met Noe-Noe and then…the car accident…and their carrier fell from the car and they were left behind. Angel! *She said 'Call me Angel'…because St. Peter sent her back.*

It was all so clear. He remembered everything. No more blank places.

"Rambo, Faith. Come to Papa."

The kittens tumbled over and skidded to a stop by his feet, like little bookends. "Yes, Papa?" Rambo blinked his bright little eyes.

"I want to tell you how I met your mother. It was earlier this summer and we were on vacation in Texas. Your mother and I…"

Faith swatted Rambo's tail and then jumped on his back.

Rambo fluffed his tail like a bottle brush and he rolled, grabbing Faith around her middle.

Guess they're not all that interested in Texas or how Angel and I fell in love.

Rambo loosened his grip on Faith, shook his black coat and looked up. "When is Mother coming home?"

"Why, soon, son—" Tires crunched in the driveway. "Listen. They're here now. Come on. Let's meet them at the door."

John carried Angel in the house wrapped in a towel. She looked like Queen Elizabeth with a big hoodie-collar around her neck. If it wasn't for the hoodie and the stitches in her head, she'd look pretty normal, but she smelled like *hospital*.

Black Cat danced at John's feet all the way across the room where he laid Angel on the blanket by the stove. Black Cat stretched out alongside her. "My dear, I've been so worried. Are you alright?"

Her head wobbled, her dilated eyes moved across the blanket. "Where's Muffins?"

Of course, her first thoughts would be for her kittens. Rambo and Faith snuggled close. Angel dragged Rambo to her side. He immediately kneaded his little paws into her belly.

Black Cat gulped, his heart aching for her. She didn't even get to say good-bye to her baby. "Officer Nina came this afternoon and took her home," he said. "She'll give Muffins a good home."

Angel nodded. She closed her eyes and sighed. "I like Nina. Muffins made a good choice."

"I have so much to tell you. Officer Nina says that Mr. Skimmer—"

Angel stood, turning in a circle, her back to him. "I'm very tired, dear. I'm going to rest for a while now."

"But, we got a call from Kimberlee. She said my name is…"

Angel was asleep.

Black Cat licked her shoulder and down her back until the hospital smell was gone. He had so much to tell her, but he'd have to wait for a better opportunity to explain her misunderstanding with St. Peter.

Chapter Thirty-Four

ohn hit the play button to listen to his phone messages.

Black Cat sat on the coffee table. *It's from my person, John. It's Kimberlee. She's the real deal.* He stood and rubbed against John's hand.

John clicked off the machine after hearing Kimberlee's message. "Well, Cindy. This sounds like the cats' owner," he said, stroking Black Cat's head.

Cindy lay huddled on the couch, her feet drawn up, a pillow clutched to her breast. "Is that lady really going to take Black Cat and Angel away?" Big tears puddled. She jabbed her fist into her eyes. Her lips quivered.

John put his arms around her. "Now, honey. Remember? This is what we hoped would happen. I'll talk to the lady, but it sounds like they really belong to her. Aren't you glad their real family called? Isn't that what we wanted?"

"But, we've had them so long, they're our cats now." Her face lit up in a smile. "Maybe it's like last time with Mrs. Stubblefield. Maybe it's a mistake." She looked over toward Rambo. "Maybe she'll take Rambo or Faith instead. Maybe Angel and Black Cat aren't really her cats."

John shook his head. "I don't think so. She saw them on the television. She would recognize her own pets. Maybe we can work something out."

"I wish that television man never told about the cats. The lady wouldn't have seen them if he didn't say all about it on television."

Black Cat lifted his head to listen, and then hopped onto the couch and lay down beside Cindy. The kittens were playing on the rug. Cindy was right. Kimberlee would never have found them if Peter hadn't called the television station and told about them finding the gold.

Isn't it strange how one simple action can ripple out and touch so many lives? If they hadn't gotten into the truck and come here by mistake, they'd never have found the gold. Maybe John would have lost his ranch. Maybe Carolyn would have taken Cindy. And if Peter hadn't called the television station, and they hadn't put the story on the news, Kimberlee wouldn't have found them. It had come full circle and now they were going home because Peter…Peter again. The elusive, invisible… Who was he anyway? John had asked God for help. Was Peter the answer?

"But, Daddy, I don't want them to go." Cindy's tears spilled over and rolled down her cheeks. "I want to keep Angel and Black Cat." She threw herself down on the sofa, and buried her face in the pillow.

"His name is Thumper, honey. He has a name. We should get used to calling him by his real name."

"I don't like that name. It's a stupid name." She clutched Thumper's long fur and pulled him closer against her chest.

Thumper licked her hand. His heart ached for Cindy. She was having such a hard time, dealing with their leaving. *This is hard.* He wished, somehow, he could make it easier.

John picked up the phone and dialed.

Thumper's heart felt near to bursting, his joy of going home one minute bumping into sorrow about leaving the next. I want to go back to my home by the lake and live with Kimberlee and Amanda…but I love John and Cindy and I want to stay in the hills with all the good woodsy smells. What are we supposed to do?

"Hello, Mrs. Clarke? This is John Goldstein, from Nevada City. I'm returning your call about the cats… Yes. Big, black and white with a white bib and four white feet… Yes. He has lots of toes on each foot." John chuckled. "She's gold with lighter stripes and green-gold eyes… Yes…together.

"You lost them near Cloverdale on Highway 101? That's not far from my mother's ranch. That must be where they got into the truck." John turned and winked at Cindy. "We thought we picked them up in Nevada City. We've been posting signs up here. We had no idea it was there, or I'd have—"

"Thumper and Noe-Noe? Yes. That's what you said on the phone. We call them Black Cat and Angel.

"I could take a few pictures and e-mail them to you… Okay, if you're sure. Of course, you can come. Oh, by the way, Angel had kittens. We found homes for two but there's two left… No, if you don't mind, I think my daughter would like to keep them." John turned toward Cindy again, and grinned. He raised his eyebrow in a question. "He's a cute little fellow…looks like Black Cat…*um*…*um*…Thumper. The female is a little tortoiseshell with an orange blaze on her nose."

Rambo and Faith are staying with Cindy? What a perfect solution! Angel will be so pleased. Why didn't I think of that myself?

Cindy sat up, and wiped the tears off her cheeks. A smile flashed across her face. She dashed across the room and sat on the floor where Faith and Rambo jumped at a blue pipe cleaner.

"Maybe you should wait a few days." John glanced over at Angel, lying by the potbelly stove, the hoodie holding her head at an odd angle.

No! No. Don't wait! Come now. Thumper hopped off the coffee table and then back on again.

"We just got Angel…*uh*…Noe-Noe…home from the vet," John said. "She has stitches in her head and she's on medication…*uh*…I'd rather not go into that right now. Let's just say, she met with an untimely accident. Perhaps you should wait until she's off her meds… Okay, if you say so. Sure, your vet can follow up. We could e-mail her medical records.

"Tomorrow, then, about 11:00 A.M. A picnic lunch would be fine. We have a nice table under the trees. Sounds like fun. Let me give you my address…"

He gave her directions to the ranch, said good-bye and turned to Cindy. "I guess you heard. They want to drive over and pick them up tomorrow." John stroked Thumper's head.

She's really coming! Tomorrow! Thumper closed his eyes and sighed, seeing in his mind's eye, the vineyard and the creek down back and the woods. Even the Emus didn't smell so bad once you got used to them.

His thoughts switched to the old Victorian house beside the lake. They were both…home, each in their own way. Thumper scurried over to where Angel lay stretched out on the blanket, beside Rambo and Faith.

He lay down beside Cindy, leaned into her hip and looked up into her eyes. How can I be happy about something when the something I'm happy about makes someone I love unhappy? And, how can I be glad to leave and at the same time sad because I don't want to leave? It sounded like one of those quiz show questions meant to trip up the contestant because there wasn't an answer. That way, the quiz show didn't have to award the big cash prize.

Angel was alive. Their family had found them and they were going home! It was all part of God's plan. *I was wrong to doubt, thinking everyone was blessed but me.*

John walked to the potbelly and stooped down beside Cindy. "What do you think about keeping Rambo and Faith? Would you like that?"

Cindy held Rambo and Faith nuzzled to her cheeks. Faith patted her hair and Rambo licked her chin. Cindy had roses back in her cheeks and a twinkle in her eyes.

"Rambo's giving me kitty kisses." She kissed the top of his head. "He thinks it's a wonderful idea. They both said they want to stay with us."

Kitty kisses, indeed. He's licking the salty tears off your cheeks. Thumper curled his front feet under his chest and blinked. I love you, Cindy.

Angel rolled over on the blanket and laid her head down with the plastic hoodie spread out across her shoulders. She put her paw on Cindy's lap. She seemed pleased with John's decision. Rambo and Faith's future was finally settled in the most wonderful way.

"Are you in pain, dear?" Thumper snuggled closer to Angel's side. She'd spent most of the time since she got home asleep, from the medicine John gave her.

She closed her eyes. "Just a little woozy. I think I'll nap for a bit, if you don't mind."

"Angel. Don't worry about a thing, now that Faith and Rambo have a home. It doesn't mean that you don't have…"

Angel's little snort left no doubt. She didn't hear a word he said.

Chapter Thirty-Five

"It's Kimberlee. She's here!" An SUV crunched to a stop outside the house."

Thumper raced from the front window to the blanket where Angel lay cuddled with Rambo. "That's Brett's SUV. I'd recognize that sound anywhere. Come and see."

Angel stood, waddled into Cindy's bedroom and crawled under the bed.

Thumper followed and peeked under the bed. "What's wrong? I thought you'd be thrilled. Aren't you coming out to greet the folks?"

"I really don't want to be bothered. My head aches." She closed her eyes and turned away.

Thumper crawled out from under the bed and sat on his haunches. What on earth was going on? She should be overjoyed, now that Kimberlee had found them and they were going home. Hadn't they talked about *going home* for months?

Car doors clunked outside. Voices from the yard carried into the house as his two families introduced themselves. Kimberlee was here. He was torn between running to greet her at the door and staying with Angel. Something was terribly wrong. He turned from the bed to the living room.

The front door squeaked open.

Kimberlee! Thumper ran to greet his family. He jumped from Kimberlee to Brett to Amanda. Between kisses and squeezes, happy tears flowed. Even Brett blinked back a few. Why, Jack was also there with Chance! *My old frenemy,* Chance. On a day like this even dealing with a dog was a pleasure. Thumper knocked *happy-heads* with the pup.

The reunion reminded him of the story of the Prodigal Son. The father said *…celebrate and be glad, for this son was dead and is alive… was lost and is found…* He didn't think he quite fit the description of a *prodigal*, but there was a parallel. He was lost and now he was found.

"You don't know what we've been through all these months." Kimberlee took Thumper by the ears and shook his head back and forth. She dabbed her eyes with a tissue.

"Please, have a seat." John gestured to the sofa. "I've made coffee and I have a few cookies. Can I get you a cup, Jack? Brett?"

"Thank you. That would be nice." Kimberlee and Brett sat.

"None for me, thanks." Jack shook his head and stood next to the sofa. "I've been sittin' for three hours. I'll stand for a bit, if ya don't mind."

"This is our daughter, Amanda." Kimberlee gave her a nudge toward Cindy.

"I'm Cindy. Come see our kittens." Cindy took Amanda's hand and led her over to the blanket by the stove.

Thumper cruised against Kimberlee's ankle, leaving black hairs and his scent on her dark slacks, marking her as his personal property. *There! Now she smells better!* His heart swelled with memories and love as he listened to his *persons'* voices.

John poured coffee and handed a cup to Kimberlee and another to Brett. "Sugar?" He set the coffee pot and plate of cookies on the coffee table.

"No, thank you. This is wonderful." She took a sip.

Where is Angel? She's missing it all. It was hard to think of her as *Noe-Noe* after calling her Angel for so long.

John pulled a kitchen chair from the table and sat. He glanced from Kimberlee to Brett, cleared his throat and fidgeted in his chair. "So, how did you happen to lose the cats?"

Kimberlee leaned forward. "We were in an automobile accident near Cloverdale. The cat carrier was thrown out and fell over the embankment. My cousin's dog's carrier stayed in the car—"

"Jack's your cousin?" John nodded toward Jack and reached for a cookie.

Brett shook his head. "Jack's our neighbor." He stirred sugar in his cup and took a drink. "Jack used to own Thumper, before… Long story, yesterday's news." He set his cup on the coffee table and stabbed the air with the cookie. "These are good."

John held the plate of cookies toward Kimberlee. She shook her head.

"So, go on. About the cats?" John set the plate back on the coffee table.

Kimberlee smiled at Amanda and Cindy, playing with Rambo and Faith. "We put an ad in the local paper, but no luck. After a while, we gave up. Then we saw the television broadcast." Kimberlee looked around the room. "Where is Noe-Noe? You said she was at the vet? She didn't…" Her face went a little pale.

John shook his head and glanced toward the stove. "I'm not sure where she is. She's usually there, with her kittens." His brow wrinkled. "Cindy? Where's Angel?" He turned to Kimberlee. "We call her Angel. And, we've been calling this one, Black Cat."

"That's odd." Jack reached for another cookie. "We used ta call him Black Cat, before Kimberlee came and Amanda changed his name ta Thumper." He wrinkled his brow and glanced between Kimberlee and Brett.

The stories I could tell you when I was called Black Cat. Why, I remember once—

"Cindy. Run to your room and see if Angel's in there. Maybe she was frightened when everyone came in. She's…*um*…been through a lot lately." John bit his bottom lip. His face flushed.

Thumper reached up to the coffee table and sniffed the cookies. *Angel's under the bed. She's having a feline female moment.*

Cindy went into her bedroom "Angel, here kitty, kitty. Where are you?"

"So, John, how did the cats get all the way over to Nevada City with you guys?" Brett glanced around the room, his gaze pausing by Amanda playing with the kittens.

Thumper turned to follow Brett's gaze. *They are beautiful, aren't they? Our children, yours and mine.*

John set his cup down. "We found the cats in the truck when we got home from Cloverdale late one night. We thought we'd picked them up at the grocery store down in Nevada City. We've been putting up posters around here. Then Angel had kittens, so we started looking for homes for them. Cindy and I are quite fond of…of Thumper and… and…"

"Noe-Noe." Kimberlee wrung her hands. "Oh, dear. We never even thought of that." She turned toward Brett. "Of course, you'd have become fond of them."

Amanda giggled and waved an Emu feather in front of Rambo's nose. "Look at the baby, Mama. "Doesn't he look just like Thumper?"

Kimberlee stood and walked to the blanket. She knelt to pet the kitten. "Isn't he a darling?"

Cindy came through her bedroom door with Angel cradled in her arms.

There she is, my darling. Isn't she beautiful? Even with a bandage on her head and the hoodie collar around her neck. Thumper hurried over to Cindy, stood on his hind feet, reached up and patted Angel's foot.

Kimberlee gasped. "Noe-Noe! You poor thing! What's happened?" She took Angel from Cindy.

Angel tipped up her head, her eyes wide. She trembled.

"There, there." Kimberlee stroked Angel's back. "You remember me, don't you?"

Angel relaxed under her gentle touch. She must have remembered Kimberlee from when they'd met in Texas.

"Now your name is Angel? I like that." Kimberlee glanced at Brett. "I never did much like the name, *Noe-Noe*. It always made her sound so naughty. I think we should call her Angel from now on."

Then Angel it is. Good decision. I like that better, too.

Kimberlee turned to John. "What happened to her head?" She ran her finger lightly over Angel's stitches.

Color rushed to John's cheeks. "Cindy? Take Amanda and the kittens outside. We grown-ups want to talk for a while."

Cindy wrinkled her nose and picked up Faith. "Come on, Amanda. They always want to talk grown-up talk. Bring Rambo. We'll sit on the porch swing." The girls got up from the blanket, each carrying a kitten.

Amanda walked carefully across the room with Rambo, as though she carried a fragile glass egg.

"Now, watch the kittens," John called. "Don't go off and leave them outside alone."

Cindy nodded and closed the front door behind her.

John's hands fidgeted in his lap. "I don't exactly know where to start. It's all so embarrassing."

"If you'd rather not discuss it, it's okay. We understand." Brett leaned toward the sofa.

"It's alright. I need to tell you what happened. She's your cat." He took a deep breath. "We've been having some trouble here on the ranch for several months and—"

"What kind of trouble?"

Leave it to Brett to zero in on the word 'trouble'.

"Well…" John coughed and cleared his throat. "How can I put this?" He peeked out the window. Probably checking to make sure Cindy couldn't overhear him. "You see, I have full custody of Cindy and my wife…*er*…ex-wife came a couple of days ago and tried to… *um*… take Cindy by force. To make a long story short, Cindy struggled with her and…*um*… well, Angel bit her."

"Angel bit Cindy?" Brett raised an eyebrow. He glanced toward Kimberlee. She stroked Angel's back.

"No. Angel bit my ex-wife." John put his hand over his eyes and rubbed his temples. "Then my ex-wife hit Angel with the fireplace poker." His words were almost a whisper. John put both hands over his eyes and rubbed his fingers into the bridge of his nose.

Kimberlee gasped. "I can't believe…" She glanced from Brett to Jack, then down at Angel. Chance stood, circled around Jack's legs and lay back down on the floor.

Thumper's fur rumpled up. *Grrr.* Just hearing again how Carolyn attacked Angel made his blood boil. *Why did I let John stop me? I should have given her something to remember me by. The old battleax!*

"I know…I know. I couldn't believe it myself." John wrung his hands. "The vet says she'll be okay in time. The stitches should come out in about a week. She'll need follow-up vet care though, if you take her home today."

"I don't know what to say, Mr. Goldstein." Kimberlee blushed. "We really didn't mean to pry into your personal business. We had no idea…" She turned to Brett. "Brett, get your checkbook. We should pay Mr. Goldstein for the vet expenses—"

"Please call me John." He lifted his head and smiled. "And I wouldn't hear of you paying for the vet. I feel bad enough about it. My ex-wife—"

"How about we split the bill?" Brett stood and pulled his checkbook from his back pocket.

"I suppose that would be okay. The vet bill's there on the buffet."

Brett stood and walked to the buffet. He picked up the vet bill, then wrote a check and tore it from his checkbook.

John picked up another cookie. "Would you folks like to walk out and see the Emus? We have a couple baby chicks, just over a week old."

"Sure, sounds like fun." Brett stood and took Kimberlee's hand. The three followed John out the door, leaving it ajar. "Put the kittens back, girls, we're going to look at the birds."

Thumper and Angel ambled across the room to the front door, watching the folks step off the porch.

Cindy hurried back into the house with the kittens and then ran after Amanda.

I'll stay with Angel and see if I can find out what's troubling her.

Chapter Thirty-Six

ark, yark! The Emus rushed to the wire, curious to see their visitors.

John led the way toward the Emu enclosure, glancing back over his shoulder toward his guests. *So this is Black Cat's folks.* Brett and Kimberlee seemed nice. He was glad Black Cat…no, what did they call him? Thumper? He'd gotten so attached to Thumper and Angel after only a few months. Felt as though they'd always been part of the family. He was sure going to miss them. Cindy was happy that Rambo and Faith were staying. Guess he'd made the right decision that time. It wasn't a hard decision. It's not as if he didn't love those little rascals too, almost as much as Thumper and Angel.

"Watch your step there by that garden hose." He turned to smile at Kimberlee as he stepped closer to the Emu gate. "Here we go. Just give me a minute." He unlocked the door and walked inside.

Kimberlee and her family stopped outside the gate.

Amanda clung to Kimberlee's skirt, peeking around her mother's legs, her wide eyes focused on the huge birds.

Cindy took Amanda's hand and tugged her out from behind Kimberlee. "It's okay. They can't get out. Aren't they funny looking?" She pulled her closer to the fence.

"Can we pet them?" Amanda reached toward the wire where one of the baby Emus peered through. It scuttled off, just out of reach.

"Maybe later, honey, if John wants to take you into the enclosure." Kimberlee took her hand and guided her away from the fence. "Right now, I think we should have Daddy Brett get our cooler out of the van. What do you say? Shall we have some lunch?"

Amanda nodded and walked back toward the house with Cindy and Kimberlee. She looked back over her shoulder. "I like the babies. Can we take one home?"

"No sweetheart. We're going to take Thumper and…*um*…Angel home. We wouldn't have room for one of the baby birds."

John grinned and pointed toward the picnic table under the trees. He called after Kimberlee. "Go ahead and set up your things over there. Cindy, you and Amanda run in and bring the sodas from the fridge and some ice. Do you need anything else, Kimberlee?"

"Maybe some glasses since you've got ice. I just have paper cups. Otherwise, I've brought everything. Brett, if you and Jack will get the things out of the van, I'll set up the table."

The girls hurried inside. Amanda returned lugging two bottles of coke. Cindy carried a tray with glasses and a bowl of ice.

Brett and Jack came back, hauling the ice cooler between them, with the picnic baskets balanced on top.

With the tablecloth spread across the table, Kimberlee took cold chicken, corn on the cob, French bread and potato salad from the cooler.

"Grab those paper napkins, girls, and we'll be ready." Kimberlee motioned for the men to sit and eat.

Lunch proceeded amongst much laughter and conversation about kids, cats and Emus. *Thank goodness we never got to religion or politics. Doubt I could hold my own with these folks.* "I'm glad the cats are going to such nice people. We're mighty pleased you've found us." John took the last bite of French bread and reached for a chocolate chip cookie.

Kimberlee nodded. "I couldn't have said it better myself. We're so happy to get the cats back and to make new friends in the process. Would you care for anything else?" She picked up the bowl of potato salad.

"Couldn't hold another bite, but thanks." John waved away the bowl. *What a pleasant afternoon. Things couldn't get any better.* He leaned back and patted his full tummy. "*Ahh.* Good food and good company. This was great. Thanks, Kimberlee."

"Can we be excused, Daddy?" Cindy took Amanda by the hand. "We want to go and look at the baby Emus again."

"Sure. Go ahead, but don't open the gate."

"We won't." She grinned and they ran, hand in hand, toward the enclosure.

John stared after the girls. *Did she just wink at Amanda? What are they up to? Maybe I should—*

"John, I just thought of something." Kimberlee grabbed his arm. "Our annual Harvest Day Festival is in mid-October. Fern Lake puts on a real nice parade and entertainment at the park. Jack's motel is sponsoring a sailboat race. It's a pretty big event. Why don't you and Cindy come for the weekend? Jack, can you reserve a room for them? What do you think?"

"Sounds fine to me. Just give me a call." Jack stuffed the last cookie in his mouth.

John's heart swelled. *What a great idea.* "Cindy would love that. She'll be begging me to come and visit Amanda and the cats, anyway. Let's make it a date."

Brett poked John's shoulder. "In fact, I'll bet you'd like to meet Kimberlee's cousin, Dorian. She's a police detective. Pretty, blonde, always on the lookout for a single guy."

"Brett! Stop trying to be a matchmaker. That's my job. Dorian's a very nice—"

Eeekke!

Cindy? John's head jerked toward the enclosure. *What's happened? She didn't open the…* John leaped up from the table, headed for the enclosure. It's one of Gilbert's babies!"

Chance barreled out from under the table and raced past John, her tongue lolling and hair flying. She bolted after the Emu chick that had just run through the open gate and headed across the yard.

Cindy stood with her hand on the enclosure latch.

How many times have I told her…? John made a grab for the chick as it ran past his legs. He missed.

A raucous screech came from the chick. He ran like the devil was after him.

Chance dogged the chick like a trailing shadow.

The chick's little wings flapped as if the extinct thought of flight had just entered his tiny brain.

John rushed after the chick, his hands outstretched. Oh, God, don't let that dog catch it. She'll kill it for sure.

Jack shot up from the table. "Chance, come back here this minute. Bad girl!"

"Brett. Do something!" Kimberlee jumped to her feet and rushed after the fleeing bird.

Amanda ran back toward the picnic table with Cindy close behind. Tears streamed down Cindy's face. "Daddy! I'm sorry. I didn't mean it."

The chick approached the end of the driveway. At the edge of the road, a car roared past and the chick turned back toward his screaming pursuers.

Chance closed the gap, each stride bringing her closer to her quarry. Gilbert's baby changed direction as each obstacle appeared in his path. He turned right at the lawnmower, left at the woodpile and veered toward the vineyard; his potential human captors close behind.

Chance zigged with each zig and zagged with each zag, keeping pace with the chick. She stumbled, regained her feet, and then thundered behind the frenzied fleeing fowl.

"Catch that blasted dog before she kills my chick!"

Jack raced behind the retriever with Brett not far behind. Jack stopped and doubled over, panting.

John cut across the lawn. The pursuers twisted and turned across the yard. *We must look like a gol-darned train, all of us running like this.*

The bird turned at the front porch and tore toward the table where Cindy and Amanda now stood, transfixed, staring at the pandemonium. Cindy put up her arms and hollered. "No! Shoo. Go away."

Gilbert's baby was not to be discouraged. With a final bound, he flapped his miniature wings and landed in the middle of the picnic table, knocked over the soda bottles and stomped into the potato salad.

John screeched to a stop and bumped into Brett, knocking him off his feet and down on the lawn. Brett rolled in the grass and burst into laughter. The others froze.

A fowl in the potato salad was the last thing anyone expected on the menu.

Chance skidded to a stop, crouched down and looked around for Jack.

Jack rushed up and grabbed her by the collar. Chance hung her head. Was she truly ashamed of her performance or only sorry she'd gotten caught?

John looked from one guest to another. His face warmed. What would these people think of him now? Bad enough his ex-wife had tried to murder Angel. Now, they couldn't even get through lunch without a disaster. He gulped, put his hand over his eyes, and swallowed. *So much for a weekend holiday at the lake. Who could blame them if they never speak to us again?* Perspiration trickled down his neck. He lowered his hand and opened his eyes.

The baby Emu pecked with wild abandon at first one delicacy and then another. Corn on the cob, French bread with garlic butter, green olives. His yellow feet squished as he stepped one foot and then the other into the potato salad. Mayonnaise smeared along the speckled feathers on his neck. A green olive stuck to his beak.

John dashed to the table. Quicker than Gilbert's baby could think *holy barbecue sauce*, John plucked him from the salad and hurried back to the enclosure, tossed him inside and slammed the door. He turned to face his guests. What could he possibly say? How humiliating! *Those girls!*

Kimberlee and the girls cheered and applauded.

Thank goodness. They're not mad? John bowed and swept out his arm like a toreador with a red cape. "Cindy? Amanda? Come here! What have you got to say for yourselves?" John balled his fists on his hips and scrunched his eyebrows together. *Now, to try and keep a straight face.* It was all he could do to keep from bursting into laughter. The corners of his mouth twitched.

Cindy looked up between her dark lashes, and then put her hand over her mouth.

Amanda giggled and ran to hide behind Kimberlee's skirt.

Jack fell to the grass, laughing until tears rolled down his cheeks. "Can't you just imagine what that chick was sayin'? *Eh? Holy mother of Phoenix…monster…dog. Run!*'" He roared with laughter as Chance hopped on his back, barking.

"Hey John, don't be mad. I haven't laughed so hard for weeks. A perfect end to an already terrific day." Brett gasped for breath and using the tail of his shirt, wiped tears from his eyes. "Let the girls off the hook. We should drink a toast to Gilbert's baby. He's the life of the party."

John strode back to the picnic table, shaking his head. "Those girls…"

"Did you see how I headed him off when he reached the porch?" Jack laughed, reached over and rubbed his hands over Chance's ears.

"I nearly had him at the woodpile." John chuckled.

"Jack, you were panting like a steam engine out there on the lawn. I've never seen anything so funny." Brett clutched his ribs, chuckling and shaking with laughter.

"I haven't laughed so hard since the house paint fell on Brett's head." Kimberlee leaned over the picnic table, grinning. She patted the girls' shoulders and reached for her glass. "A toast to Gilbert's baby. May he never find himself the main course at another picnic! May he always be as happy as he was in the middle of the potato salad."

"Hear! Hear! Should I bring Gilbert's baby to Fern Lake when we come for the Festival?" John pulled Cindy into his arms and swung her in a circle.

"No!" The guests cried in unison.

Thumper stretched out on the bedroom floor. The sound of raucous laughter outside finally died down. *About time they stopped their foolish jocularity. Shouldn't they be getting ready to leave?* As much as he loved John and Cindy, he was anxious to get home and show Angel all the neat things at the Fern Lake house and on the dock. "Now that they've settled down out there, Angel, let's take one last walk down by the vineyard, like we've done so many times before."

His Angel slipped out from under the bed, her hoodie scraping the bedframe.

He trotted to the door and meowed.

The door creaked open. "Oh, Black Cat. You missed all the fun." Cindy stooped to stroke his head. "Daddy looked so funny chasing Gilbert's baby."

I guess that's what the whoop-la was all about and we missed it all. Drat! He rolled his eyes. "Come on Angel."

Angel ducked her head, swinging the hoodie to the side and stepped out the door onto the porch. She followed him across the grass and past their *persons* still seated at the picnic table.

Thumper wandered down the path toward the Emu cage with Angel at his side.

"I want to say good-bye to the Emus." He paused beside the gate. This was likely the last time he'd see the awkward birds that had become so familiar over the past months.

The baby birds danced up to the fence and peered through the wire. "It's hard to believe, but I think I'm actually going to miss them." Inside the wire, naughty Gilbert's baby, now the epitome of obedience, followed his papa, pecking bugs left and right, as though his escape from confinement and the Wild Emu Chase had never happened.

"Are we about done here?" Angel turned back toward the house. "I want to spend every minute we can with Faith and Rambo. We don't have much more time with them."

Thumper flicked an ear. "What's going on with you? We haven't been gone five minutes. You don't seem very happy about going back to our real home."

Angel looked back at the porch where Cindy and Amanda were giggling on the swing. She turned toward Thumper, her ears pulled down inside her hoodie. "You mean we're going back to *your* real home, don't you? What about me? I lived in Texas and you took me away. Now, we live on an Emu ranch in Nevada City, and you want to take me away again. Maybe I just don't belong anywhere."

"Why Angel, how can you say that?" Thumper sat back on his haunches. "We belong together with Brett and Kimberlee."

Angel turned her nose up in a pout, the hoodie surrounding her head like Queen Elizabeth's collar. "I'm used to things here. Maybe I don't want to go. Maybe I want to stay here with John and Cindy. Maybe I feel like this is *my real home*." She looked toward the house, moving the large plastic hoodie as she turned her body.

Thumper dropped his head. How could he have been so blind? It hadn't even entered his head how Angel might feel about leaving John and Cindy.

But, about her not wanting to come with him to California? That wasn't exactly true. She wanted to come with him; she'd more than made that clear. He wouldn't argue that point right now. After all this time on the Emu ranch, it was understandable that she'd become devoted to John and Cindy. Did she think it was easy for him to leave?

He shook his head to clear his mind. She was right about one thing. No one asked her how she felt about returning to Fern Lake. She was lying in the vet's office with her head smacked in when Kimberlee called. She had no sooner come home from the hospital when here comes Kimberlee, someone she barely remembered, taking her away from her last two kittens and *her* new *persons*. No one had asked what she thought about any of it.

He opened his mouth to speak. What could he say? Would it make any difference to tell her, yet again, how much he loved her? She knew that. She'd opened her heart and bared her soul, sharing her deepest feelings. Wouldn't his vows of undying love or any amount of begging invalidate her feelings? He wouldn't negate her pain by arguing. He closed his mouth.

Angel turned and stomped back to the house.

Thumper followed through the door and found her lying on the blanket by the stove.

"Wait. Angel, listen… I…" His gaze moved from Angel to the kittens playing under the table. No words of wisdom had popped into his head between the vineyard and the house. Her concerns were valid and his heart ached, knowing that she was unhappy with the decision made behind her back and without her consent.

Rambo scurried across the room and hopped onto the blanket, where he began to nuzzle his mother.

Angel hissed and boxed his ears.

Rambo jumped back, his eyes bright, his little tail bushed out like a tiny bottlebrush.

"Man up, Rambo!" Angel rolled over and turned her back to the little fellow. "You're seven weeks old. Go eat from the Friskies bowl. I can't be your lunch wagon forever!"

Rambo shook his head and hunkered down on the blanket next to his mother. What a painful, first *life-lesson*. No more free lunch. He waddled over to the Friskies bowl, took a couple of mouthfuls and then lapped water from the water dish.

"Angel. Weren't you a bit hard on the boy?" Thumper's ears tingled. They'd be leaving soon and they'd never see their babies again. How could Angel be so cruel? Was that the last thing she wanted Rambo to remember about his mother?

"Hard on the boy? You don't understand. Apparently, we're leaving in a few minutes, whether I like it or not and he isn't coming with us. The hardest thing a mother can do is tell her son to *man-up*, that she won't be there to help him any longer, that there's no more *tittie-milk*. He'll be on his own for the rest of his life. Do you have any idea how much that hurts? Do you have any idea how it breaks a mother's heart to pretend she doesn't care, so her son has the courage to turn away, often in anger, and stand on his own four feet?"

"Angel. What can I say? I…I didn't understand. Forgive me." Thumper hung his head, the lump in his throat almost choking him. "I think I understand now." He slumped on the blanket and swallowed hard. "You don't want to come with me."

Angel rolled over, turning her back. "Don't say that. I…I don't know what I want." She sighed. "I'm so confused. The last thing I want is to hurt you. Maybe I should hide somewhere so they can't find me when they leave. I don't have that much longer, anyway. It might be easier for you if we made a clean break now…instead of later…when *he*…calls…and I have to go." She put her head down on the blanket. The hoodie smacked the rug. She twisted. "I hate this thing!"

Now, what is she talking about? It didn't make sense. His thoughts were still muddled by Angel's rejection of Rambo and her heart-wrenching confession. Then her words came back to him. *It might be easier to make a clean break now…instead of later…when he calls…*

Angel… He crept closer to her, still trying to make sense of it. When he calls? St. Peter? They never had a chance to talk about this. *She's thinking of me. She wants to spare me the pain of watching her die.* She still thinks she's going to die. *Oh, my darling!*

"Angel, listen to me." He lifted her hoodie with his paw until their eyes met.

She closed her eyes.

"I said, listen to me. If St. Peter was ever going to take you, don't you think it would have been when the mama hit you with the poker? You almost died then, but you didn't! You misunderstood what St. Peter meant. Think a minute. Tell me his exact words."

"He said I could come back until the babies were born and had homes, until you got your memory back and for as long as you needed me."

"For as long as I need you? Don't you understand? Angel. I'm *always* going to need you. He didn't mean you only had a little while on earth to accomplish an assignment. He gave you back your life, another chance to live, to raise the kittens, to help John rescue his ranch, to bring Peter into our lives so Kimberlee could find us. He meant that you could be with me always. You're so special. You've touched so many lives, and you have so much more to give. You're not going anywhere. You do understand, don't you?"

She opened one eye and peered into his face.

He nodded, his heart thumping. Please, God, help me make her understand.

She opened the other eye, her black irises enlarged, the hoodie lifting from the blanket. "Oh!" Her whiskers twitched. The troubled look in her eyes melted away. "Are you sure that's what he meant? I'm not going to die?"

"Not any time soon. Listen. Come back with me to Fern Lake. John and Cindy will come to visit. Before long, you'll love Kimberlee as much as John and Cindy, and she'll be your own special *person.* We'll have new adventures. Instead of a horse ranch, or an Emu farm, we'll live next to the lake. We'll watch the sun rise over the hills all pink and yellow and watch it slide into the lake every night all red and golden.

"What about Rambo and Faith? How can I bear to leave them? They haven't found their forever homes yet."

"Didn't you hear John? Rambo and Faith are staying right here on the ranch with John and Cindy where they'll be loved. We've taught them all they need to know. They have the ancestors' memories to guide them, just like the other two girls. All our babies have good homes, now. They'll all have long and happy lives."

Angel's eyes glowed in the afternoon light.

"Listen. I hear Kimberlee and Brett and John coming onto the porch. They must be about ready to leave. Run, get your favorite toy and kiss the babies good-bye."

Angel nuzzled the kittens, and then raced into the bedroom. She returned with her favorite squeaky mouse gripped tight in her teeth. "I'm *weady*." The fur rippled down her golden back. Even with the hoodie restricting her movements, she wiggled with joy.

A patch of sunlight shined through the window. The rays bounced off her golden head and shined like a halo. *A halo around my Angel's head.*

Kimberlee opened the front door. "Thumper? Angel? Are you ready?"

Thumper licked Angel's cheek. "We're ready. Let's go home."

About Elaine Faber

Elaine Faber is a member of Sisters in Crime, Inspire Christian Writers, and Cat Writers Association. She lives in Northern California with her husband and four house cats. She volunteers at the American Cancer Society Discovery Shop and is a board member of the Elk Grove Friends of the Library.

Elaine started writing poetry and short stories as a child. She has completed five novels. Many of her short stories are published in magazines, on-line weekly magazines and in at least eight short story collections (anthologies). She favors writing in the cozy mystery and humorous mystery genre.

Black Cat and the Accidental Angel is the third Black Cat Mysteries, featuring Thumper, (Black Cat) the cat who, with the aid of his ancestors' memories, helps solve mysteries and crimes. Elaine's novels are available on Amazon in print and e-book.

(Books)
Black Cat's Legacy ~ http://tinyurl.com/lrvevgm)
Black Cat and the Lethal Lawyer ~ http://tinyurl.com/lg7yvgq
Black Cat and the Accidental Angel

(Coming Soon)
Fall 2015—A humorous WWII mystery. Mrs. Odboddy, an eccentric elderly lady, fights the war from the home front. When ration books go missing, Mrs. Odboddy's conspiracy theories run afoul of reality. Before long, she's up to her neck in mortuaries, chickens and chicanery when an old lover returns and involves her in the CIA's search for missing Hawaiian money.

Elaine welcomes your comments. Write to her at:
Elaine.Faber@mindcandymysteries.com
Elaine's Website ~ http://www.mindcandymysteries.com
Share your thoughts about the Black Cat series on an Amazon Book Review.

Also by Elaine Faber

Black Cat's Legacy

Thumper, the resident Fern Lake black cat, knows where the bodies are buried and it's up to Kimberlee to decode the clues.

Kimberlee's arrival at the Fern Lake lodge triggers the Black Cat's Legacy. With the aid of his ancestors' memories, it's Thumper's duty to guide Kimberlee to clues that can help solve her father's cold case murder. She joins forces with a local homicide detective and an author, also researching the murder for his next thriller novel. As the investigation ensues, Kimberlee learns more than she wants to know about her father. The murder suspects multiply, some dead and some still very much alive, but someone at the lodge will stop at nothing to hide the Fern Lake mysteries.

Cover photo *Boot's Eyes*: © Elaine Faber

Black Cat and the Lethal Lawyer

With the promise to name a beneficiary to her multi-million dollar horse ranch, Kimberlee's grandmother entices her and her family to Texas. But things are not as they appear and Thumper, the black cat with superior intellect, uncovers the appalling reason for the invitation. Kimberlee and Brett discover a fake Children's Benefit Program and the possible false identity of the stable master. To make matters worse, Thumper overhears a murder plot, and he and his newly found soul-mate, Noe-Noe, must do battle with a killer to save Grandmother's life.

The further Kimberlee and her family delve into things, the deeper they are thrust into a web of embezzlement, greed, vicious lies and murder. With the aid of his ancestors' memories, Thumper unravels some dark mysteries. Is it best to reveal the past or should some secrets never be told?

Cover photo *lawyer with cat* © CURAphotography,shutterstock.com image 19277278